SEXY
LITTLE
Liar

Also by Noire

Natural Born Liar: The Misadventures of Mink LaRue

Maneater
(with Mary B. Morrison)

Lifestyles of the Rich and Shameless
(with Kiki Swinson)

Published by Kensington Publishing Corp.

SEXY LITTLE

Liar

NOIRE

Kensington Publishing Corp.
http://www.kensingtonbooks.com

DEDICATION

This crazy misadventure is dedicated to all my loyal friends and readers who jump on the urban erotic train every time it pulls into the station. Thank you for riding with me as I lead you through mysterious doorways and drag you down twisted paths, and for trusting the creative fiyah in my pen to deliver a sexy and unique story every time it hits the paper. My creative writing skills allow me to explore different styles and write in different voices, on many different topics, and I'm amped that y'all are having just as much fun reading about the scandalous Mink LaRue as I'm having writing about her!

As usual, leave a review when you're done and message me at Noire Black on fb.

Muahh :))) I lub y'all!

ACKNOWLEDGMENTS

Like always, I give all props to the Father above for blessing me with an original voice and a creative mind. Big thanks are going out to Missy, Black, Nisaa, Man, Jay, Reem, Ree, and my entire UET team for all the little things you do behind the scenes to help make me a success. Big ups to my UETBC fam, and all my loyal readers and friends. Be sure to check me out on Facebook in the Urban Erotic Tales Book Club so we can chat about con-mami Mink LaRue!

Muah:)))
Noire

WARNING!

This here ain't no romance
It's an urban erotic tale
When Gutta hits the bricks
Mink's gon' sho'nuff catch some hell!
It started out as just another ordinary scam
Until Mizz Mink discovered
They might really be her fam!
Mink is seeing dollar signs
She thinks she's got it made
She's counting up her duckets
Hoping Viceroy's 'bout to fade!
But when a chick from Philly shows up
Lookin' like her twin
The competition's on,
So may the sexiest liar win!
A grip is on the line
Yo, what's Harlem chick to do?
Here's another misadventure
in the life of Mink LaRue!

CHAPTER 1

New York City was my shit! Our plane had just landed at JFK, and after lying our way through a wild and crazy misadventure down in D-Town, me and Bunni Baines, my partner-in-grime, were hyped as hell to be back in the Big Apple!

We had dipped outta Manhattan with nothing up our sleeves except mad dreams and devious schemes, and after working our ghetto grind and flipping the state of Texas upside down, we were rolling back in town with more dough than we had ever baked before.

"Taxi!" My best friend hollered as an airport worker wheeled our luggage outta the crowded terminal. Bunni was posted up in a bright pink cat-suit and a matching pair of silver-buckle gladiator sandals. I was rocking a platinum-white Glama-Glo wig with bright orange streaks down the bangs, and an orange and white striped tank top that I'd tucked into a skimpy white tennis skirt that barely covered my apple ass.

For two hood-bound Harlem chicks me and Bunni had crazy suitcases everywhere, and every last one of them was busting at the seams with mad jewelry, crazy shoes, and the hottest designer gear that stolen money could buy.

I had recently become an official member of the Dominion oil family of Texas, and using my new status as the once-missing and now-found oil heiress Sable Dominion, me and Bunni had hit the rich folks' mall in Dallas and killed every store in sight. I mean we ransacked that joint like a pair of greedy cat burglars, oohing and aahing as we touched and admired and scooped up damn near every stitch of gear that had a hot label on it. We shopped like fiends for hours and hours, and we didn't come up for air until we were broke-down tired and every corn on our toes was crackin'.

"Now see there, Mink." Bunni rolled her eyes and sucked her teeth as she struck a funky pose on the sidewalk outside the baggage terminal. Bowlegged Bunni had a real stank shape and she always dressed to show that shit. Almost every dude who zipped into the terminal stole a quick peek at her round titties and bouncy ass as he passed by. "We gon' hafta splurge on us a fly whip or something, baby! We packin' mad ends now, ya heard? How in the hell we gonna look pulling up around the way in some beat-up yellow cab?"

Bunni had that shit right. Image was everything in our hood, and I was damn sure tryna elevate mine. I was *not* the same con-mami Mink LaRue from the 'jects who had skied up outta New York just a few weeks ago. After chilling in a huge Texas mansion and ballin' around town in half-a-million-dollar whips, I had the head and it was sho'nuff big too.

"Don't worry," I told Bunni. "We gotta roll with this setup for right now," I said and grabbed her arm as I pulled her toward a waiting cab. "But trust and believe, this is gonna be our last time slumming around the city in a whooptie, okay? We's *paid* now, mami! Our pockets are *swole*! As soon as we hit Harlem I'ma lease us a limo and a driver too, bet?"

We climbed our booties in the back of the cab and left the driver and the baggage dude standing outside tryna figure out how to cram all our shit in the trunk. It seemed like just yesterday that me and Bunni had climbed in a cab at the Dallas International Airport and headed toward the Dominion Estate where we were on a mission to pull off the biggest con caper of our grimy little lives.

Our crazy misadventure had kicked off when Bunni went shopping at the Food Land up the block from her crib and saw my picture on the back of a carton of milk. The National Center for Missing Children had just started a new campaign aimed at solving some of their biggest cold cases, and a three-year-old girl named Sable Dominion—a rich little oil heiress who had been kidnapped from a midtown drugstore—was one of the missing kids they were featuring. Dollar signs had started cha-chinging in Bunni's greedy little eyes, and she swore all out the missing chick was *me*.

"Hey now! We gots'ta go to Texas and get up on that loot!" Bunni insisted as we checked out Sable's age-progressed photos on the Internet. "For real, Mink! You look *just like* that chick! Your own *mama* couldn't tell y'all apart!"

Me and Bunni were a slick pair of part-time pole twirlers and full-time con artists, and for the past few years we had been using our scheming wit and banging bodies to pull off ganks and rack-up bank in every borough in the city of New York.

We had jumped on the computer and did a few Google searches, and both of us damn near flipped out when we found out that not only was Miss Sable about to come into a hundred grand inheritance on her twenty-first birthday, but if Bunni pretended like she'd found me, she could get a crack at the twenty-five-thousand-dollar reward money that the Dominions were offering too.

Well, desperate times called for a sho'nuff desperate hustle, and me and Bunni almost burnt the house down tryna cook up a scheme to get our hands on that Dominion cheese. We were broke as hell and we needed that loot. Not only was Bunni and her brother Peaches about to get booted outta their tenement apartment and have their shit tossed on the curb, but a throwed-off drug dealer named Punchie Collins was tryna slump me for ganking him outta some ends, *and* I had a shit-load of court-ordered fines to pay up real quick, or else a warrant was gonna be issued for my arrest.

And if that wasn't enough to light a firecracker under my ass, my gangsta boo Gutta was finishing a lil bid upstate and he was about to be back on the streets in a minute, and I do mean on the *streets* too. See, when Gutta went to jail he left me sitting on his stash of twenty-five g's and he warned me not to touch that shit. He was planning on using that money to rebuild his drug empire as soon as he hit the bricks. But a cheese-chasing rat like me just couldn't help nibbling. A grand here, five grand there, shoes, wigs, chronic, Krug, jewels, and wild parties . . . *shiiit* . . . me and Bunni had burned through Gutta's cash so fast that before his bid was even halfway over his laid-out crib was a wrap and so was all his paper!

So I had been stuck between nothing and nothing, and pulling off a hustle to steal Sable's hundred grand was my last crapshoot, my final shot at street redemption. I was a con-mami, a grifter, a fraud master to the highest degree, and me and Bunni had used every flimflam in the book to convince those super-rich black folks down in Dallas that I was really the kidnapped daughter that they had lost so long ago. We had busted up in their mansion in the middle of their Fourth of July barbeque, and trust me when I tell you we popped off a New York-sized explosion up in that joint!

Shiiit. Them Texas folks didn't know what to do with me as I laid my slick Harlem flow on their asses. In no time at all I had Sable's mother, Selah, eating outta the palm of my hand, and my fine-ass play-uncle Suge Dominion had done a damn good job of eating out the rest of me!

Bunni had played her role like a champ too. She'd scammed her way up on a freaky pain slut named Kelvin Merchant who worked at the DNA lab, and in return for whipping his ass and pinching his balls, Kelvin had hooked us up with a fake DNA report that guaranteed me a slice of the Dominion family pie.

With the DNA results on the table, I had rolled outta Dallas with a hundred grand in my bank account, and Bunni made out like a street bandit with twenty-five large in reward money for all her hard work too. All in all, it was the biggest hustle of our guttersnipe lives, and we were amped up and feelin' ourselves for pulling off a gank so lovely. And now, all I had to do was pay my fines to the city of New York, tear off some ends to crazy Punchie Collins, and stash twenty-five grand in Gutta's safe to keep that fool from murking me when he came home from jail.

After that, life was gonna be one big freaky-ass party, and as long as I handled my bizz I could get as wild and loose as I wanted to! *Hell yeah.* My blood surged with hood excitement as our rickety taxi pulled up outside of Bunni's building and the hater-bitches on the front stoop got to peeping all in the windows. *Handle ya bizz, Miss Mink LaRue!* That's all a paid-out-the-ass hood chick like me had to do!

CHAPTER 2

Barron Dominion hopped out of his white-on-white 2012 Maybach and slammed the door behind him. He had dropped his so-called sister Mink off at the airport earlier in the day, and he had been damn glad to get rid of her ass too. But even before Mink's New York–bound plane could take to the skies, Barron had gotten a phone call hipping him to her shiesty game and bringing him back to the same DNA lab that had fucked him around in the first place.

Striding boldly across the street, Barron eyed the front door of Exclusively DNA and frowned. Them bastards up in there didn't know who they were fucking with today. As the oldest son in the Dominion dynasty and a cutthroat young corporate attorney, Barron was holding the reins as the acting CEO of Dominion Oil, a highly prosperous empire that his slick, self-made millionaire father, Viceroy Dominion, had built from the ground up.

For the past few months Viceroy had been drifting in and out of a coma after sustaining serious head trauma in an oil rig explosion, and the task of keeping his clan together and protecting their vast, multi-million-dollar fortune had fallen directly into Barron's lap.

Barron stepped up to the front door of the lab and yanked at the door handle. The last time he had to come down here shit had gotten real ugly. Half-drunk and zooted up on some damn good 'dro, he had gone in hard on a lab technician and broken his fuckin' nose. And it was all because of that chick Mink LaRue, the hot-ghetto scam artist from New York City who had tried to run a game on his family and con them out of a hundred grand and a share of the Dominion trust fund.

Mink had connived her way into their inner circle by pretending to be his kidnapped sister Sable, and somehow her DNA had come back a perfect match for the missing little girl too. But Barron had been two steps ahead of the shiesty Harlem diva, and he'd slipped a lab tech named Kelvin Merchant fifteen big ones to not only make that matching lab report disappear, but to slide him a bogus report showing Mink as a negative match for Sable instead.

But somehow the dumb-ass clerk had fucked around and let the truth leak out. Barron had been on a big one as he sat at the dinner table with the rest of his family and listened to his mother read from a DNA report and announce that Mink LaRue was definitely Sable Dominion, the long-missing member of their family. Barron had jumped straight up and disputed that shit as hard as he could, but no matter how many suspicions he cast on Mink and the report, his mother had been holding all the evidence she needed right in her hands.

So Barron had tossed back some Hen dog and wilded straight out. The next morning he had busted up in the lab head-butting niggas and throwing killer blows, and by the time it was all over he had beaten the dog shit outta the incompetent lab technician whose stupid mistake had cost Barron a hundred yards.

But karma really was the muthafucka everybody said it was, and today, just minutes after dropping Mink and her ghetto sidekick off at the airport, Barron's cell phone had buzzed and Kelvin Merchant had been on the line. And the crazy-ass story that rolled outta the lab tech's mouth had jabbed Barron hard in the gut and completely blown his mind.

We had another specimen come in this week from a young lady from Philadelphia. I was asked to run tests on her sample and compare the results to your sister Sable's DNA . . . I know you probably don't wanna hear this but . . . umm . . . we've got another match.

Mink, Barron's eyes had immediately narrowed. *That scheming little bitch!* His collar got real tight as a hot image of her sexy body and conniving eyes flashed through his mind. That chick was nothing but a hood leech. She would suck your pockets dry if you let her. Her and that skank sidekick she rolled with had gotten away with over a hundred grand of Dominion cash, and Mink's slick game of trickery was so on point that she had fooled almost everybody she met.

Almost everybody, Barron reminded himself as he strode across the threshold of Exclusively DNA and slammed the door shut behind him. Because no matter how many smooth lies flew out of that gutter chick's mouth, and no matter what the fuck some doctored-up DNA report said, Barron hadn't been fooled by the crookedness of Mink's tongue or by that little-girl-lost act she had put on for his family. Yeah, he mighta lusted after those ripe, perfect titties she had on her, and yep, his nose was open on those wide, swinging hips the girl rocked, and *hell yeah* he had beat his shit off and fantasized about that lusciously plump booty perched above Mink's perfectly shaped butterscotch thighs, but he hadn't been fooled by her scheming ass at all. Nope. Not at all.

CHAPTER 3

"*Really*, Madame Mink?" Bunni's brother Peaches fussed at me as he peered into the mirror and plucked a few stray hairs off his muscled-up chest. Peaches was six feet five and his chocolately body was rock hard and buff as shit. He was sitting at the kitchen table looking real special in his lacy pink half-slip and sexy lime-green stilettos, and the boosted nine-hundred-dollar diamond ring glistening on his finger was definitely to go to jail for.

Me and Bunni had lit through a whole lotta money while we were down in Dallas, and we'd splurged on a bunch of fly gear for Peaches too. We'd hit a huge drag queen store and racked up on the kind of frilly, nonsensical shit that a prissy dude like Peaches loved to style, but there was no way me and Bunni could get our big brother the two things he was feening for the most: a pair of lumped up titties and a nice fluffy ass.

"I mean, *really*!" He side-eyed me and smirked as I repeated my request into the phone. "Who does that?"

"Who does *what*?" I sucked my teeth and cradled the phone against my shoulder. The last thing I wanted was Peaches and his common sense bringing me down to earth when I was *so* feeling myself up in the sky! I had dialed up one of the biggest limo services in the city and I was waiting on hold as they checked to see if they could scramble around and find me exactly what I wanted.

"Mink." Peaches frowned. "Be for real now, baby girl. You really want them people to send you a stretch Hummer *and* a thugged-out driver who can rap? Ere damn day? For a whole goddamn month?" Peaches pursed his glistening lips and then made little popping sounds as he worked his shiny lip-gloss around. "That damn money is burning a hole in your push-up bra, girl. I don't see why you and Bunni can't just catch a cab or take the train like you been doing." He frowned at me, then rolled his eyes. "That's a whole lotta good money you about to toss off, if you ask me. And after all the drama and hard knocks you done been through, please don't tell me you ain't learned your lesson yet."

I frowned right back at his ass. Peaches could be a real buster sometimes. He was just like somebody's grandmama. He had practically raised me and Bunni from the time we were thirteen years old, and even though I was hardheaded and couldn't nobody tell me shit, when Peaches spoke I usually listened.

Usually. But not this time.

"C'mon, now, P," I whined. "Get wit' it! Me and Bunni worked like crazy down there in hot-ass Texas! *Shiiit*, we deserve to floss! Don't worry, I'ma get straight with everybody I owe, but a bitch just turned twenty-one and it's my time to shine, ya feel me?"

Peaches smirked. "I feel Punchie's fist busting you in ya mouth, that's what I feel. But go 'head witcha grown-ass self. I know one thing, you and Bunni better keep a real tight count on all that money, you hear? Or y'all gonna look up one day and find every single dime of it *gone*."

It took about an hour for our limo to show up, and by that time me and Bunni had already fought over the mirror in the tiny bathroom and slid our luscious bodies into our very best gear. We pranced down the pissy staircase and outta that raggedy-ass tenement like we were tipping out of a mansion, and when I peeped the shiny stretch limo at the curb and the bangin' dude who was pushing it, I just couldn't keep the grin off my face.

Our driver was tall and fine and looked like a pussy-killer dressed up in a suit. His eyes were popped open just as wide as mine were, and he started drooling the moment he got a good look at the package I was holding.

"Ooh-*wee!*" he exclaimed as me and Bunni pranced outta the building. "What's your name, baby?"

"Mink." I giggled and smoothed the top of my perfect-peach Glama-Glo wig. "Mink Minaj."

The heat in his eyes burnt up the tassels on my peach and purple go-go skirt as I switched my freaky hips toward his gleaming ride.

"Yeah, you got that Nicki groove on lock," he growled, eyeballing my cleavage like he was a vampire kitten who wanted to suck my milk. "But your back pockets is even fatter than hers."

I giggled and made sure he got a good look at my plump yellow thighs as I slid onto the plush leather seat. I was used to turning dudes on, and fucking with their heads was nothing but a big game to me. It was all part of my hustle, and I didn't care if a man was in high school or strapped down to a bed in a nursing home, if he had swole pockets then his ass was a mark in my book, and I hit him upside the head with my wicked sex appeal every chance I got.

Dude had just slammed the car door when a shiny-black psycho wearing a doo-rag tied over his cornrows bust outta the front door of the building eyeing me like he was an assassin. My heart banged in my chest. It was crazy Punchie Collins. He was a local drug-slanga that I had ganked for about a grand. Word that I was back in town musta gotten back to him, and I could tell by the way he was grilling me that he wanted his cash.

"Yo, whattup!" he hollered, holding his hands up high in the air and shooting me gang signs as he eyeballed our flashy setup. "Yo, I see you got whips and mad jewels and new rags . . . but where the fuck my package at, Mink?"

"I see you, Punchie!" I hollered out the window and fronted him off. "I got you, boo!" I winked and gave his throwed-off ass two thumbs-up. "Be'lee that, papi. I'ma tear you off and treat you right!"

And I was too. I was gonna pay off Punchie Collins, take care of my court costs, pay the bill on Gutta's storage so they wouldn't auction all his shit off, and then find me a way to flip the rest of my money and make it last a long, long time. Yeah, all that shit was definitely gonna happen, I told myself as the limo pulled away from the curb and Punchie launched a round of hot bullets outta his eyes, but first I was gonna get my head right and do Mizz Mink Minaj tonight!

Me and Bunni were back on our old stomping grounds! One hundred and twenty-fifth Street was still live as hell and Club Wood was still the place to be! We rode in the whip with the music blastin' and the sexy driver rappin' us a hot stripper song by that rowdy Reem Raw.

Lil Mama I can see it in ya eyes we can ride if you ready to roll!
I got the Caddy double-parked outside we can slide if you ready to go!
The way she grind pop it back, make it wind
Got my mind goin' outta control . . .
Other bitches they don't wanna see you shine
She get by 'em when she droppin' it low!
I just wanna see you take it down lowerrr!
Break it down!

Let them haters see you make it roll overrr!
Break it down!
It ain't nothing these other bitches can show her
She the shit ,and she know it, but I'ma show her just how to
Break down!

Our limo pulled up directly outside the front door, and me and Bunni got ready to make our grand entrance at the strip club where we used to trick off customers, swindle squares, and dominate butter bitches on the poles.

"Wait!" I slapped Bunni's hand as she reached over to open her door. "Don't get out yet! You know them fools are probably peeping all out the damn windows," I stunted. "You gotta learn how to floss your shit properly, Bunni. Let's chill for a few minutes and give these niggas a chance to appreciate our status, ya heard?"

With the music blasting, we sat in the back of the limo and got tipsy on the bottle of liquor that came with the ride, and even though he wasn't supposed to be doing no drinking on the job, our fine ass driver tossed back a few right along with us.

"Them pole bitches ain't gonna believe it's us," Bunni squealed when we finally slithered outta the whip about ten minutes later. Just like I predicted, faces was pressed up all against the front window as the strippers and hoes tried to figure out which rich celebrity baller was about to bless Club Wood with his pocket stash tonight.

I cracked up at all the hater eyes that swept over us as we walked through the door. These hoes were disappointed as hell that it was me and Bunni rollin' in instead of two paid-out-the-ass NBA ballers looking for a lap dance and a little bit of licky-lick.

"Mink!" my fake-friend Punanee ran over and tried to hug me like she was glad to see me back. Punanee thought she was the shit because she used to headline on the main stage over at the G-Spot, but I couldn't stand her ass. "Girl where y'all been? Niggas been asking about your ass for weeks! I been showing off your double-hump moves and wracking up on *all* your customers, honey!"

I shook Punanee off as the crowd parted to let me and Bunni get to the bar. That trick could keep my damn customers. Mizz LaRue was paid now, and all that ass shaking and pole humping was in the past for me. Uh-uh. I was done with that type of physical labor. Didn't no self-respecting daughter of Viceroy and Selah Dominion have to grind her pussy around up on no stage and make it rain for her greenbacks no more. Hell, nah. I was a Dominion now, and I was real proud to say that me and my rich play-daddy down in Dallas was just alike. Both of us had gotten our paper the easy way.

We stole it!

CHAPTER 4

Kelvin Merchant liked to make it hurt. Especially when he could do it on the sneak tip. Secret sexual sadism brought him the utmost erotic pleasure, and the agonizing thrill of the leather scrotum-scruncher that he had twisted tightly around the base of his fuzzy nuts had him erect and moaning and squirming all over his work stool.

Exclusively DNA was one of the busiest labs in town. Kelvin was responsible for a high volume of genetic testing, and he was sitting at the counter rubbing his throbbing erection and trying his best to formulate the summary of a report when suddenly the front door of the lab burst open and a raging black ass-kicking stormed in.

"Mr. Dominion!" Kelvin stammered and leaped nimbly to his feet. Despite the sweet pain that pulsated in his groin, the look of fury in Barron Dominion's dark eyes made Kelvin's erection go limp. He stared at the handsome, athletic-looking rich man, and as his fat cheeks jiggled in fear and surprise, the memory of the beat-down ol' boy had put on him was fresh in his mind.

"Mr. Dominion, my black ass," Barron spit as he strode up

to the counter and leaped over that shit like he was a regular gangsta from the streets.

Kelvin put his fat hands up to fend off the brutal blow he knew was coming. He liked pain, but the last thing he wanted was another head-butt from this fool, and he knocked over his stool as he stumbled backward trying to get out of range.

"Now what was all that bullshit you were talking on the phone?" Barron got up in his face and demanded as the pain freak standing in front of him trembled in fear.

"It's not b-b-bullshit," Kelvin stuttered. "I don't know how it's possible, but we were sent another DNA specimen from a lab in Philadelphia. A man named Sam George called and told me to look out for it. He said it was just a routine test, and he told me not to bother you with the results. But I ran it personally. I ran it *twice.* And just like the sample we ran on Mink LaRue, this one came back a positive match for your sister Sable too. I thought you would wanna know about it."

"Yo, hold the fuck up," Barron said. He took a small step backward and shook his head. "Who the hell submitted a sample from way in Philly? We made it a rule that all DNA tests have to be performed right here in this lab."

Kelvin nodded quickly. "That's right. The *testing* has to be performed here. But Sam George had the sample collected in Philly and then sent to us by express courier. I'm sorry, Mr. Dominion, but whoever this girl is, her DNA is a perfect match for your missing sister Sable."

Barron felt his blood get hot. He knew exactly what time it was, and he wasn't up for no more games. Scheming tricksters! There was no way in fuck that the DNA from two different girls could both come up a match for Sable's, and since Barron truly believed his adopted little sister was long dead and long buried, then that meant somebody's slick ass was lying. Or maybe even *two* somebodies.

★   ★   ★

Pilar Ducane rolled up to the gates of the Dominion Estate in her custom-designed luxury Lexus coupe. Spritzed in a light cloud of Chanel No. 5, her lace-front weave perfectly framed her face and she tapped one expertly manicured fingernail on the steering wheel as she waited for the huge, ornate gates to slide open.

She glanced at the car's center console as her cell phone rang and the display lit up. Her so-called fiancés name and number flashed on the screen and she pushed the decline button and smirked as she rolled her eyes. No matter how raggedy her life was right now, Ray was such a buster that he was the last person she wanted to talk to.

While it was true that the cunning Dallas diva had been knocked down by her father's recent financial troubles, she damn sure wasn't knocked out. No matter what angle you approached Pilar from she was sharp as a sword. From head to toe, every single detail of her attire had been selected with the utmost taste and elegant attention, and the total cost of today's ensemble, including her authentic designer handbag, was well over twenty grand.

Pilar drove through the gates and parked her whip right outside the mansion's front door. She'd gotten a crazy phone call from her adopted cousin, Barron, and the cockamamie story he'd told her had her bottom lip twisted with anger and envy.

Mink LaRue.

That slimy bitch was still trying to run game. Why that sleazy Harlem hoodrat couldn't get hit by a city bus or fall in front of a goddamn subway train was a freakin' mystery. Pilar was family, and Mink was a fraud. There was no way in hell she should have been riding around broke and busted while Mink dug her fingers deep down in the family cookie jar. Pilar had always thought of herself as a ruthless and cunning go-getter, but after watching a professional slicksta like Mink sashay away with a nice slice of the Dominion fortune stuck up her ass, Pilar knew it was time for her to tighten up her hustle and get her own game back up to par.

As the spoiled daughter of Selah's brother Digger Ducane, Pilar wasn't used to coming in second best to *anybody*, and she damn sure wasn't used to being denied anything she had set her eye on. Her father had been one of Dominion Oil's largest contractors, and Pilar had been raised in the lap of luxury, that is, until the economy fell off and took Digger's once-prosperous oil transport business right down a shit-hole with it.

Almost overnight Pilar had gone from splurging on clothes, jewels, and every other luxury item a beautiful high-society diva could ask for, to having her credit cards melting at every store in town. Pilar had cried and blamed her father for damn near sending them to the poorhouse but, she silently admitted as a servant opened the mansion's front door and she stepped inside the cool, elegant parlor, she had blamed her super-rich relatives too. The goddamn Dominions. They had a shitload of money and Pilar was dying to get her hands on their cash and their last name too.

And to make sure she got both of those things, Pilar had worked herself up a real slick plan. She'd always been moist between the legs for her fine-ass cousin Barron, and since he had been adopted by the Dominions when he was a baby and wasn't really blood family, she saw nothing wrong with laying her whip appeal on him every chance she got. She'd already sent Barron's sniveling white fiancée, Carla, running out the door, and if it went down the way Pilar schemed for it to go down, Barron was gonna forget he'd ever known that skinny white bitch and put a big fat ring on the luscious ba-donka-donk that Pilar was laying on him.

Yeah, all the fuck-me flirting and the horny little sexcapades that Pilar had been pulling on Barron had been working like a charm. That is, until some New York skeezer named

Mink LaRue showed up outta nowhere and dropped a big load of urban shade on her bright Texas shine.

"Trifling bitch!" Pilar muttered under her breath. Her heels click-clacked on the stone floors as she strode through the large sitting area and headed toward Barron's office. Somehow Mink had schemed herself into the exact position that Pilar had been aiming for—wearing the Dominion last name—and not only had her aunt Selah fallen for the girl's fake-ass act, Barron's horny eye had zoomed in on her big, thunked-out ghetto booty too.

It was pitiful, Pilar thought, the way brainless chickens like Mink had nothing but the shape of their asses to fall back on. Barron was a real smart dude, and he was used to being around some of the most beautiful women in the state of Texas. But there was something about that funktified skank Mink that had put a mean rock in his stuffy silk drawers. Yeah, he tried to hide it and he was way too bougie to admit he wanted to fuck her, but Pilar knew lust when she saw it, and her cousin B, the rich dude that she was trying her best to hook up with for life, was lusting like hell after his adopted sister Mink.

Just thinking that shit made Pilar get evil, and she couldn't keep the wicked glint out of her eyes or the smirk off her lips when she walked into Barron's office and closed the door, then sat down across from his desk and crossed her sexy legs.

"Now tell me that story again," she demanded as her cousin glanced up from a document he was reading. The look in Barron's handsome dark eyes went from surprised to seduced in two seconds flat. Pilar giggled inside. This nigga was sprung. Smelling her vapors. His gaze roamed all over Pilar's deliciously shaped frame, and she knew he was remembering that bomb jockey hump she had put on him just two days ago.

"It's just like I said on the phone," Barron said slowly as his eyeballs roamed up and down her shapely legs, "I got a call from the DNA lab. They claim they've got another match for

Sable's DNA. It came from a girl somewhere in Philadelphia. That's all I know."

"See, I knew it!" Pilar shrieked and jumped to her feet. Her firm breasts jiggled beneath the fine fabric of her short Pucci dress, and she saw Barron's eyes zoom toward her erect nipples. She walked over to him and perched her heart-shaped ass on the edge of his huge wood desk. Everything in Barron's office was sleek and polished and required maintenance, and Pilar knew she fit right in.

"I told you that bitch Mink was lying! Her scheming ass was lying the whole damn time. I knew she wasn't Sable right from the jump. That chick didn't have me faded for a minute!"

"Yeah, Mink is definitely a fraud, and some shady shit is definitely up," Barron agreed. "And she's stupid too. You just can't have two sets of DNA come up a match for one person. That shit is impossible. But on the real, whoever this Philly girl is, she must be scheming too."

"Why do you say that?"

Barron shrugged and stood up. He looked like a million dollars coated in creamy milk chocolate, and he was worth a whole lot more than that. He thrust his hands down in the pockets of his William Fioravanti suit and shook his head.

"Sable is dead, Pilar. If you ask me, she's *been* dead. Probably since the day she got snatched. All of this searching we've been doing for her, and all this head banging and fighting off her wannabes . . . It ain't been nothing but a waste of time and money. I've been looking for a way to break it to my moms that there can't be any *real* DNA match out there for Sable, because there is no *Sable* out there! Not anymore. For real, my sister is dead. Gone."

Pilar slid her butt off the edge of the desk and stepped up closer to her cousin. Her nose was level with the knot in his tie, and she inhaled the very rare scent of his ultra-expensive Clive Christian's Imperial Majesty and swallowed hard.

"Well if you thought Sable was dead then why in the hell

did you let Mink get away with all her inheritance money? Hell! I could have used that mo—" she started, and then bit her tongue and walked her mouth back. "I mean, *the family* could have used that money on other stuff."

"See there." Barron grinned and slid his big hands around her tight waist. He knew damn well Pilar was supposed to be off limits, but ever since he had broken up with Carla, his cousin had been sliding all over his dick like syrup on a pancake stack. "That's where you're wrong, Pilar. I knew Mink was gaming, but she had my moms blinded. It didn't matter what kind of charges I brought on the girl, or what I could prove, Mama just didn't care. She said she blamed herself for how Mink's life turned out, so whatever grimy shit Mink did couldn't have been her own fault."

"I understand how your mother feels, but you still shouldn't have let Mink get that money! She didn't deserve it because she's *not* Sable!"

Barron let his hands slip down Pilar's waist and cup her soft, round ass. "Listen, baby," he said. He pressed his nose into her neck and then ran the tip of his wet tongue over the rim of her ear. "We're running a business here, and one of the first things you learn about money is, if you gotta pay somebody a couple of grand to keep from paying them a couple of million, then you pay 'em. That little bit of money was nothing compared to what Mink might get if Daddy is kicked off the board and the trust fund is activated at Dominion Oil. That's where all the *real* money is, and *that's* what I've gotta find a way to stop Mink from getting."

"And how are you going to do that?" Pilar asked, enjoying the way his strong fingers felt rubbing and stroking all over her ass. "What you gonna do? Kill her?"

Barron laughed again and pressed his lips to the tender meat of her neck. "Nah, I'm ain't gonna kill her. But I *am* gonna clip that ass. Cut her off at the knees."

"How?"

He shrugged. "I don't know yet. But if she ever comes back to Texas holding her begging-ass hand out, I'ma handle her."

Pilar sucked her teeth loudly and pulled out of his arms. Barron was talking all that good shit now, but when Mink was here she'd seen him suck down the girl's funky vapors every chance he got.

"What do you mean you're gonna handle her?"

"Just what I said. If she comes back then I'll handle that ass."

"But what kind of sucker move is that, Bump? You can't wait for Mink to just bust up in here again! This is a *fight,* baby. You gotta take it to her and toss her on the mat! That chick is from the streets of New York, and trust me, the next time she comes out swinging she's gonna go real gutter with it. Mink has to be declared ineligible for the trust fund money! Forget about sitting around and waiting for her to throw the first punch. Man-up and let's take this fight straight to the ring!"

"Yo, what do you want me to do, Pilar?" Barron smirked. "Send a hit man after the girl?"

"No," Pilar said after thinking for a moment. "Not a hit man. I want you to hire a private investigator. Find somebody good who knows New York. Find him and let him dig all up in Mink's nasty ass."

Barron shrugged that off. "I already thought about that one. It would work, but like I said, no matter what they dug up on her Mama just ain't gonna buy it."

"So? Who said anything about your mother?" Pilar asked slickly. "*Aunt Selah* might not wanna hear about all the low-down shit Mink has done, but the board members at Dominion Oil sure as hell will."

Barron raised one eyebrow and then chuckled. "Damn girl!" he said as he backed Pilar toward his desk and cleared everything off that shit with one sweep of his arm. "What'd you say your last name was again?"

She giggled. "Ducane. Why?"

Barron cupped her thighs and slid her designer dress up over her ass, then lifted her hips onto the desk and leaned her back. " 'Cause," he said as he unzipped his pants and maneuvered his hard dick outta his silk drawers, "the way you talking you sound like you got some Dominion in you, baby. That's for real."

Pilar giggled again as she fingered her wet pussy and then reached for the thick chocolate bomb pop that he was stroking up in his fist. "I know I *want* some Dominion in me," she whispered, licking her lips and hoping like hell Barron was too turned on to even think about putting a wrapper on his pretty brown wood. "Oh hell yeah," she moaned from deep in her throat as he slid his thick black dick up inside her hot tunnel and started pounding her nice and raw. "I damn sure want some Dominion *in* me."

CHAPTER 5

"Ain't no party like a New York party!" Bunni slurred as we sat up in Club Wood getting toasted up to the max. As usual the club was packed out with ballers and hustlers, and chicks with plump titties and huge asses were workin' their pockets all the way down to the last lint ball.

Me and Bunni were on one! We were ballin' our asses off, and mad party-goers were giving up the props and paying us our righteous respect. I started off buying rounds for all the chicks that I usually stripped with, and by the time the getting got good my ass was flying so high I bought the whole damn bar out!

Them long-throated chicks was guzzling Krug and tossing back Hen-Hen like every liquor store in the city of New York was about to go bone-dry. I chugged down my share of alky too, but I was careful to watch my shit being poured from the bottle because the last time I got tipsy up in Club Wood somebody had slipped me a tab and I got caught up in a serious flimflam.

See, Bunni and Peaches had bagged a cross-dressing principal of a prestigious boys' school in a blackmail scam that we were charging him twenty-five large to get out of. They had sent me out to pick up the loot, and me and the principal had agreed to meet at Club Wood and conduct our little transaction right there in the club. But as soon as I gave him the blackmail pictures and he handed over the brick of cash, that slick old skeezer had trapped me in a cross-con. Some fine nigga named Dajuan Latrell Sullivan, aka Daddy Long Stroke, had slipped something in my drink when I wasn't looking and then he fucked me hard and robbed me blind.

Getting stole like that was one reason I had let Bunni talk me into going way down to Texas to gank those rich folks in the first place, and now that we had pulled off our slick grimy lick and we were back in our own territory, I was damn glad that I had gone.

"*Girlll*," Bunni drawled in her deep-fried ghetto twang. "Lil Bang and them got some real good shit flowing in the back," she told me. "Chronic, sess, 'dro. Shit, they got some good X back there too, girl. It's our first night back in the city. Let's go for broke and get all the way live!"

Free head banga? Bunni didn't have to tell me twice. I almost broke my damn neck climbing off the barstool and hauling ass toward the back of the club. My swagger was on one hundred as I shook my hips in my tiny-tasseled purple go-go skirt, and niggas who had seen me rock the poles buck naked a thousand times still couldn't keep their hands off my bangin' hips as I sashayed by.

We danced and grinded and got so lifted that we broke daylight up in that camp, and when we finally crawled back up to the front of the club all dry-mouthed and zooted, Perry and his cleanup crew were putting the barstools up on the counter as they got ready to mop the gritty floors down.

"Goddamn!" Our rap-a-licious limo driver said as the three of us stumbled outside and he squinted into the early-morning sun. He had hung hard with us the entire night and probably

puffed more yay and drank more liq than me and Bunni put
together. He dug in his uniform pocket and came out with his
limo keys, then wobbled on his feet as he held them shits up in
the air and let 'em dangle. "I'm fucked up like a *mutha*fucka!
Which one of y'all nasty bitches wanna drive?"

Life for me and Bunni was turning out to be one big-ass
party, and I swiped that bank card they gave me in Texas so
many times that I got a crook in my damn wrist. Regardless of
all the stores we had hit while we were down in Dallas, the
best shopping in the world was right here in New York City,
and we sho'nuff dropped some dollars in the Big Apple too.

I had always had a good eye for hot fashion, and it seemed
like having money just made me appreciate the finer shit even
more. I spent mad loot adorning my body from head to toe in
stylish shit from designers like Brian Atwood, Vera Wang, and
Tracy Reese. I became a real label whore, and as long as something sounded expensive and exotic, I plunked down my bank
card and snatched that shit right up.

"Madame Mink," Peaches warned me one night as our
limo driver carried a truckload of bags and boxes inside the
crib from every major store in the city, "you're trying to do
too much, baby girl. You're gonna wake up one morning and
every dime you got is gonna be spent."

Deep inside I knew Peaches was talking true shit, but I was
having way too much fun to hear all that. Me and Bunni had
just splurged on a penthouse suite at The Plaza for NBA
weekend, and right now we were getting dressed to head
down to Chelsea to take one of those real crazy Urban Desire
party cruises up and down the Hudson River. Peaches could
go 'head with all that noise he was talking. Besides, I mighta
been a real big spender but I was nobody's big fool. Gutta's
cash was already tucked away to the side for when he came
home, and I was planning on tearing Punchie Collins off a

hunk of dough in a minute too. On top of that, Bunni had found a dude who was gonna sell us some cut-rate crack at a real stupid price, and the way we figured it we would triple our investment on every transaction.

I igged Peaches. My shit mighta looked funky from the outside, but on the real tip I knew what I was doing. And Peaches needed to stop all that stuntin' any damn way because he was benefitting from the money too. Not only was his rent paid up for the next six months, but me and Bunni had gotten down fifty-fifty on a bunch of back-alley estrogen shots for him so he could get ready for his sex change operation. He was shooting them female hormones in his ass left and right, and damn if there wasn't two wubby little titties tryna pop out on his hairy, muscular chest.

"Madame Mink are you listening to me?" he demanded.

"Yo, I got this, P," I told him as I finished getting dressed for the party cruise. The boat held four hundred people and I wanted to make damn sure I stood out as the numero uno bitch in the crowd. I was rocking a lemon-ice Glama-Glo with long spiral curls down the back, and a skin-tight lemon-ice mermaid dress with silver jewels glittering everywhere. "I'ma pay my fine on Monday and take care of business like I'm supposed to, Peach, okay? So quit all that damn worrying. Mizz Mink Minaj has all this shit here under control."

"Errrm-herrrm," Peaches said, twisting his lips as he looked at me sideways. "*Errrm-herrrrm*. Yep. Whatever you say."

I didn't mess around too tough with no water, but the boat scene was all the way live! Me and Bunni got there a little bit late but we was still right on time. It was one big floating party going on and there were fine niggas ballin' every damn where. But there were some hater bitches on the scene too. Especially the ones who were from around our way. One lil come-up in particular had followed me around all night shooting me dagger looks and tryna throw salt in my game 'cause she'd heard I was holding and she couldn't stand to see a bitch who was paid.

"Watch ya pockets!" she screamed on every dude who so much as looked at me. "She's a live one! A true tricksta! Schemin' Mink is in da house!"

"Igg that bitch," Bunni warned me as the young chick who lived on our block kept right on following us around flossin' about how I wasn't nothing but a liar and a big ass thief.

"Nah, Bunni!" I said, getting heated. "I oughtta fly her big, water-head right off her scrawny neck," I fumed. Didn't *no* guttersnipe hater get to flounce around putting Mizz Mink's game on blast! "Yeah, I should walk right up on her and fuck her lil ass up!"

Bunni hand-checked me. "Remember now, you ain't paid ya fines yet so you still got a *W* hangin' over your head. Fuck her lil ass up and the cops are gonna come. And if the cops come your ass is going to jail. Just igg that crazy bitch, Mink. I don't mind beating her ass, but she just ain't worth poppin' off no bullshit drama tonight."

I knew Bunni was right so that's what I did. I igged what was comin' outta that raggedy trick's mouth and laughed every time she walked past me talking shit with her gigantic dome wobbling around on her scrawny neck. I was pissed off though. This was the same chick who used to bum Pamper money from me for her baby, and now she was smellin' herself and tryna come at my throat. *Sheeiiit.* Mami must didn't know she wasn't slick enough or fine enough to compete with a prime stunna like me! She didn't have the body, the mug, or the skillz!

I had forgot all about her lil ass when I went upstairs and saw my sherm friend Borne chillin' up on the top deck. Borne was my little emergency-fund friend. We fucked around some-times and I could always count on him to come to my rescue whenever I was in a tight spot. Borne looked a'ight in the face, and even though he had a nice big dick he was a square and he was skinny, and he definitely wasn't in the hustling game.

"My girl Mink!" He got up and hugged me real tight. He stepped back and looked me up and down with mad appreciation, and I stood there and took it, knowing I looked fuckably delicious, like I was about to go floating up the Hudson in my skimpy little mermaid dress.

Borne grabbed my arm and kinda yoked me up a lil bit as we walked along the deck. My eyes was everywhere as I checked out all the playas and hustlers on the scene, but Borne was busy doing that jealous-nigga thang. That thang weak nigs did when they had fucked you real good a few times and wanted to make sure everybody knew it.

And the lil hater bitch who was talking noise acted like she knew it too.

"C'mon." I grabbed Borne's hand when I saw her coming my way again. We ducked into a little room that was full of toilet paper and cleaning supplies. I could tell Borne was horny as hell, and a hottie like me was always down for some good dick. I let him kiss all over my titties and then I unzipped the bottom of my mermaid dress and hiked it up around my waist and let him bang my shit out. It was kinda good and yeah, he made me get all wet and gushy, but after it was all over my high was blown and I realized that this wasn't the dick that I had really wanted.

"Was that shit good for you?" Borne whispered as he tore open a pack of toilet tissue. He rolled up a ball and stuck it between my legs and patted my coochie dry.

All I could do was shrug. I'd gotten me a nut, but something had been seriously missing from that fuck! I mean, yeah, Borne was a piper and all that, and yeah, he had stamina and could push it pretty good, but on the real? My ass was spoiled! I had gone down to Dallas and gotten me some Texas-sized dick, and no matter how much meat Borne was packin' he wasn't no kinda match for Uncle Suge!

★ ★ ★

If all it took was a couple dollars to burn a hole in your pockets, then I could see why my entire plump apple ass was flaming on fire! Peaches had jinxed my flow in a real bad way, because just like he predicted, somehow I woke up one morning broke as shit, with only the money I had stashed away for Gutta left to my name.

"Girl, where in the hell did all that money go?" Bunni had the nerve to stunt on me like she wasn't the one right by my side helping me spend up every dime.

"Bitch stop playing!" I told her. "You know where all the damn money went." I was ashamed to even think about the way that dough had disappeared into thin air, let alone count it up. But on the real, most of it was gone. Forget about the thousands I had spent getting tips on liquor and drugs, I had also bought enough new clothes to last me all the way to forever. Shit, my ass had shopped feverishly, like a junkie who needed to be in rehab. Fashion changes on a daily basis in New York, and a chick like me didn't know nothing about a budget. As long as something looked good, cost a gwap, and had a foreign-sounding label on it, I had grabbed it and paid for it. You woulda thought my boosting days were over the way I was dropping dollars. I had bought out the entire new line of Glama-Glo wigs too, and Neiman Marcus, Bloomingdale's, and Bergdorf Goodman had become my favorite new hangout spots.

Of course I had slid the city of New York ten yards for my court costs so I could keep my ass outta jail, and I gave Peaches almost ten grand to help him get his titty shots and whatnot too. But between shopping, renting limos, throwing hot-ass parties, rocking fabulous jewelry, and sucking down lobster dinners at expensive restaurants and buying front-row tickets for a few bangin' concerts me and Bunni wanted to see, I had burnt up more than fifty grand.

"So how much you got left in the bank?" Bunni demanded like she was my damn accountant or something.

I shrugged and admitted, "I ain't hardly got nothing left in the bank, but I still got thirty in Gutta's safe. Twenty-five g's for him, and the other five I was sitting on so me and you can get down and flip some weight. You still got your ends to put in, right?"

"Um, hell yeah," Bunni said, looking all shifty-eyed and guilty in the mug. "Yeah, girl. I still gots some of mine. But um, even if we put our money together, ten grand ain't enough to get no real weight so we might need to borrow some of Gutta's cash too. Don't worry, though. We can put it back once our product starts selling."

"Hell *no*, Mink!" Peaches screamed on me. "Don't you touch not one damn dime of Gutta's money! Bad enough that fool is gonna come home and find out you got kicked outta his crib and all his shit is stuffed in a storage bin! If you mess over his money too that nigga is gonna put your lights out, baby. For *good*!"

"Awww, *fuck* Gutta!" Bunni barked as she channel surfed on the flat screen she had bought that was so damn big it covered half the living room wall. "Fuck him up his jailbird ass!"

"Oh, so now it's fuck Gutta?" I stared her down, peeping her game. "Oh, I get it now. I see how you living, Bunni. Your ass is broke too. Broke *and* crazy! Talking about diggin' in Gutta's stash and fuckin' him up the ass at the same time! You singing loony tunes, Bunni, 'cause you broke and your pockets is full of lint."

"I ain't broke, baby! I already told you I gots minez! But check this out," Bunni said as she clicked off the television and walked up on me with her chunky monkey leading the way. I busted the twisted lil twinkle in her eye from all the way across the room, and I knew she was thinking hard on a brand-new scheme. "We can still make some moves and rack up on some cash. I finally heard back from my boy uptown. He got in touch with the connect who's gonna hook us up with the product. Don't worry, his prices are real good and he said he got us."

"Okay, he got us but *when*, Bunni? That dude been ducking you ever since we got back from Dallas, and you still don't even know who his connect is. If we gonna make a big move and get at some big money, then we need to make it now."

Bunni waved her hand. "Don't you worry about nothing, Mink. Leave the move-making to me. You holding five racks for yourself and twenty-five for Gutta, right?"

"Yeah."

"Well there it is," she said like playing the drug game was real simple. "All we gotta do is slide my dude the twenty-five, and then we triple-flip our first batch of product and we can pay Gutta back and put some dough in our pockets at the same time."

"Whoa, hold the hell up," I said and shook my head. "Where's your loot? How much you putting in?"

She threw up her hands. "Okay, damn! You got me, Mink! I spent my shit! I'm broke. You busted me. I spent it. You know good and damn well I spent it!"

I shook my head at that shit. "Well I guess the plan is dead then. I ain't tryna mess up none of Gutta's money, girl. You heard what Peaches just said. That nigga will straight wild out and press his tool to my head if he comes home and I'm broke."

"But you not *gonna* be broke, Mink!" Bunni insisted. "It's not like we gonna hang out and spend his shit up partying or nothing! The only thing we doing is using some of his paper so we can stack more paper. Besides"—she smirked and twisted her lips—"Gutta ain't the head-case you need to be worried about right now. That fool Punchie Collins wants that money you stole from him, and you ain't gonna be able to keep ducking his ass forever. And on the real, once you pay him and Gutta off and get you a little yay and some yak, then your ass is gonna be just as broke as minez."

I thought about it for a minute and then I nodded. Bunni was right. Gutta was on lock in an upstate prison, while psycho Punchie Collins was right outside lurking in the staircase and looking to sneak my ass. If running a little street hustle could bring in enough quick cash to dig myself outta the hole I had once again fallen into, then I was all for it.

"Okay," I said as Peaches looked at me and rolled his eyes in disgust. "I'm down. But you sure we can triple-flip our money real quick, right? I mean, your dude is on the up and up, word? You know him like that for real?"

Bunni yawned and nodded. "Yeah. I know him. We used to fuck back in the day. Trust me, Mink. All we gotta do is get him the cash and he'll deliver the product. We'll put our shit out there with a couple of corner boys who scramble uptown, and before you know it our pockets will be real knotty again."

"Cool," I said as I stared down at the letter I had just got out the mail from Gutta that morning. "The sooner your boy can hook us up, the better."

CHAPTER 6

Bunni had made contact with her boy named Light and we held a meeting in the stairwell of a project building down the block. He was a scary-lookin' yellow dude with light green eyes, and he sounded like a real killer when he laid down his rules.

"I'm telling you right now"—he pointed his finger in my face—"don't go jumping off in no water that's too deep, ya heard? You wanna play with the big boys and rake in the large bills? Then you gotta bone-up to the risks and pay ya fuckin' dues! Ain't no mercy out here on the streets, ladies. You gimme twenty-five racks and I'll give you enough shit to flip and make back fifty large in profit, dig? Now, you stick me for my product and I *promise* I'ma stick you in a garbage bag. But if you play this shit the right way there might be some opportunities for you to make even more in the future."

I turned my head and smirked at that one. I wasn't tryna become no female drug czar. All I wanted to do was make my money and get gone, but Bunni's eyes got real big when she heard the words *future opportunities* and I could tell she was already sold.

We turned over the cash and ol' boy told us where we

could pick up our product. He said his manz was already there waiting for us, and he even drew up a little sketch map so we would know which part of the warehouse to go to. I almost shit when we turned around to leave and he licked his lips and said in a low voice, "You know, y'all are two fine-ass bitches! A nigga like me don't usually fuck where he eat, but if I did, I'd take a quick go at both of y'all. Together. In a sandwich." His gleaming eyeballs turned the corner on our curvy hips as he tried to check for our bootys. He shook his head in delightful admiration. "Damn. I hate I'ma have to pass on all this good looking pussy, but it was nice meeting you jawns anyway."

"Nice *meeting* you?" I elbowed Bunni all in her liver as he got in his whip and pulled off. "What the fuck is he talking about nice *meeting* you? You said you *knew* this muthafucka! You said y'all used to *fuck*!"

Bunni had the stupid look on her face. "Naw, that ain't ex-actly what I said, Mink! I said I knew the dude who was down to make the deal with us. Me and *him* used to fuck. I think this guy is his cousin."

"His cousin? You *think*? You mean we just gave the last of our money to some nigga you used to bang's so-called *cousin*?"

"Um, yeah," Bunni said, looking even stupider in the face. "Pretty much."

The address Light had sent us to pick up our product at was in a warehouse on the Lower East Side of the city. I was scared as shit when we got there, and I kept praying he hadn't set us up to get knocked. Me and Bunni both looked right ridiculous in our designer shit and high-heel shoes as we crept up the rickety stairs and followed the map that ol' boy had sketched out for us.

"You go first," Bunni whispered as we stood outside a door that had a whole bunch of graffiti scrawled on it in different colors.

"Hell no!" I frowned and pushed her in front of me. "This was your idea, your fuckin' scheme, and *your* fuckin' friend!"

She turned around and gave me the evil eye.

"Uh-huh. But it's *your* fuckin' *money*, remember?"

Bunni smirked, then crossed her arms and backed up until she was leaning up against the wall. She wasn't about to move another muscle. I could see it all in her face. I was mad as hell, but since my money was on the line I had no choice but to open that door and go through with our plan.

I took a deep breath and twisted the knob, then pushed the door open. A rush of foul, musty air flew up my nose. I squinted into the darkened room. The first thing I saw was a whole bunch of wooden crates stacked up real high.

The second thing I saw was big-nose Moolah Jenkins, one of my childhood enemies. Moolah slang dope for Punchie Collins, and my heart banged at the sight of him swigging from a naked bottle of Old English malt liquor.

"Sup, Stink Mink! I knew I smelled something rotten up in here! Why you looking so surprised to see me, mami?"

"What's up, Moolah," I said suspiciously. "What the hell are you doing here?"

"Oh, I'm doing what I do best, shawty. I'm representing for my boss, bitch!"

And that would be scary Punchie. A tight knot of fear swelled in my stomach.

"Look, we ain't in the third grade no goddamn more," I barked on him. "Me and Punchie might got us some bizz we need to handle, but that ain't got nothing to do with you. It's between me and him."

"Oh, Cool P already know how you do bizz, baby. You said you was gonna hook him up, right, Mink?" Moolah took a swig from his Old E and laughed real loud and crazy. "Yeah, I know, I know. Check this out." He put one hand on his hip, stuck out his butt, twisted up his lips, and started imitating me in a high-pitched voice. "I got you, Punchie!" he said, walking back and forth and switching his skinny booty the same way I switched mine. "I'ma tear you off *proper*! I'ma take real good care of you, boo!" He shot me a thumbs-up sign and winked.

"Come on now, Moolah, baby." Bunni came to my rescue and tried to help me out. She shimmied up on her crazy-ass neighbor and made sure he got a good look at her stank camel toe. For somebody who was just acting real damn scary on the other side of the door, Bunni sounded swole and in control right now. "Fuck Punchie!" Bunni talked that shit. "Mink ain't been ducking no damn Punchie! She just had a little cash-flow problem, that's all. She's still gonna take care of him. Right now she's tryna handle her business so she can hook him up with a little extra when her ends get right. That's what's up."

"When her ends get right?" Moolah quit grinning and exploded. He grilled us like he wanted to smash our foreheads in with his beer bottle. "Y'all bitches been flossin' all over town in a stretch fuckin' limo! Ya driver prolly got a fuckin' hernia tryna carry all ya packages up the stairs! Oh yeah." He laughed. "I got ya fuckin' cash-flow problem, baby!" Moolah clapped his hands and bent over, cracking the hell up. "While you busy looking for ya lil connect, all your product done flowed right outta your pockets and straight into minez!"

"What?" I said as he kept right on laughing. I didn't see shit funny, and I didn't like the way that fool was looking at me neither. Like he was a slick rat that had just swallowed a fat hunk of cheese. "Where's the dude who was supposed to meet us up in here? You tryna say you got my package, Moolah?" I shrieked over his loud-ass laughter. I licked my lips and glanced at Bunni in a panic. "Girl what the fuck is this nigga talking about?"

"I'm talking about your grimy-ass getting *jacked*, bitch!" Moolah barked. "The same way you was catching our customers on the stairs and collecting our cash? Well I just caught your connect and collected on your ass too!"

"*Moolah!* You stole my product?"

"Uh-huh," he said, chuckling. "About fifty bills worth, baby."

My whole face broke apart as tears sprang to my eyes. "Uh-uh, Moolah. Don't do that. You know that shit ain't right. We was about to flip that. Lemme talk to Punchie and get this shit straight. All I owe him is a grand or two at the most. How y'all niggas gonna beat me outta a whole fifty large?"

"What the fuck?" Moolah smirked. "I'm supposed to feel sorry for your silly ass or something? Didn't my boy Light explain this shit to you? There ain't no mercy in this game!"

"But I was gonna turn that money over to pay Gutta!"

"*Fuck* Gutta! That nigga ain't no real G! If he don't know how to handle a trickster like you then he deserves to get ganked! You got a lotta shit to learn, so welcome to the game, Miss Stink Ass! Now, I'ma hit you with some real good advice so don't say I ain't never gave you nothing okay? Pay attention, shit head. The first rule of the drug hustle is, *don't trust nobody you don't know!*"

I stared at that fool and his eyes were glistening with laughter and glee.

"Guess what the second rule is?"

Like I gave a damn! I wanted to smash that nigga and I wasn't about to play no guessing games with him.

"What is it?" Bunni bust out and asked over my shoulder.

Moolah laughed even louder. "The second rule is, don't trust nobody you *do* know neither!"

I had a headache that just wouldn't quit.

"For real, Mink, I'm sorry," Bunni said as I laid on the couch with a frozen bag of jumbo shrimp pressed to my throbbing dome. "Come on now, damn! How many times do I gotta say I'm sorry?"

I closed my eyes and ignored her ass. Gutta was gonna be home real soon and my head had been hurting like hell every day. I was so mad behind big-nose Moolah's thievery that I wanted to kill his ass. But on the real, what was I gonna do about it, huh? I mean, I couldn't just call the cops and tell 'em that Moolah had ganked me out of a package I was planning to flip, and I damn sure couldn't roll up in the projects and tell my cousins to catch Moolah and take my cash outta his ass neither. Hell no. I could see that scenario now. I would have to do a whole lotta 'splaining about how I had walked up on twenty-five g's to buy drugs in the first damn place, and knowing my corrupt family they would end up tryna shake me down for the last few little dollars I had left.

I didn't know what to do or where to turn. All I knew is that once Gutta rolled into Harlem my ass wasn't gonna have too much longer to live.

"Mink!" Bunni called my name real loud. "Did you hear me? I said I'm sorry! Damn! I don't know what else to say, girl. I'm sorry."

I was mad as hell at Bunni on the real, but deep inside I knew it wasn't all her fault. There was no way I shoulda agreed to dip in Gutta's stash in the first place. Peaches had tried to warn me about letting all that money run through my hands like water, but my ass had been burning up with a fever. All that cheddar had me high as hell. I had been straight outta control, floating on a cloud of endless green, and no matter what Peaches said, I had been too stupid and too damn greedy to even try to come down.

"Mink," Bunni said slowly, and as I hid behind my icy pack of shrimp, all I could wonder was why this chick was still blabbing in my ear. "I know you probably don't wanna hear this but . . ."

I turned over and groaned. She had that shit right. Whatever it was that was about to roll outta Bunni's mouth, I didn't wanna hear it.

"Girlfriend, my left titty is *itchin'*."

I jumped up and flung that bag of shrimp dead in her grill.

"Bunita fuckin' Baines! If you don't get your nasty-ass, rashy-tash, itchin' little ball of a titty up outta my face . . ."

"But it's a sign, Mink!" she protested. "Some kinda signal-sign! Girl you know when my titty itches it's tryna tell me something!"

"Uh-uh. I don't know shit about no paranormal titty signs, Bunni! All I know is that my ass is about to get murked because *you* trusted a fool with my money, and *I* trusted *you*!"

"I was just tryna *help* your ass, Mink! All my money is gone too, and you don't see me whining and bitching and dragging my ass all over the floor about it! Damn, girl. This ain't the first time we been broke. I can feel it, Mink. For real. My left titty ain't never led me wrong yet. Something good is gonna happen for us, girlfriend. I know it will."

I plopped back down on the couch and slapped a pillow over my face. I hated to admit it, but Bunni was right. We had been way broker than this before. At least I still had a couple of dollars left. I could at least buy Gutta some fresh sneakers and gear and put a few ends in his pocket. Thank God for that!

"On the real, girl. I got a feeling," Bunni insisted. "Something real good is about to happen."

"Yeah, okay." I sucked my teeth and tried to stay mad even though Bunni had the slickest con game in Harlem, and just the thought of a good gank was starting to give me a rush. "Something real damn good better happen real damn quick, Bunni. It sure as hell better."

CHAPTER 7

It was a hot, rainy day in Texas and the light mist of water falling from the sky turned into steam as soon as it bounced off the pavement. "A'ight," Barron said as him and Pilar rode in the backseat of a champagne-colored Rolls-Royce. They'd just had lunch at an exclusive Italian restaurant in Dallas, where Barron had been called away from his baked ziti by one of Viceroy's neurologists, who was checking in to update him on his father's condition. Viceroy seemed to be getting a little bit worse every day, and Barron was almost at the point where he hated taking the doctors' calls.

Flashing Pilar a quick grin, he flipped open a folder and took out a few sheets of paper. "I got an email from a dude named Dutchy Gaines today. He's a private investigator from Harlem who's itchin' to take the job."

"How did you find him?" Pilar asked as she sat beside him smelling delicious and looking right luscious with her sexy legs crossed at the knee.

"One of my frats from college put me on to him. He said dude's whole family works in law enforcement. Dutchy is a probation officer who recently started his own PI firm."

"Oh really?"

Barron nodded. "Yeah. It looks like he's pretty good, too. He's been finding all kinds of muddy footprints that Mink left behind, and he said I might wanna take a quick trip to New York so we can go over a few things in person."

Pilar sat up straighter and a look of excitement flashed in her gray eyes. "So, are you gonna go? I think you should. I mean, you never know what kind of devastating information might be out there on her. You said this guy Dutchy is supposed to be good, right? Well, if he's following Mink's footprints then they'll probably lead him straight to a garbage dump. I think you should go, Barron. I really think you should go."

A sexy look entered his eyes. "Ay, wassup? I thought you wanted to be with me all the time? You trying to get rid of me now, or what?"

"Oh, you know better than that," Pilar joked, and then she leaned over and laid her head on his shoulder. She slid her hand up his thigh and let it fall on his crotch. Sighing softly, she massaged his dick until it started to rise. Inching his zipper down, she inserted her fingers through the front hole of his boxers and stroked his thickening shaft.

Barron gripped her slim shoulders. He clenched his ass cheeks and thrust his pelvis toward her. He breathed deeply through his nose and slowly out of his mouth.

"Yo, roll the window up, Charlie," he instructed his driver. The smoked panel of glass that separated the Rolls' front seat from the rear compartment slid up noiselessly. And as soon as it did, Pilar went to work.

With her cheek resting on Barron's chest, she slid his monster out of his pants and held it in her hand like it was her favorite pet. It was big, black, and beautiful and it stood straight in the air. Pilar gently fisted it, then let her palm glide up and down its length, masturbating him like an expert while he moaned and fucked up at her.

"Ahhh, shit," Barron muttered as he flung his head back and pumped his hips.

As they sped down the highway with the sound of rushing traffic in their ears, Pilar stuck out her tongue and licked the tip of Barron's dick. She loved the way he tasted. The way his balls smelled. She sucked a sweet glob of cum from the head and gathered it around in her mouth before swallowing it with joy.

Barron reached for her breast and fingered her nipple into a pebble. He squeezed her firm flesh in his hand, and then palmed the back of her head and urged her to go lower, to take his dick and even his balls inside the warm wetness of her mouth.

"Baby . . ." he whimpered as her head bobbed in his lap. "You sure know how to suck some good dick," he praised her. *Damn right,* Pilar thought as she felt sparks shoot off deep inside her pussy. She grunted as her head jutted up and down and a trail of saliva dribbled from her bottom lip. "Yeah, you can suck some damn good dick!"

Pilar was trying to suck that dick morning, noon, and night. Hell, once Barron put a ring on her finger she would slob on his knob multiple times a day if he wanted her to.

Determined to get him hooked, she moved in double-time now. Pilar jacked and licked, then tightened her lips and blew that dick until her cheeks collapsed and she felt the head swell up in the back of her throat. And then she hummed on that baby like she was about to break out in a song.

But Barron was the one who started singing as he banged up in her throat and his balls clenched and felt heavier than two giant stones.

"Oh, yeah!" he urged her into deeper, longer strokes as the wet fire in her mouth set a tornado swirling through his nuts and straight up in his bone. Pilar was giving up that wet-neck, and that shit felt so, so damn good. "Gimme that pussy," Barron started chanting to the beat of his thrusts. "Gimme that . . . gimme that . . . gimme that good-ass neck pussy dammit!"

Pilar let the head of his dick slip past the trapdoor in her throat, and then she clenched down on it like she was trying to swallow. The soft, hot pressure on his tip sent Barron over the edge, and he slammed her head with his palm, then cried out as a powerful jet of cum spurted up from his balls and splashed straight down Pilar's throat.

"Ayghgagyhhh!" he cried out as his orgasm sent the nerves in his dick and his toes into overdrive. He held Pilar's head tightly in place as endless streams of hot liquid pulsed out of his jerking dick and filled her still-sucking mouth.

Pilar's lips trembled as she struggled to keep them gripped around his slowly shrinking dick. As Barron ran his fingers through her hair and massaged the back of her neck, she swallowed the warm semen in her mouth and gently squeezed his balls.

"That was good, baby," he said when she finally sat up. Gazing into her sexy gray eyes, Barron reached out and caressed the side of her face. "That was real, real good."

Pilar flashed him a smile and reached for her purse. "If you play your cards right, it can get even better than that," she told him smoothly as she rubbed lip gloss on her perfectly shaped lips. "Stick with me, Bump, because it can get way better than that."

I was crashed the hell out in my panties and bra, sprawled flat on my stomach and snoring my ass off, when outta the darkness something heavy landed square on my back and pinned me down on the bed. *Ouch!* Pain exploded behind my eyes as my ponytail got yanked and my head snapped back on my neck. Something cold and hard dug into my neck, right under my jawbone.

"Whaaa?" I opened my eyes and stammered in the pitch blackness of my room. I had spent the whole night getting my drank on down at Club Wood, and for the last two hours I had been lost in dreamland and slobbering puddles of leftover Erk and Jerk on my extra-plush pillow.

"Uh-huh, *bitch*," a cold, deranged voice muttered in my ear as rough fingers slid around to my throat and squeezed. "I got yo slick ass now! Who the *fuck* you thought you was runnin' game on, Mink? What? You thought I was one of them ol' *la-dee-da* niggas you be frontin' off in the streets, right?"

He was straddling my hips. Rough-riding my ass. Trapped under his weight, I broke out in a cold sweat as my windpipe was crushed and the name *Punchie Collins* exploded in my brain.

My skin got clammy. It was burning the hell up in that room. New York City was smack in the middle of a scorching-hot heat wave, and since me and Bunni was late on the electric bill I had left the window open so I could catch a little piece of the late-night breeze. But instead of a cool breeze slipping in my window, that crazy-ass Punchie Collins had pulled a straight-up cat burglar move on me. That psycho fool had crept up the fire escape and caught me sleeping, and I gagged like hell as he sat on my booty and choked the shit outta me.

"Don't *no* fuckin' body play Punchie and get away with that shit!" he growled in my ear and dug his fingers all up in the meat of my throat. "I want my *paper*, bitch!" He smushed my head in with the butt of his SIG. "And I want that shit rat' fuckin' *now*!"

"Wa-wa-wait!" I hollered, tryna stall him. I was caught out there all by myself. Peaches and Bunni had dipped to DC to visit their aunt, and I gasped and clawed at Punchie's rock-hard hand as I tried to buy myself some room to breathe.

"Hold up, P-P-Punchie, *wait*! Your boy Moolah already got me for my product, boo. I paid twenty-five large for a package and that fool stuck me up! Yo Moolah *got* me!"

That nigga igged me and swung his gat from way down in Alabama. He cracked me in the dome hard enough to make a thirty-man drum line boom in my head. A trickle of blood splashed from my temple and rolled down into my eyes. He mushed my face deeper into the pillow and laughed again.

"You must think I'm some kinda fuckin' sherm, huh, Mink?" He started bouncing up and down on my ass like he was riding a pony. "I oughtta fuck the shit outta you! I oughtta shoot you right in ya stank pussy! I oughtta give you some of this big black dick you been wantin'!"

"But Moolah got meeee . . ." I hollered all in my pillow as that nigga cracked my tailbone under his weight and bitch-slapped me upside my head with his tool over and over again. Even above the sound of the gun splitting my skull I could still hear Peaches' voice in my head warning me about the dangers of gankin' a throwed-off drug-slanga like Punchie:

You better watch yourself, Mink! You fucked with Punchie's money and he ain't going away, you know. I tried to tell you and Bunni that lil "catch-a-crackhead" scam was way too risky, but y'all just didn't wanna listen.

Peaches ain't never lied. Punchie was a fool for real. This dude was bent. Straight-up mental. I could feel the crazy rolling offa him and I knew he had snuck in my window to do way more than just ride my ass.

Something told me I was gonna have to scheme my way outta this trouble. If begging for mercy woulda made Punchie raise up offa me I woulda begged my sweet ass off, but Punchie wasn't the forgiving type and mercy wasn't in this nigga's nature. It wasn't even about the money with him no more. It was about giving him his propers and maintaining his street cred, and whether Moolah had given him the package I had dropped twenty-five large on or not, this nigga was fixin' to straight-up slump me. Yeah, by the time Peaches and Bunni got back home my cold body was gonna be stretched out right on this rickety little cot, and Punchie Collins wasn't gonna be nowhere to be found.

I cringed as the butt of his tool kept raining down on me fast and furious. "I should go up in your ass," he bitched some more. He gripped my hip with one hand and started grinding and humping on my half-naked booty real hard. "*Yeah!* Uh!

Uh! I should run my dick straight up your big donkey-donk ass!"

He started popping his hips, rubbing his crotch all over my ass, and then he got to gun-busting me again. "Slick *bitch!* You round here shoppin' "—*whack!*—"and stuntin' "—*whack!*— "and flossin' in limos and tossin' mad paper in the gutta." *Whack!* He pounded me. "Fuck my nigga Moolah gettin' you! This *me!* I know you got some more bank on you! I know there's a whole lot more where you got that shit from! Now WHERE THE FUCK IS IT?"

"Okay!" I yelled as he pistol-whipped the hell outta me. I pressed my nose into the pillow and tried to cover both sides of my face with my hands. Punchie might break my fingers and dent my skull, but this nigga wasn't about to fuck up my mug if I could help it. *Don't fuck up my face,* I screamed inside as he beat me.

"Okay, I'll give it to you!" I shrieked. "You can have it, Punchie! Whatever I got left you can have that shit!"

That maniac went completely still. "Well where it at, then?"

I knew I had fucked up the moment the words flew outta my mouth. For a second I started to tell Punchie to just continue on cracking my dome because all I had left was about five measly grand, and I was planning on laying that and some kinda bullshit sob story on Gutta when he got out. *Shiiit,* I was so scared of what that monster was gonna do when he found out I had spent his money that I woulda *much* rather let Punchie beat me to death than face Gutta empty-handed when he got sprung up outta the joint. Hell no. Death by Punchie would be way better than death by Gutta!

But all that whacking musta scrambled my brains 'cause suddenly I heard myself blurt out, "It's in the safe! Let me up and I'll open it!"

Punchie scrambled offa me in two seconds flat, and I cried out with relief as the crunched-in bones of my lower back

snapped back in place. I rolled over and fell off the bed, land-
ing hard on the floor at his feet. That idiot dug deep into my
ribs with the thick toe of his boot and barked on me again.

"Where's the fuckin' safe, bitch?"

"Under the bed," I squeaked and wiped a dribble of blood
off my chin. "I'm getting it, Punchie, *damn*! I'm getting it!"

I scooted forward on my knees and crawled halfway under
the bed, wishing like hell my ass had a loaded gat stashed under
there. I woulda cocked that shit and fired right through the
raggedy foldout cot and blasted Punchie's monkey-ass straight
to hell!

But instead, I pulled out the small safe that Gutta had left
with me before he got knocked. Now that it was almost empty
it wasn't all that heavy, and it had a round dial on the front that
I fumbled with in the darkness.

"I can't fuckin' see," I complained as blood trickled from
the gash he'd opened up in my hairline and dripped into my
eye.

I heard him move toward the doorway where the light
switch was, and flip it up and down a couple of times.

"Yo wuttup with the goddamn lights?" he demanded
when they didn't come on.

"They cut off. We ain't paid the bill yet."

"Trifling bitches!" Punchie cursed in the darkness. "You
mean y'all three bitches got two stank pussies and one hairy
asshole farting up in here and can't nobody turn enough tricks
to keep the lights on?" I heard him snort with contempt.
"Skank-ass gorillas! Last week you and Bunni was cruising
around in a limo flossin' like you was fly. And this week your
shit is cut off and you walking around in the dark! Stupid
bitches!"

Punchie stuck his gun down in his pants and pulled out his
cell phone. He clicked on a flashlight app and then crouched
down beside me and pointed the beam at the safe's silver dial.

"Spin that shit," he demanded as he pulled his gat out again and pressed the tip right under my ear. I glanced up and saw the outline of his face in the cell phone's back glow. Sweat dripped from his chin and craziness darkened his eyes. "You got ten seconds, bitch, or I'ma start poppin'. Get it open."

My hands was sweating like a mutha as I turned the dial nervously. Numbers had never been my thing, and right now I was so damn shook I could barely remember my own name.

Twenty-one to the right, thirteen to the left, and eighty-seven back to the right, I spun.

Nah, hold up, I corrected myself. It was twelve, thirty-one, seventy-eight. I jiggled the handle.

That shit didn't work either.

"Biiitch . . ." Punchie growled.

Thirteen, seventy-eight, twenty-one!

I heard a click and the shit popped open!

I reached inside the safe and closed my hand around the small stack of crisp bills. I knew better than to let Punchie peep the last of my stash, so I skimmed two grand off the top and held it up in the air for him to see.

"Here, goddammit!" I shouted. "Two racks! This all I got left! Y'all niggas done already beat me outta a gwap! So take it, niggah! Take it and get the fuck outta here, Punchie!"

At first I thought I had shut his ass down with my little two grand in cash, but there was an evil glint glistening in Punchie's eyes as he pointed his flashlight, crooked his neck, and tried to swing his eyeballs all up inside Gutta's safe.

"Yo, what else you got up in there, girl?"

"None a' ya damn bizz!" I snapped and tried to slam the door real fast, but Punchie's greedy hands were much quicker than mine. He reached out and swatted the safe and tipped it over, sending the last little bit of my cash scattering out on the floor.

For a split second we both froze.

And then we dove. Me first, and then Punchie's big ass landed right on my back.

"Get the fuck offa me!" I screamed and covered the scattered bills with my sweaty, half-naked body. "This is *Gutta's* shit!" I shrieked and flattened myself out like a pancake as Punchie tried to slide his hands between me and the floor and snatch up as many bills as he could. "This all I got!" I fought hard as hell tryna protect the last of my dough. "Get the fuck outta here, nigga! Y'all already stole me!"

Truly, I didn't have no wins over big Punchie Collins. That nigga stood up and grabbed me by my ankle, then dragged my ass across the room caveman style.

"Punchie, *nooo*!" I shrieked into the floor as he stomped back over toward the bed and headed for the scattered greenbacks on the floor. "Asshole I'm tellin' you that's *Gutta's* money! That nigga's coming home in a minute, and when I tell him you stole on him he's gonna *fuck you up*!"

"Nah." That fool laughed, and I could hear him scooping up my last few hundred-dollar bills off the floor. "Gutta's gonna fuck *you* up, Mink. Neither one of y'all don't deserve this stash no fuckin' way. Gutta shoulda known not to trust a sexy little liar like you, and you shoulda known not to fuck over a G like me." He flicked off the light coming from his phone and once again the room was pitch black. "Yeah, fuck Gutta," Punchie said and cracked up laughing. "That nigga been in the joint lickin' balls for a whole year. He bring his ass out here making any noise and I'ma make him lick minez."

"Punchie." I sat up in the darkness and begged in a soft voice. "Please don't do me like this." Closing my eyes, I leaned against the wall and pulled my knees up to my chest. I pressed my fingers to my temple, and even though I wasn't bleeding no more my head was still bangin' like a mutha.

"Look, that's my last bit of money, Punchie. My *last*. And if I don't have at least a lil sumthin' waiting for Gutta that fool is gonna kill me. For real. I'll tear you off something better than money, okay? Fuck it. I'll give you something you really, *really* want. Something you been wanting for a long, long time. Just gimme my fuckin' money back, Punchie. Gimme my money back and I'll let you eat my pussy out, okay? Okay? OKAY?"

Punchie didn't even answer. And when I opened my eyes and saw the white curtain flapping in the window, I knew why.

That nigga had dipped. And he'd taken every dime of my money with him.

I sat there trembling and defeated. I had been caught up in some pretty fucked-up misadventures in my life, but this shit right here was about to bake the cake. I wished like *hell* I could put my life on rewind. If I coulda, I woulda took back every dime I had thrown away on senseless bullshit since me and Bunni had brought our happy asses back home from Texas. If I coulda, I woulda hit all those hot nightclubs and fancy designer stores, and gave back all the stupid clothes, fancy jewelry, expensive liquor, and designer drugs that I had blown my once-in-a-lifetime hundred-thousand-dollar inheritance on!

Hell yeah! If only I coulda, I most definitely woulda!

Once again my ass was damn near broke.

Gutta was gonna be back on the streets real soon, and I had sat up racking my brain all night wondering exactly how that maniac was gonna serve me. I had thought about hiding out at my conniving grandmother's house, or with one of my crazy aunts who lived in the projects, but I didn't trust none of them trifling LaRues to look out for me. Shit, they had never liked me anyway, and all Gutta had to do was toss a twenty-dollar bill up in the air and every last one of them woulda squealed on my ass before the money could hit the ground. And that went for Granny's scandalous ass too.

Fear was gnawing at me all down in my bones, and it kept me frozen like a cockroach caught under a bright light. I didn't know if Gutta was gonna shoot me, slit my throat, or choke me out until I took my last breath, but I knew he was gonna do me. I knew that shit for sure.

I had already written out my obituary and picked out my funeral gear. It was a powder blue sequined mini-dress with fluffy blue feathers around the plunging, low-cut neckline. It was short enough to show off my banging banana legs, and I had a sweet page-boy-style Glama-Glo deluxe wig with powder blue and silver-streaked bangs that went perfectly with it. I was sitting with my feet propped up on the coffee table while Peaches polished my toenails in the exact same shade of blue, when my cell phone buzzed and a number with an 817 area code popped up on my screen.

"Dane!" I hollered as soon as I answered the phone. "What's good in your hood, big brother?"

In a flash, Bunni was all up in my face jumping up and down. "He wanna talk to me, right? Uh-huh, his fine Domino ass is tryna holla, ain't he?"

"Hell no he ain't!" I said, laughing as I pressed the phone to my chest so Dane wouldn't hear me. "If he wanted to holla at your stank ass he woulda called *you* and not *me*!"

I was kinda happy to be getting a call from Texas. Dane was the second-oldest boy in the Dominion family, and me and him was real cool. He was one of them laid-back college boys and he could rap his ass off, and me and Bunni had spent many nights getting lifted off his trees and tips off his liq. Dane's style was usually smooth with just a thin layer of street grime on it, but right now his easygoing voice sounded kinda pressed out coming through my telephone line.

"I'm good, baby. Chillin'. But Pops ain't doing so hot," Dane said. "He got real sick again right after you left town. It's been pretty touch and go with him ever since then, but the hospital called this morning and said he just took a big turn for the worst and he definitely won't be running the company anymore. Hell, he can't even communicate with us no more.

The whole family is about to hop on the jet and get down to Houston, and I just thought you should know."

"Oh my goodness," I said forcing a rush of fake sympathy into my voice. I didn't give a damn about Viceroy Dominion! That rich old man scared the shit outta me with his one-eye self. Viceroy had been drifting in and out of a coma for months now, and when I had visited him in the hospital with my play-mother Selah, I felt like that old hustler had put his one good eye on me and seen right through my pretty smile and straight into the heart of my devious grind.

"I'm real sorry to hear that," I told Dane. "How's your mo—" I clamped my teeth down on my stupid tongue. "I mean, how's Mama Selah doing? Is she holding up okay? I been meaning to call her and stuff . . ."

"Mama's hanging in there. You know how she is. Always trying to make things work out for the best. But I'm telling you, Mink. You might wanna think about coming back down here real quick. The shit is about to hit the fan, baby. Barron is tryna make some real grimy power moves. He's about to call a board meeting so he can take over Dominion Oil. And you know what that means."

"Uh-uh, Dane." I shook my head. I didn't understand none of that oil board stuff and I didn't want to. If it didn't involve some money greasing up my pockets then it didn't have shit to do with me, and I didn't wanna have shit to do with it neither. "You know I love me some Uncle Suge," I told Dane, "and you's a real chill nigga too. But I can't come back down there right now. It ain't nothin' personal, but Texas just ain't my bag."

Shit, Texas was way too damn hot, and for a New York City slicksta like me Dallas was way too slow. What I really wanted to tell Dane's ass was that the only way those Dominions was getting me back down there is if they were willing to drop another hundred grand in my bank account so I could pay Gutta off and save my damn life.

"Oh, so Texas ain't your bag?" Dane asked with a chuckle. "Not even if it means you'll get Sable's share of our multimillion-dollar trust fund?"

Cha-ching! My eyeballs had mad dollar signs stamped on them as they rolled around like little pinballs in my head.

"You mean that trust fund thing is back on the table?" I blurted out. "That's the three-hunnerd-grand hustle, right? I thought y'all said we had to wait until your father was dead and buried before we could get our hands on some of that?"

"Pops has to be dead or declared permanently incapacitated, and that's why Barron is calling for a meeting. Pops is sliding and sliding fast. If his doctors say he can't understand what's going on around him, or he can't think straight enough to handle his own affairs, then our trust fund gets activated and Barron steps in and takes over the company."

"Barron?" I twisted my lips. I couldn't stand his ass! "Why does he always get to make all the damn decisions?"

"Because," Dane said simply. "He's the oldest. He knows the oil bizz better than everybody else besides my father, and he's gonna do everything in his power to make sure we don't lose a dime of what Pops worked so hard to build."

"Well ain't no need in me coming, then," I told him in a huff. "Because there ain't no way in hell your brother is gonna give up a dime when it comes down to me."

"He doesn't have to give it up, Mink. You're already entitled to it. You passed a DNA test, remember? That trust fund belongs to every last one of us, and that includes you. But the way Bump is trippin' we all might get fucked. We might not see a dime of that money if he gets in there and convinces the board to let him change the trust's terms. Barron has all of Pop's old friends in his pocket, and believe me, he's gonna try to short us. Me and Uncle Suge got a few things on the burner, though. We're tryna to stack us a heavy team so we can vote against Barron and make sure he doesn't fuck us outta our money."

"So what do y'all need me to do?"

"We need you to vote with us, Mink. We're about to get Jock and a few other board members on our side. But we need your vote too, nah'mean?"

I was trying real hard to understand. "And all this voting stuff is so we can get that three hunnerd grand every year, right?"

"Damn right," Dane said. "*Every* goddamn year. Now you can stay up there in New York and let Bump pocket your share of the family's cash, or you can bring your ass back down here to Dallas and help me and Uncle Suge get you a slice of that sweet green pie. Either way, you got a decision to make."

CHAPTER 8

Decisions, decisions, *decisions!*

Me and Bunni damn near broke our necks tossing shit into our designer suitcases as we beat feet outta Harlem. Once again Peaches had come up outta his bra to give us some money, and as hardheaded as I had been I was almost ashamed to take it. But I did. I bought us the last two seats on a red-eye flight outta JFK that was stopping all over the damn place before it finally landed in Texas, but we didn't care. We coulda had a layover in West hell someplace, but were gonna have our butts on that flight regardless.

"Slow the hell down, girl!" I fussed as Bunni stuffed her clothes all down in the corners of her suitcase. "Luggage don't fly for free no more you know, so we can only take one bag each this time, okay?"

Bunni stared at me like I was tryna sell her some bad crack. "One bag? Mink how the hell we gonna fit all our stuff into one bag? You got more gear than me, so tell me how the hell we gonna do that?"

"Easy. All we gotta do is pack real light. We only take the stuff we really, really need."

"I don't know about you and your stuff," Bunni said as she

dragged another suitcase out from under her bed, "but I needs all minez, okay?"

"Uh-uh, Bunni! We ain't getting outta no taxicab lugging thirty suitcases behind us like we did the last time we went down there! We're part of the family now, so let's roll up in that mansion like we got some sense this time. Whatever we don't take with us, we can shop for when we get there. Remember, the Dominions got accounts at all the fly malls, and as long as I sign my name on the account we get to buy anything we want, okay?"

I could tell Bunni wasn't cool with leaving none of her outfits behind, but she had no choice but to go along with my program. I picked through my stuff and chose only my very best gear to take with me, and I made sure I had the right accessories to match every single stitch too. I packed my wigs in a separate carry-on bag and stuffed about ten pairs of cute summer shoes in there too.

Peaches had borrowed his friend's car to take us to the airport, and since our flight wasn't leaving until late that night and we had plenty of time to kill during the afternoon, I asked him to give me a ride to the nursing home where my mother lived. I couldn't stand hospitals, and just thinking about going up in one had my head in a bad space. Wasn't nothing good or glamorous about a place where sick people laid around waiting to die, and visiting my mama here was always a mood buster for me.

I had ditched all my makeup and I looked real regular as I jumped in the car with Peaches. There was absolutely no designer labels on my ass today. I had on a pair of navy blue sweats and a plain white T-shirt. Instead of my usual six-inch fuck-me pumps, I had slid my feet in a pair of regular old Nikes. I had ditched my Glama-Glo too. There wasn't no reason to plop no outrageous wig on my head and make my scalp get all sweaty. Instead I styled my own hair, and brushed it down my back in soft shiny curls.

I had been coming to the nursing home to see Mama for a long time, but no matter how many times I visited I would never get used to seeing her looking so hopeless or helpless. I was only thirteen when my mother got up one morning and drove her car straight into the Hudson River. She had been trapped in her seat belt under all that cold water, and by the time a bunch of strangers were able to pull her out she had gone without oxygen too long and she suffered some brain damage. My aunts and cousins liked to talk a lotta shit and say Mama had brought her situation down on herself, but I wasn't tryna hear none of their high-and-mighty project blab. Who the hell was they to judge her, and where the hell was they when she was down in the gutter and coulda used a little help?

"You straight?" Peaches asked as he stopped the car and let me out near the front door of the rickety old nursing home. "I ain't gonna have to come in there and put my foot up nobody's ass, am I?"

I smiled and shook my head. "Nah," I said softly. "I'ma be good today."

Back in the day I used to raise all kinds of hell every time I went to the nursing home to see my mother. I didn't give a damn what Jude Jackson had done, or why she had ended up all twisted up in that bed the way she was, she was still my mama and I couldn't stand to see her being disrespected and ignored by the workers who got paid by the state to take care of her. It used to fuck my heart up to have to pull off her nightgown and change her grown-woman diaper while she cried and looked embarrassed, and the only way I knew to express the helpless rage I was feeling was to get all loud and start a knockdown drag-out fight with one of her attendants.

But I was past all that useless fighting now. Mama's care was something that I couldn't do a damn thing about, and even though I still wrote letters to the state sometimes and I barked on the staff when I needed to, for the most part I had learned to roll with it and hope for the best.

But there was some different kind of shit waiting for me at the nursing home today, and I got the shock of my life when I came around the corner and walked into Mama's room.

"What the . . ." I muttered under my breath as I froze in the doorway. My mother had company. In the eight damn years that she had been laying up in here I could count the number of visitors she'd had on three damn fingers, and when I saw this chick sitting on the side of Mama's bed and brushing her hair it messed me up and sent hot sauce shooting through my veins.

"What the hell are you doing here?" I spit as the light-skinned woman with the buzzed stud haircut and the plaid dress shirt leaned over Mama and wiped some dribble from the corner of her mouth.

"Sup, Mink," my aunt Bibby LaRue said real casually, like me and her had just been hanging out together yesterday. She was my father's favorite sister, and the last time I'd seen her was four years ago when the cops was dragging her manly ass off to jail. "How you doing, baby?"

"Don't worry about how I'm doin'," I snapped. I knew my moms and Aunt Bibby had been real tight back when I was younger, but after my father died all of that had changed.

I walked up on her real close. "Why you up in here alone with my mother?"

She glanced at me. "What you tryna say? Jude is my friend. I can't come see her?"

"You ain't *been* coming."

I was posted up ready to defend my mama with my last damn breath. And I needed to be too, because Aunt Bibby was cutthroat and would pop off on your ass in a Harlem minute. Back in the day she was known to be good with a straight razor. She had carved up plenty niggas on the streets of Manhattan, and right now she looked kinda aggravated, like she was tryna keep herself from getting slick with me. But instead of jumpin' funky, all Aunt Bibby did was grill me a little bit.

Like I was still some kinda child she could whip with an extension cord, or a roach that she could smash with her house shoe.

I grilled her right back. I wasn't scared of Aunt Bibby but I didn't trust her ass neither, and just like the rest of Harlem's "Bad News LaRues" I didn't want her hanging around my mother. At least ten of my aunts, uncles, and cousins still lived in a three-bedroom project apartment with my grandmother, and every last one of them grimy fools had blamed my mother for causing my father's death.

Aunt Bibby shrugged. "I just got out the joint not too long ago and I wanted to see Jude," she said. "That's all."

"You wanted to see her for *what*?"

Even though my lip was poked out I couldn't help but notice how much the two of us favored. We had the same light complexion, the same soft hair, the same big smile and the same hazel eyes. It was a LaRue thing. We got our looks from my grandmother, except most of the females in our family were shaped up like wide-bottom Coke bottles, and Aunt Bibby and all the dudes were big and tall and built like battleships.

"Chill out, little girl." Aunt Bibby shrugged her man shoulders. "Mama told me Jude be laying up in here by herself all the time. I just figured somebody should come by and check on her."

"I don't know how Granny told you that lie," I said, swelling up as I stepped to her, "because I'm *always* up here checking on my mother!" I didn't give a damn how many niggas Aunt Bibby had carved up on the streets! She didn't put no fear in my heart and I was ready to get at her mannish ass when it came down to my mom-ski!

"Oh yeah?" she said like I was just a barking lil pup. "Well that ain't what I heard."

"Well you heard wrong then! My mother don't need none

of y'all to do shit for her! Ain't none of y'all *been* coming around to see her, so I don't know why you all of a sudden coming up in here *now*."

"Like I said, I just got out the joint and I wanted to show some love to Jude," my aunt said calmly. "I been knowing your mother for a long time, Mink. We was friends long before you showed up on the scene. Me and Jude go way back, and there's a lotta shit I could hip you to if you wasn't so damn grown and hardheaded and quick with your goddamn mouth."

She looked at me like she wanted to backhand me, and then she shook her ugly bald head. "Shit, I know stuff you would pay good money to find out."

I smirked and fronted her off. "You don't know a damn thing about me, Aunt Bibby. And even if you did, there ain't nothing I need you or anybody else to tell me about my mother, okay? Y'all turned your backs on us when she had her accident and every last one of y'all tried to blame her for Daddy—"

"Not me," Aunt Bibby cut me off with a raised hand. "I ain't *never* blamed her for what happened to Big Moe! The only thing I *ever* blamed Jude for was the crazy shit she was responsible for! And that was for not telling you that—"

"You blamed her too!" I spit. "I ain't tryna hear a damn thing you gotta say!"

"A'ight. That's cool," she said and stood up to leave. "I could hit you with some knowledge, but cool. Go 'head and stay blind, deaf, and dumb, Mink."

"I already got knowledge!" I hollered. "I got all the knowledge I need!"

She sucked her teeth at me in stank disgust. "Ig'nant ass!" she hissed. "Y'all lil young bitches today wouldn't recognize a stick of knowledge if it was ten inches long and had cum shooting out the tip."

★   ★   ★

Tears started rolling down Mama's face as soon as Aunt Bibby walked outta the room. I felt like shit for arguing over her head like that, but I wasn't the one who had started it.

"Hey, Mama. How you feeling today?" I asked, and sat back down next to her. She had her eyes closed tight, but with all that water seeping outta them I knew she wasn't sleeping. I stared down at those closed eyes and admired my moms. I had the LaRue genes so I was the spitting image of my father, but mama was a real pretty woman too. She had soft hair and clear skin in a deep shade of caramel that was real gorgeous and attractive. Her eyes were big and brown, and back in the day when she used to smile a lot, her bright-white teeth would light up a room.

I loved my mother all the way to the bone, but no matter how hard I tried, I just didn't get it. I gazed into the sadness of her face and tried to figure out how deep a nigga's pocket had to be and how low his dick had to swing to make a woman amp out and do the type of crazy shit that my mama had done.

Run up on Lenox Avenue and tell your daddy to bring his ass home, Mama used to all the time tell me. Or, *Wait 'til your daddy drives past and tell me which ho he got riding around in my goddamn car.*

I watched all the crazy changes she went through tryna keep up with Big Moe LaRue, and I swore all out I wasn't *never* gonna love no man the way my mama had loved my daddy. Fuck all that! Let a nigga get sprung and love all over *me.*

I leaned down and kissed her on the forehead. Even though Aunt Bibby and her shit-talking ass had gotten my temper up, I wasn't gonna let it ruin my little bit of time with Mama, so I did like I usually did when I visited her. I brushed her hair and put a bunch of colorful, pretty clips in it, and then I took her clawlike hands and straightened her fingers out one by one so I could cut her nails and polish them up real nice.

The whole time I worked on Mama I talked to her just like she could understand everything I was saying. "Remember the last time I came to see you and I told you I was going down to Texas? Well, I went and it was wild as hell, Mama," I told her. "I acted a pure fool down there, and them country folks loved me so much they want me to come back again. But this time," I said, "they're gonna be paying me a whole lot better."

Mama started making that funny noise again. Like she was crying. Her crooked hands shot up in the air and a look of fright rose in her eyes.

"Don't worry." I hugged her and comforted her through her moans. "I'ma tell them nurses they better not let Aunt Bibby back up in here no more, okay? If she brings her big ass around here again I'ma roll up in Taft and wear her out, for real!"

Mama cried and tried to reach out for me. "You gonna be okay," I told her. "Texas ain't that far, you know. I'll be back in a couple of weeks, okay?" I kissed her hands and then her forehead. "Peaches said he's gonna check on you while I'm gone, and if you need me, Mama, he'll call me, okay?"

I kissed her again, and then I got up outta that stuffy little room in a hurry because I didn't want her to see me crying. I got in the car with Peaches and slammed the door, and I didn't say a word all the way back to Harlem. All I could do was lean against the car window with tears running from my eyes, and instead of babying me like he usually did, Peaches gave me my peace and let me have my space.

When we pulled up on the block and he parked the ride, I turned to him and swallowed hard. "Peaches," I said softly, "you gonna see about Mama while I'm gone, ain't you? You gonna look out for her, right?"

He nodded and turned his hand over and wiped away my tears with his big old ashy knuckle. "You damn right I'ma look out for her, Mink. And I'll kick all of them muthafuckas' asses up in there if they don't treat her right too."

"Okay, thanks," I said, feeling some kinda way inside. Here I was about to jet my money-grubbing ass outta town and get my hustle on by pretending to be somebody else's damn daughter while my own mama was layin' up in a nursing home all by herself for twenty-four hours a day. "One day I'ma get my mama up outta there," I swore under my breath. I knew I sounded stupid, like a little kid who still believed in fairy tales, but I couldn't help it. "Hell yeah. One day I'ma stack enough bank to set my mama up lovely so she can live the rest of her life around people who gon' treat her right."

Peaches touched my arm, then leaned over and kissed me on my forehead. "I believe you, Madame Mink. Word up. I believe you."

CHAPTER 9

It was black as midnight when we left New York, but by the time the plane zipped to about a million other cities and then touched down at DFW International Airport, the sun was rising high in the summer sky. The last time me and Bunni had rolled in to Dallas we'd been slumming so hard we barely had enough ends to scrape together to pay for a taxi, but when we walked out of the terminal this time a big, bronco-busting Texas-sized truck was waiting outside for us and my play-uncle Suge Dominion was posted up and leaning against the bumper.

Superior "Suge" Dominion was a six-foot-five big chocolate banga! This nig had my mouth wide open and my pussy moist as fuck. He was Viceroy's smooth, criminal-minded younger brother, and his gutter game was all day long and all night strong. Suge was one of them real tall and beefy-built gangsta cowboys. Everything about him was big and thick, and I do mean *everything*. We had a sizzling hot sex thang going on between us, and hitting the sheets with him was like wrestling with an alligator. I loved that shit!

"Uncle Suge!" I hollered and ran over and jumped right up in his rock-hard arms. He cradled my soft booty in his big hands and I wrapped my legs tightly around his waist and squeezed my thighs, happy to see him again and wishing he could fuck my lights out right where we was standing.

"Wus good, Mink baby," he said in his deep Houston hood-drawl, nuzzling my neck and tickling my skin with his curly black moustache. I wrapped my arms around his neck and he palmed my ass and held me like I weighed about two pounds. "Umph . . ." he grunted sexily and pushed his nose down into the cleavage between my ta-tas, sucking up my fumes. "You smell real sweet, baby girl. I missed your fine ass."

He lifted his head and licked my chin, then pressed his mouth to mine and let his hot tongue snake into my mouth. I met him head up, thrusting my tongue into his mouth too, and sucking all over his gorgeous cocoa-pop lips.

"Yuck!" Bunni hollered from behind me. "Get a damn room, why don'tcha! All that face sucking and tongue twirling y'all doing looks nasty as hell!"

Me and Suge both laughed, and when he went to put me down I pressed my titties to his chest and made sure my entire body rubbed against him as I slid down his front. He tossed our suitcases in the back of his silver monster-truck, and then held the door open as me and Bunni both climbed in the plush front seat. His Ford truck was a custom-designed beast, and it smelled like straight-up luxury inside. The first time me and Suge ever kissed had been inside his truck, and the last time we fucked had been right here on this same front seat with me leaking mad puddy juice everywhere!

"So what's been happening down here in The Big D?" I giggled and asked Uncle Suge as he pushed his silver bull-buster toward the Dominion Estate. I was sitting in between him and Bunni, and he drove with one hand and rubbed all over my thigh with the other one. "Who you been chillin' with since I left?"

"Viceroy," he said, and frowned. I knew Uncle Suge was real close to his brother, and I could tell how bad he was hurting because everything about him changed when he said Viceroy's name. He took his hand off my leg and put it back on the steering wheel. "The doctors are getting kinda worried. All this fuckin' money we got and them clowns can't do a damn thing for him."

"I'm so sorry," I lied with a straight face. "I thought he was getting better when I left."

Suge nodded. "He was going up and down for a good minute. But he's pretty bad off these days. He's just a shell right now, baby girl. It's almost like he's not even there."

I touched his arm like I had some sympathy. "Yeah, Dane told me. That's why I came back. I kinda wanted to be here if he . . . you know, just in case something happened to him."

"Well it's a good thing you came back, Mink. My brother might not pull through this time and I hate to say this shit, but if Viceroy bites the dust then me and Dane are gonna need you to help us kick the dog shit outta Lil Bump."

The gates to the Dominion Estate were closed when we pulled onto the property, and when Uncle Suge clicked a button over his rearview mirror, those babies slid open real wide, the way a good stripper does when she spreads her legs on a nice hot pole. We rode down a manicured tree-lined strip, and my eyes feasted on the sight of the ice-cold mega-mansion that sat at the top of a long, circular driveway.

"We's home!" Bunni hollered, sounding all country-ghetto, and I couldn't help but grin right along with her. After slummin' around in the grimy Harlem projects and the pissy stairwells and polluted hallways, it felt real damn good to be rolling up on some highly polished luxury. I peeped the Bentleys and the Rolls-Royce parked in the driveway, and the Mercedes and Dane's bangin' Hummer were both up under the awning. Off to my left, I could see the *Diva Dominion* Business Jet sitting off in the distance under an aluminum-top awning all its own.

Right off the bat I noticed that Barron's ultra sleek 2012 Maybach Landaulet was missing, and I was glad his tight, stuck-up ass wasn't around to be a buster on everybody's mood.

Durant, one of the young security dudes, musta heard the gate open because he came outside in his hot little uniform holding his walkie-talkie and tryna look real important. I giggled like hell when I thought about how he had tried to shoo me and Bunni the hell off the property when we drove up in a yellow cab looking broke and sexy and trying to crash the Dominions' Fourth of July barbeque. Bunni had been rocking a pair of coochie-cutter shorts that made that nigga drool all over his shiny little silver badge.

"Baby D!" Bunni screeched and hopped outta the truck before Uncle Suge could even put it in park. She ran across the wide driveway and jumped all over the security dude, hugging and kissing him like they went way back.

"A'ight, now." Uncle Suge chuckled as Bunni's tits and booty jiggled all over the poor young'un. "Don't hurt him, Bunni. The boy's got a job to do, so don't hurt him now."

Something was jiggling in me too as I looked up at the beautiful house that was so damn big my eyes couldn't take it all in at once. There were butterflies in my stomach that were flipping and fluttering, and making me wonder what the hell I was doing coming back here to dip my greedy little fingers in these folks' honey-pot once again.

The first time I'd bust up in the mansion everything had been just a big game to me. A hustle. A challenge. A great big con that if I could pull it off, was supposed to solve all my cash-flow problems and leave me sitting pretty for a good minute. But this time it was different. It wasn't a simple hit-it-and-quit-it type of thang no more. I didn't have a problem lying or manipulating or scheming to get what I needed outta life, but some kinda way this whole grimy caper had turned into building relationships and fuckin' with other people's feelings. I guess it felt harder this time because I knew these people now, and they thought they knew me too. Especially Selah.

Two servants came out to get our suitcases outta the back of the truck and I turned to Uncle Suge and stepped up on him real close.

"Thanks for coming to pick us up from the airport."

He looked down at me and nodded, then touched the brim of his dope Stetson hat. "You can ride with me anytime, baby."

"Am I gonna see you later on tonight?"

His sexy eyes twinkled and the grin he flashed me made my thick nipples ache.

"You wanna see me?"

"Hell yeah I do," I told him, and I said that shit real bold too, 'cause Mizz LaRue had no problem telling a nigga what she wanted.

Uncle Suge nodded again, and I could tell by the hungry look in his eyes that if we hadn't been standing outside his brother's house in broad daylight he woulda snatched me up and stuck his tongue down my throat. He probably woulda tossed me back in his truck and fucked the shit outta me too.

Biting his lower lip like he was holding himself back, he tapped me lightly on my ass and turned away. "I'll call you later. It won't take me long. Maybe an hour or so, okay?"

I grinned and nodded. " 'Kay. I'll be ready for you. Later."

One of the servants told us that Selah and Fallon had gone out shopping but that didn't stop me and Bunni from invading the joint. The mansion looked even better inside than I had remembered. Everything about it was sleek and shiny and expensive as hell. The parlor had glistening marble floors and high ceilings. A light floral scent was in the air, and I could smell the polish they had used to shine the countless end tables and leather furniture.

"Miss Dominion, your suites are ready," an older servant

named Big Grownie, who I remembered from our last trip, swished her wide hips into the room and told me. Like the security dude Durant, she was dressed up in a monkey suit too, but hers was a big black dress with an apron and a lacy white bib-thingy on the front, and she had on a pair of hot-ass stockings that put her thick thighs on loudspeaker with every step she took.

"How you doin', Miss Grownie!" I said and hugged her with mad respect like I did with all the older black women I knew in the projects. "You doin' all right today?"

She smiled at me and looked all shy, but she looked happy too as she hugged me right back. "I'm doing just fine, baby," she said, coming up outta that subservient shell that the Dominions and all their millions of dollars had her in. "It's good to see you back."

Bunni tried to pull a slick one. She jetted up the stairs in front of me and tried to take the room that I had stayed in the last time we were here.

"I got this one!" she hollered and jumped on the bed just like a big-ass kid.

"Uh-uh, Bunni!" I fussed. "Hell *no*. Same, same baby. This was the room they put me in last time, and this is the one I'm staying in this time too!"

"Why you always gotta get the best shit, Mink? Huh?" she pouted. "Why's it always gotta be about *you*?"

Here we go again, I thought as my girl twisted up her lips and shot daggers outta her eyes. Bunni could get real stank and funky sometimes. If she got pissed off and salty for the slightest little reason, then she would throw a bone in a plan regardless of the consequences. I smiled at Miss Grownie real quick, and then I pushed Bunni inside her room and slammed the door behind us.

"Don't start none, won't be none, Bunita!" I pointed my finger dead in her face. "It ain't all about *me*! But it ain't all about you neither! Now, your ass is just as broke as minez is.

We came back down here to get this dough real quick so we can get paid and get the hell gone. It don't really matter who sleeps in which room. I'ma need you to just go along with the program so we can get up on this loot, okay?"

Mad or not, I saw two gigantic dollar signs flash in Bunni's eyes, and they were even greener than the contact lenses she was styling.

"I don't know why you tripping, Mink," she smirked. She shrugged her shoulders and turned away from me, switching her bowlegged ass around my room before heading into hers. "You can keep your old funky-ass room! This one over here is better any damn way. I just wanted to see what you was gonna say."

"Really?" I shrieked, giving her a shitty look. "All that drama and that's the one you really wanted anyway? The rooms are just alike, Bunni!"

She bust out laughing and bent over and unzipped her suitcase. "Girl, shut up. We ain't gonna be stuck up in these rooms any damn way. We came here to put in work, goddamn it. Now let's get after it."

Neither one of us had slept a wink on the airplane and we were tired and hungry as hell. The maids had put out a tray of crackers and pretzels in our suite, but we wanted us some real food, so after taking our showers, me and Bunni went downstairs to the kitchen to see what kinda grub we could munch on until Selah and Fallon got back home.

The Dominions had a cook named Miss Katie, and she was one of those old black women who fixed almost everything from scratch. We sat right in the kitchen with her as she hooked us up some grits, turkey sausage, and fried eggs, and me and Bunni both had a slice of homemade pineapple upside-down cake when we finished eating our food.

With my stomach nice and full, I hit Dane on his cell phone to see what he was up to. During the summer when he wasn't in school, Dane chilled in a private little fuck-pad above the Dominions' ten-car garage. He sounded sleepy when he answered the phone, but he told me and Bunni to come right on up anyway.

Bunni acted a pure-ass fool as soon as he opened his door. "Oowweee! Dane-*Daaaane*!" She pressed all up against him and meowed his name over and over, sounding just like an alley cat in deep heat. Dane stood there naked except for a pair of low-slung basketball shorts. His eyes were red like he was already smoked-out and zooted. His ebony dreads looked sleek and freshly twisted, and his smooth chocolate skin and crazy muscles sent Bunni over the edge. By the time she finished molesting the nigga, running her hands all over his chest and grinding her fur mound all up on his thigh, Dane was grinning and he had a big piece of wood rocking up the front of his drawers.

"Get y'all fine asses up in here!" Dane said, adjusting his bone and then reaching out to hug me. We followed him inside his cute loft apartment that was five times bigger than the crib me and Bunni lived in with Peaches. There were two real big bedrooms and two luxurious bathrooms, a loft, a living area, and a kitchen that the servants kept on jam.

Dane Dominion was a regular ol' dick swinger. He was one of those rapper dudes who wasn't never gonna grow up, and at twenty-four years old he was still in college and still running around town DJ'ing at clubs and parties. Dane was street smart, and he kept him some kinda hustle going, but his main grind was getting high, laying tracks, and banging all the lil groupies and honeys who lived in his college dorm.

From the first day we met, me and Bunni had been vibing with Dane right off the bat. He wasn't nothing like I thought a rich dude would be. Not only was he all about partying, smoking trees, and getting tipsy just like I was, Dane had treated me real righteous when I bust up in the joint claiming

I was a long-lost family member. He had accepted my word that I was his sister Sable, and left it at that.

"What's going on?" I said as the three of us went into his large bedroom. Dane hopped up on his elevated loft bed, and me and Bunni both took off our shoes so we could get up on there with him.

"Yo, hold up." I hand-checked Bunni before she could fly off into parts unknown, and then I grilled Dane with my nose in the air. I waved my hand toward his blankets and said real snooty-like, "Your shit is proper up in there, ain't it? I mean, I hope you ain't been hot-sheeting no freaky-ass chicks 'cause I ain't tryna land in nobody else's puddle, ya heard?"

Dane laughed. "Nah, baby sis. I got it nice and fresh for y'all. Word, I ain't bounced nobody around in at least two hours."

Dane pressed a button on his console and a sick beat under DJ Kay Slay blared through the expensive studio speakers that were positioned all around the room. He reached up on his headboard and pulled down a stick of yay rolled with Big Bambu, and he passed it over to Bunni so she could spark it up.

"It's a good thing you brought your ass back down here," Dane said as the three of us puffed, passed, and grooved to the sounds. "Bump is tryna get extra with his shit, for real."

I shook my head. "Look, Dane, I get everything you told me, and Uncle Suge even says the same things, but y'all know Barron can't stand my ass. How is me being down here gonna help everybody get paid?"

"That's the easy part," Dane said. "All you gotta do is show up. Show up at the board meeting with the rest of us and let it be known which team you're batting on and we should be set."

I took a deep toke on the joint and squinted through one eye. "How you figure?"

"Check it out," Dane explained. "Like I told you before, Pops is sliding fast. The doctors don't know how long he's gonna be able to hold on. But even if he does manage to make it, there's almost no chance in hell that he's gonna get back to a point where he can run the business again. And that's where Barron comes in."

I nodded. "Right, I get that part. If your—I mean if *our* father can't do his job no more, then Barron gets to take over the company."

"Yeah. But not only does B get to run the company, he gets two shareholder votes on the board, and that means he can take control of all the money too. And that includes the family trust fund that Pops started. He organized it so all of us could get three-hundred-thousands yards a year for life, but if Bump gets his finger on that trigger we could all end up with our pockets shot full of holes."

"And how am I gonna be the one to stop him?"

"C'mon, now, girl. You ain't stupid so add shit up. When Sable was missing Pops always had control of her vote. If Pops is outta the picture and Barron is in charge, then *Barron* gets control of Sable's vote. That nigga gets to vote *twice*. But now that your DNA test came back you're automatically a member of the board and you get to cast your own vote. We just need you to throw it in the same pot with ours so we can stop Barron from taking over in the first place. But don't forget, Mink," he cautioned, "you gotta make sure your shit looks squeaky clean, baby sister. At least on paper. If Barron digs up any kind of grime on you and passes it off to the rest of the board members, then they can say you violated the terms of the trust and snatch up all your money. I mean you still get to vote either way, but whether or not you get paid is up to them."

I bit my lip and thought about that shit real hard. I had been pulling cons and capers practically my whole damn life. If Barron dug deep enough he could come up with enough dirt on my behind to fill up that big-ass pond they had out back. Twice. That nigga was already sniffing on my tail and coming up with small stuff. How the hell was I supposed to keep him from finding out about all my most diabolical criminal capers?

"So who's down on whose team?" I asked, my mind whirling like a computer. I needed to know how long the odds looked before I got in any deeper. "Who's in your corner, and how many people can we count on to have our back?"

Dane took a swig from his bottle and said, "Right now we lookin' kinda light. It's just me, Uncle Suge, you, and maybe Jock, if we keep leaning on his ass."

"What about Fallon? She ain't gonna be down?"

Dane shook his head real quick. "Hell nah. She's Bump's baby. He's been daddying that girl since the day she was born. Wherever Barron leads, that's where Fallon is gonna follow. So are you down wit' it or what?"

I nodded. "Yeah," I agreed. I was gonna need a real big mop to wipe away all the dirty tracks I had left behind, but three hundred grand a year was more than a grip, and I was down for almost anything if it meant padding my designer purse with that kind of loot.

"Hell yeah," I said real quick. "I'm down to the ground. Count me in."

CHAPTER 10

We laid up in the bed smoking yay with Dane for a little while longer, but then Bunni started getting all freaky and shit. She slid her foot up the leg of Dane's shorts and started teasing him, stroking his dick with her toes, and when he grabbed her ankle and bent over and got to sucking on her crusty big toe, I knew it was time for me to dip.

I left them getting naked under the covers and went back inside the main house to look for my baby brother, Jock. For him to be the baby boy and the only biological son in the Dominion clan, it seemed like Viceroy and Selah had slacked off when it came to raising his little ass. Jock was only eighteen but he was a dro-head to the max, and he sagged and styled hood shine like he came outta the trenches of Brooklyn or something. He looked just like a younger Viceroy in the face. He was tall and built damn near as cut as Barron, and he had a thug-a-licious look about him that kept plenty of young girls sniffing on his dick.

Upstairs in the mansion I took my time walking to Jock's room. He lived on the wing opposite from mine, and I couldn't believe how shiny all the banisters were, how plush the miles of carpet felt under my feet, or how luxurious and beautiful the Dominion home really was.

There was loud music blasting from the room when I knocked on Jock's door, and I could hear him in there throwing his lil weak rap lines down over a slick beat by a hot producer named Ken Will who was blowing up on Facebook for his hit-making beats.

"What's up, baby brother!" I squealed when Jock opened the door.

"Mink." He greeted me with a grin and reached out for a hug. "Wussup?" he said, opening the door wider so I could come in. "What you doing back in Texas, girl?"

"I came back to check you out," I said, looking around the room with my eyes bucked open wide. Jock was a pussy freak. There were crazy pictures of monster-booty chicks in erotic poses all over his walls. Some of them jawns looked just like racehorses from the back, with their humongous muscled-up asses hanging halfway down to the ground. That shit was scary. I knew I had a sweet ass and my tail-feather was nice and round, but the asses on these nasty beasts looked like birth defects. They were outrageously freaky and damn near obscene.

"What?" he said, laughing at the look of disgust on my face. "What's the problem?"

I shrugged. "I ain't got no problem. I just don't know how you sleep in here with all that scary-looking ass up in your face all night long."

He cracked up. "Ass is a good thing, Mink! Ass is a real good thing!"

"Uh-uh." I frowned and rolled my eyes at him. "All ass ain't good ass, honey. And don't believe the hype neither. You *can* get hold of too much of a good thing."

Jock kept right on laughing with his crazy self. "Only a female would say some shit like that. Only a female."

"Yeah, whatever." I waved my hand as I sat down on a

beanbag and crossed my legs. "So besides chasing donkey butts in your dreams, tell me what you been doing since I left?"

Jock opened his little fridge and took out two beers and passed me one.

"I been straight, man," he said. "Just tryna chill and have a little fun while I can, ya dig? Before you know it the whole summer is gonna be over and it'll be time for me to go back to school."

I nodded. "For real. It seems like just yesterday we were getting blasted at the Fourth of July barbeque and it looked like Viceroy was getting better."

Jock shrugged and kept at his beer like he didn't wanna talk about his father.

"You think he's gonna get better?" I pushed him.

Jock shrugged again. "He comes and goes. One minute it looks like he's doing better, and then the next minute the doctors are saying he ain't gonna make it. I don't really know."

"Well, I heard he's even sicker now than he was when I was down here before. You been to Houston to see him recently?"

"Yeah. We flew down there the other day."

"Oh really? So how did he seem to you?"

He chugged back some brew. "He seemed a'ight. The same as usual. You know . . . just laying there."

"Yeah, that's what I heard. I also heard Bump is tryna slide in ya pop's seat so he can take over. He called a meeting with the board, you know."

Jock shook his head and stood up. "I see what you getting at, but I don't fuck with none of that business stuff, Mink." He tossed his empty beer bottle in a small garbage can. "Dane and Uncle Suge already came at me about all this. If you're trying to scope out some info on DO, I ain't the one."

"How are you not the one, Jock? Shit, yes you are! You get a vote on the board just like everybody else do."

"But I ain't never voted before. You gotta be eighteen and

I just crossed that line last week, ya dig? Besides, I'm on the fence with this shit. My father always votes for me. Whatever's good with him is good with me."

"That's what I'm saying though!" I jumped up and touched his shoulder. "You need to get off the fence because your pops can't vote for you this time. Hell, he can't even vote for his own damn self."

"Then Barron'll do it. He's my brother, and he's down for the family bizz. Whatever Bump wants to do, I'll ride with him."

"Why?" I demanded. "Just because he says so?"

"Nah, it ain't just that. He's my brother, Mink. My *brother*."

"Hey now!" I said, getting all up in his face. "I'ma ya damn sister, too? Remember?" I stared him down, silently reminding him about the little understanding we was supposed to have.

Jock's eyes mighta been red and chinky from all the weed he had smoked, but I could still see the smart-ass look that flashed in them as he smirked at me and then laughed out loud. "That's some funny shit, Mink. Know what? New York chicks like you got a rep for scheming. Your whole shit is funny though. You's a real funny girl."

Oh, okay, nigga. So you wanna go there?

"Nah," I said, stepping across the line and smacking the shit outta him with my trump card. "Funny was the color of that white chick's face when Uncle Suge dragged her dead ass outta the pool house and stuffed her into the back of his truck that night! Yeah," I said when those slanted red eyes of his got real big and round. I could see his lil young, pea-sized brain twisting and turning, shocked as hell that I was about to blow his spot up. "That shit was *mighty* fuckin' funny! Matter fact, it was so damn funny that you forgot to laugh. If I remember that shit right, you was out there *crying*, nigga! *Waaa! Waaa!* What exactly did you and your little friends do to that silly white girl, Jock? I mean damn, she looked totally fucked up, nah'mean? High, drunk, straight toasted to a crisp. But she was way overdone, nah'mean? That bitch was cocked-out cold, and something tells me she still ain't came to yet."

Jock's cute lil face looked like a slab of concrete. Hard and frozen with fear. "Yo, Mink. Chill with all that. Everything got all fucked up that night. That girl was crazy. It wasn't my fault."

I blasted on him. "Tell that shit to the po-po, baby! That white chick was *dead*!"

"Shhh!" Jock said and pressed one finger to his lips. His young ass was shook. Straight up petro. "Not so loud! Chill the fuck out, all right? A'ight." He licked his lips and his beady eyes darted back and forth. "You shaking me down and that's fucked up, Mink. So what do you want? Huh? What the hell do you want?"

Now that's more like it! I thought and flashed him a sly grin.

"What do I want?" I asked innocently. I pursed my lips and looked up in the air like the answer was plastered somewhere on the ceiling. "Well," I said as I twirled my hair and put my hands on my hips. I narrowed my eyes and shot his little ass a round of hot bullets from my eyes. "You can start by fixing your damn face and checking that 'tude when you talking to me. And after that," I told my shook little play-brother, "I want you to climb your ass off that voting fence you straddling and make sure you jump down on the right side."

Five minutes after I got back to my suite my cell phone buzzed. It was Uncle Suge, and he was parked outside waiting for me. I bounced down the stairs in my stark-white skin-tight Birthday Cake shorts and frilly ribbed halter, looking and smelling like something good to fuck.

And that's exactly what Uncle Suge wanted to do to me when I jumped up in his truck and gave him a real hot tongue kiss.

"Ummm," he moaned as he reached for my halter and rolled it down until the tops of my swollen titties was showing. I ain't have no shame. I did him one better and pulled that shit *all* the way down! My twins jumped free and sat up looking bold and ripe, bouncing around like two hot, suckable water balloons.

"I missed these," he said and took one in each hand. My clit started blinking as he thumbed my erect nipples and squeezed my titties with just the right amount of pressure. I made up my mind right then and there. I wanted that nigga. I went straight for his dick, reaching into his lap and gripping the big bulge of prime Texas meat I knew was waiting for me in his pants.

"Hold up, hottie"—he laughed and pushed my hand away—"before somebody sees us." I backed away a little bit as he put his truck in drive and pulled off. My naked titties was jiggling under the hot sun as he drove around to the back of the mansion and parked under a big oak tree. The cool shade felt good and it took the heat in the truck down a notch, but my coochie was still burning on fire for Big Suge.

He rolled up all the windows and turned the air-conditioner on. I rolled my halter down around my stomach, and he damn near tore my belt and my hot little designer shorts off tryna get to my pussy.

And when he finally did get my gear off my stuff was soaking wet for him. He urged me back on the seat until I was leaning against the window, then he stared down into my neatly-trimmed naked pussy and grunted real hard.

That dude took the plunge! He had his tongue up in me before I knew he had moved. He grunted and slurped as he licked my pussy meat like it was a gourmet affair, nibbling on my wet flesh and flicking his stiff tongue back and forth over my clit as I screamed and creamed in delight.

My body trembled and I sweated with my first nut, but I wasn't through yet. I raised my knees until my lower body looked like a giant letter M. Suge slid his big rough hands under my ass and lifted my hips up to his mouth again, and ate me like I was his favorite-flavored pie. I squealed and jumped as he slid his finger up my ass and gently fucked my back door, and I reached up and held onto the overhead handle and rode that shit like a wave.

I don't know how he got his weapon wrapped up, but somehow he did.

"Lemme see that ass," he begged me as he gripped his long dick in both his hands. "Turn over, baby. Lemme see that ass."

I rotated my body on the seat until I was up on my knees with my ass facing him. I looked over my shoulder and saw the way he was staring at my bold double cheeks, and got more turned on than ever. I knew I had booty for days, but I loved the way Suge looked at my body, like it was the finest one he had ever seen.

He scooted outta his seat and placed one palm on each of my ass cheeks. I felt his breath on my neck as he massaged my flesh, squeezing and stroking my buns until heat started surging in my clit again. My naked titties was pressed up against my window as he breathed hard and played with my ass. I wanted to feel that dick up in me, but Suge wanted something else.

I gazed at him over my shoulder as he removed the magnum from his enormous dick. He gripped it in one hand, then went up on his knees and started rubbing the head of it all over my ass. That shit felt spectacular, and between the cold glass on my hard nipples and the way he was slapping the head of his wet dick all over my sweat-covered ass, I lost it. Sticking two fingers deep inside my hot pussy, I fucked myself deeply as I poked my ass out and enjoyed the sensation of his hot, rubbing dick.

Suge parted my left ass cheek a little and held me open. He pushed the tip of his dick against my asshole, and when he gave a little push I pulled my fingers outta my pussy and played with my throbbing clit until I came. And the moment he felt me let go Suge busted him one too. He slapped all over my sensitive booty with his hard, squirting dick, and by the time his nuts was empty we were both exhausted.

I was slobbering on the window when he opened his glove box and took out some wet wipes. I stayed on my knees until he wiped the cum and sweat off my ass cheeks, and then he pulled me back and held me gently in his arms.

"Ahhhh." He sighed as I snuggled with my back against his chest. His rock-hard forearm was around my neck, and I lowered my chin and kissed his chocolate skin.

"So, did you miss this or what?" I asked him boldly.

He chuckled behind me. "Hell yeah. I missed *you*. So don't you leave me no more," he growled as his curly moustache nuzzled my ear. "Matter fact"—he turned my face toward him and kissed my lips—"your sweet ass better not never leave the state of Texas again."

Me and Uncle Suge stayed in his truck talking and kissing for a little while longer, and then he dropped me off around the front of the mansion and promised to get up with me later. I went upstairs and took another shower and then laid down on the bed, and some time later my head was floating on my plush pillow when Bunni busted up in the room disturbing my damn peace.

"Mink, get up. Your play-daddy's main squeeze is back from tricking off his moolah. You gonna prolly wanna go check her out."

"Wh-what?" I squinted through one eye and lifted my head up off the pillow. "Bunni, what in the hell are you talking about?"

"Damn." She sighed. "Take you outta the hood for one damn day and all of a sudden you don't speaka no English no more. I *said* Selah is back from shopping. She just went upstairs to her room, so you need to get up there and get your ass to work."

I sat up and wiped the drool off my face. My eyes burned and felt gritty from too much weed and not enough sleep, and I blinked real fast until they stopped hurting.

"A'ight," I said, dragging my ass up out the bed. "I'ma go see her."

I went into my private bathroom to wash my face and brush my teeth. Even the bathrooms in the Dominion mansion were beast. The counters were made of beautiful granite, and the cool floors were tiled in natural stone. The mirror sparkled without a single streak on the glass, and all the faucets and sink fixtures were done up in gold.

I pulled my shit together, then changed into a cute pink summer dress with one slim shoulder strap, and took my hair down out of the bun I had stuck it in before I laid down. I was the queen of crazy, outrageous wigs, and I owned the entire funky-elite Glama-Glo collection. But I knew Selah liked seeing me in a certain innocent light, and part of my hustle involved making sure the mama bear of the Dominion clan thought of me as her sweet little long-lost cub.

I untwisted my natural curls and let my dark hair fall down my back, then I finger-combed it until it lay soft and wispy around my shoulders, making me look like somebody's sweet angel. A little pale-pink gloss on my lips, and a stroke or two of mascara, and I was ready to be about it. I slipped my feet into a cute pair of pink and black sandals, and then I set off to see how deep I could get into Selah's motherly little head.

I walked up the carpeted stairs and crossed the mansion to get to the west wing of the house. Everything about this joint screamed *moolah*, but the suite that Selah and Viceroy shared could only be described as ten tons of gwap and a shit-load of glamour rolled up in one big knot.

Their doorway was deeply recessed, and a spray of colorful fresh-cut flowers grabbed hold of my eyeballs. That thing was so damn big and pretty it looked like it had taken somebody hours to get all of those different kinds of flowers into such a dizzying pattern. There were two big gold knockers on the highly shined double cherrywood doors, and I lifted the one on the right and gave three tiny knocks. Not the kinda nigga-knockin' folks did when they were bammin' down your door in the projects or nothing, but just three quick little polite knocks that said, *Somebody is here to see you.*

I started grinning as soon as Selah opened the door, and the instant she saw me standing there in all my cute bubblegum pink, an explosion of light just brightened up her eyes.

"Sable!" she squealed and threw her arms around me and held me real tight. "Praise God! Thank Him, *thank* Him! It's so good to see you, baby! I missed you so much! Oh, I'm so, *so* happy you decided to come back home!"

All I could do was grin and nod. The last time I'd seen Selah Dominion she was crying her eyes out in the back of her limo as her, Barron, and Dane dropped me and Bunni off at the airport so we could fly back to New York. My pockets had been full of loot so I was kinda feeling myself that day, and even though Selah's tears had dripped all over my guilty conscience, I damn sure didn't feel bad for breaking up outta Texas and leaving her behind.

But everything was different now. I was broke as hell again, and I needed to plant myself real deep in Selah's heart again in a hurry. I could tell how bad she had missed me just by how tight she held me, and I played that shit up like a pro.

"I really missed you too," I lied as I pushed my face into her breasts and let her smother me in her toned arms. Selah's perfume was a light but expensive scent that reminded me of Halston, and the fabric of her white dress was so crisp that I knew it had to have cost a grip. When she finally let me go I saw that it was a high-end design by Dior, and I knew it had set her back more cream than most black folks made in six months.

She took my hand and pulled me deeper into her room. Her spread was sick and gigantic, with huge windows and high ceilings where four ornate gold fans all spun in the same direction. I thought about the night that Selah had read my phony DNA report out loud to the entire family. She had been so damn happy to have her little girl back that she'd gotten tore-down drunk and asked me to spend the night with her in her bed.

I had slept with Selah that night. I let her hold me and clutch the ugly little ducky doll baby of Sable's that she had held on to for all those years. And when we woke up the next morning I had felt real shitty for perpetrating such a big fat fraud on such a nice lady, but hey. I was a con-mami and a grifter. What the hell did she expect a hood chick like me to do?

"You know I wanted you to come back here, Mink," she said, calling me by my right name. Her voice was real serious as she kicked off her jeweled Dior croc sandals, and a worried look entered her eyes. "But not under these conditions. After you left it was almost like all the fight seemed to go out of Viceroy. He had been doing so good while you were here! But then all of a sudden he just stopped communicating with me, and I just couldn't seem to reach him, you know what I mean?"

I nodded my head, but on the real I was seriously thinking some other shit. The last time I'd seen Viceroy he was laying up in a hospital bed wrapped up like a mummy. One of his eyes was covered with a bandage, and the other one was bigger than a hardboiled egg. Selah had stood next to me and had a long conversation with him like he could hear and understand her, but I had caught a fucked-up vibe from that old man, and blown up or not, I sensed a slick old gangsta laying there underneath all that crusty gauze.

"I heard," I said, faking sympathy. "And that's why I came back as soon as I could get a flight. I felt like the right place to be was right here with my family," I lied real smooth outta the side of my neck, "and I just didn't want to miss out on any more important moments with y'all."

Selah melted behind that lil slice of bullshit talk, just like I knew she would.

"Oh, Sable. Baby, there were so very many moments that

you missed." Her eyes glistened with tears, and she took a deep breath before giving me a small, sad smile. "I wish I could put them all in a great big basket and tie a bow around it. I'd give you the gift of the memories that were stolen from us when I lost you, and I hope you'd find enough forgiveness in your heart to accept it from me."

Please don't start that crying shit, I thought as her misty eyes turned into waterfalls. The last thing I wanted was for Selah to take another guilt trip halfway around the world behind the fact that she had been toasted up outta her skull when Sable got kidnapped. I mean I definitely felt for her, and I felt for her little girl too, wherever the hell she really was, but my role was to get up on the Dominion dough, and get it the best way I could.

"I already told you," I said in a sweet-little-white-girl voice as we sat down together on a plush sofa. "I forgive you, and whatever happened in the past, I think we should leave it there. I'm just happy to have a family who loves me right now. That's all."

Selah took my hand and I could see her tryna pull her shit together and get a grip on her emotions. Even though I knew she really, really believed I was Sable, it was still kinda crazy to me, this insane and intense love she seemed to have for me when she didn't even know shit about me. Especially when you consider the fact that her and Viceroy had adopted Sable when she was just a few days old, and the girl had been snatched when she was almost four.

I just didn't get it. Was four years enough time to get your heart so wrapped around a damn kid? Especially one that wasn't really yours? I had lived with my mother for thirteen damn years, and she had pushed me right outta her very own ass. And still, she had never been as bent over me as Selah was over Sable. I felt kinda jealous over that.

"You're right," Selah said finally. "You are home with family, and we do love you. All of us do. And that's why it's so important that you have a chance to visit with your father while there's still time. We'll be flying down to Houston the first thing tomorrow morning. Let's just pray that things don't get any worse for him until we get there."

I sat with Selah and listened to her chatter on and on about how good a man Viceroy was, and how her kids had been blessed to grow up with a father like him. The only thing I knew about the man was what I had read on the Internet and what I had heard from other people, and if you let Dane tell it Viceroy wasn't nothing but an old G. He had been born and raised in the slums of Houston, and even though he had always been smart and ambitious, the grime of the streets ran thick through his blood.

I'd found out that Viceroy had built his family fortune by stepping on the neck of one of his good friends, and after making some shrewd and cunning oil deals, he had stockpiled himself a major share of crude oil and became one of the country's major connects. Shit, what his hustling ass had done was no different than what any good kingpin in the drug world would do. Start out small, shit on ya friends, annihilate your enemies, and then gain control of your market and watch the dough roll in.

Matter fact, I was willing to bet that Viceroy had done damn near all the grimy, illegal shit he banned his kids from doing in the terms of his trust fund. There was no way his hands could be squeaky clean, because a self-made dude like him who did bizz with rich white boys just had to be dirty all under his skin. Selah was originally from Brooklyn so I knew she could get gully too, but she had trained herself to look and sound real sophisticated, and I figured that was part of Viceroy's ploy to dust off his gutter image.

But whatever. For a rich Brooklyn chick Selah was real easy to like, and if I wasn't such a hardcore con-mami and she wasn't such a soft and easy mark, I woulda really been into her. So, while Suge was handling his bizz and Bunni was off banging Dane every chance she got, I tried to spend a little bit of time with Selah.

I stayed up under her for the rest of the day, and it tickled the shit outta her when I went up to her room real early the next morning and climbed up in that big old bed with her. We laid around and watched mad episodes of *Survivor* and some of the other reality shows she had taped, and then we called downstairs and ordered up breakfast in bed and ate like crazy. Both of us had a thing for cinnamon French toast so we got our plates stacked real high. I got mine with turkey sausage, and Selah got hers with some of that nasty corned beef hash that came outta the can. That shit was hood as hell but she loved it!

I kinda liked what I had going on a lil bit too. You woulda thought I had been raised with boo-coo money the way I fronted like I wasn't straight-up gaga over how the Dominions was living. I could actually picture myself getting used to having endless dough and every little thing I wanted brought to me at the snap of my fingers. Between all the good get-high Jock and Dane kept on supply, and that good wood that Uncle Suge was plunging me with, I was starting to think, fugg grimy-ass New York! I could get real comfortable down in hot-ass Texas!

I had already spun Selah all kinds of fairy-tale lies about my life in New York, and when we were done eating our French toast we got comfy on her big bed and she started telling me about her childhood in Brooklyn.

"My father was a longshoreman and a big-time gambler," she confided. "He raised us in the Bedford-Stuyvesant section of Brooklyn. We lived in a cold little apartment on Broadway. Right over a Chinese restaurant, with the el speeding past my bedroom window twenty-four hours a day."

It turns out that Selah was the oldest child. She told me she had grown up with her brother Digger, who was stank Pilar's father, and a sister who was a whole lot younger than her.

"Oh you got a sister?" I asked. "I always wanted me a sister. What's her name? Why isn't she around here?"

I saw her lips get tight and a hard look fall over her face.

"She *is* around," she said and flung the plush comforter offa her as she got outta the bed and walked toward the bathroom. "Somewhere."

I was quick to catch on to the change in her temperature, but I knew better than to push her. Instead, I filed the words *Shady Sister* under Selah's name in my mental Rolodex and tucked it away just in case I needed to whip it out and use it one day.

"You know," I said softly when Selah came back from the bathroom. As a Harlem con-mami I was well schooled on the art of *give a little, get a lot*. People would usually let their guard down some if you gave up a bit of juicy dirt on yourself first. "I wasn't telling you the whole truth when I told you about my past. I left out some of the juicy parts."

I saw a bolt of tension shoot through her and a worried look clouded her eyes. "What do you mean? What weren't you honest about?"

I shrugged and pulled the covers up under my chin, and tried to look all sweet and innocent in the face.

"Just . . . stuff. Mostly about my childhood, you know? I mean, I was too embarrassed to come down here and tell you all the crazy things that happened to me when I was a little kid. But now that I know you're gonna love me no matter what my life was like in the past, it's a lot easier for me to share my secrets with you. You get what I'm sayin'?"

Selah walked over and sat down on my side of the bed. Tears sprang to her eyes and her bottom lip actually trembled.

"You can tell me anything, baby. Anything. And I promise not to judge you. Ever."

I hated to twist the knife in her open wounds, but me and

Bunni were on a money-making mission and Mizz Mink had a job to do. I knew Barron was gonna try to make me look bad, so I wanted to dish my dirt to Selah first so she could be prepared for all the foul shit she was bound to hear.

"Well," I started, "my life wasn't nowhere near as happy as I tried to make you believe it was. I was raised around winos peeing on the stairs, dope fiends shooting drugs in the hallway, rapists tryna catch young girls alone in the alleys, and there was more petty thieves living in my project building than roaches," I said, telling her the whole truth for once.

"Day in and day out there was a whole lotta grimy stuff going on all up in my face, and by the time I was ten or eleven I had seen so much that my eyes were already about ninety-years old."

Selah looked straight-up horrified at the words that were rolling outta my mouth, and I took a deep breath and went in for the kill. "You know, sometimes when a child gets hurt when they're real young it can leave a mark on their soul that only love can erase. And if the child never gets the kinda love and understanding she needs, then those marks can have a lot to do with the decisions she makes later on, you know?"

Selah damn near leaped on me and crushed me in her arms. I didn't know exactly what I had said that was so damn slick, but whatever it was I could tell she really liked it.

"Oh, Mink!" she cried and moaned. "Baby, truer words have never been spoken. We all do things when we're hurting that we regret later. Lord knows I have, so Mama understands. Mama understands!"

I held still while she cried big tears and got to rocking me and patting my back with her delicate fingers. She was treating me just the way I always thought a mother should treat her daughter, and even though I wasn't used to being hugged on by no woman, I sat there and took it because on the real tip, it didn't feel that bad at all.

CHAPTER 11

The door to Selah's suite was open just a crack when Barron walked up, but what he saw through that little slice of light was more than enough to piss him off.

Mink!

Scandalous hoochie! Why the hell was she back in Texas, and what the hell was she doing up in Selah's suite? Funking up the joint! Hugging all over his mama with her tiny little pink dress hugging all over her bombastical ass! He watched as Selah walked into the bathroom, and then his eyes jumped right back on Mink. Barron took a slow, deep breath. Fuckable bitch. The sexy thrust of Mink's hips fucked his head up, and all the nasty words he wanted to spit at her got stuck somewhere near the tip of his rising dick.

She raised her arms and yawned and stretched.

Barron's blood pressure shot up as she arched her back. Damn that bitch was hot. She was like a virus and she gave off some kinda voodoo scent. There was something about her body that turned him way the fuck on and kicked up vapors in him whether he wanted it to or not. Out of all the girls he'd boned, including his cousin Pilar, Mink was the only chick who had ever rode him in his sleep. He had fucked Mink in all kinds of delicious ways, and in a hundred different positions. He'd shivered through countless erotic dreams where he'd be sliding his hard meat way up in her guts and licking out the deepest parts of her pussy, and he'd wake up with his dick jerking and spurting into his sheets, cumming like a muthafucka, and embarrassed as hell. Barron had no idea why his body was so sexually aroused by the sight of Mink LaRue when the rest of him couldn't stand to be anywhere near her ass.

His dick jerked, and he stuck his hand in his pocket and squeezed it tight.

"Cut it out," he whispered under his breath as he tried to push back his hateful lust. He adjusted the thick piece of meat in his pants, then walked boldly into his mother's bedroom.

"Mink," he spit coldly, like he hadn't been eye-fucking her up the ass two minutes ago. "What the hell are you doing here?"

Her plump titties jiggled as she spun around and flashed him a sexy little grin. Her eyes darted toward the bathroom where Selah could be heard running water in the sink.

"Hi, Barron. I'm sorry it took me so long to get here but I caught a flight as soon as I heard."

Barron frowned. "Heard what?"

"Heard your ass got kicked to the curb!" She busted out laughing. "Man, where's Carla? Why you let your kissing-cousin Pilar scare that white girl off? I thought y'all was gonna have a great big Texas wedding?"

"Shut your ass up!" he barked. "Don't worry about me and Carla. Worry about your damn self, okay?"

"Barron?" Selah called his name as she came out of the bathroom pressing a washcloth to her eyes. "Hey there, son. Were you yelling about something? Is everything okay?"

Barron covered her questions up with concern. "What happened, Mama? What's wrong with your eyes?"

She waved her hand and gave him a small, reassuring grin. "Nothing, baby. I just got a little emotional, that's all. I'm just so happy to have Mink back at home that my feelings got the best of me. Happiness will do that to you, you know."

Barron wanted to knock Mink on her ass as she stepped up on his mama and gave her a great big hug while shooting him a sly, devious smile. "Well, if having me here makes you so happy, Mama Selah, then this time I might stay for a long, long time."

"Yo, see there? You talk shit about a gold-digger and she slides right under the crack of your door," Barron said as he strode into his uncle Digger's plush backyard. It was hot as hell outside and Pilar was chilling alone in the Jacuzzi. She had an icy drink in her hand and some smooth R & B cuts were flowing from the outdoor speakers.

"What are you talking about?" Pilar lifted her alligator-framed Moss Lipow sunglasses and pushed them up high on her head. She had on a skimpy cream-colored Martinique string bikini, and the tops of her breasts were puffed out like fresh-baked corn muffins.

"I'm talking about *Mink*," Barron said as he loosened his tie and unbuttoned his starched designer shirt. He kicked off his imported leather shoes and set them up on a beach chair, and then unbuckled his belt and let his tailored pants fall down around his ankles. He took off his watch and peeled off his socks, and then stood there posted up in his sky-blue silk drawers looking like one big chocolate-covered muscle.

"She's back," he said as he lowered himself into the bubbling water next to his cousin. She passed him her drink and he guzzled the whole shit down in one gulp and then said, "I walked into Mama's room today and damn if she wasn't standing there." *Looking sexy as fuck,* he wanted to add.

"That bitch," Pilar said, feeling her stomach clench into a knot. "You know why she came back. She ran through all her money and now she's broke again."

"Damn right." Barron nodded. "Broke as a joke. Why else would she bring her ass back down here?"

Pilar shrugged and narrowed her eyes. "Maybe somebody told her to come back. Maybe Dane or Uncle Suge got with her. She might have heard about the board meeting and the vote that's coming up."

"Yeah, she might have," Barron agreed, "but it don't really matter." He let his hand wander under the water until he found her erect nipple. He rubbed it gently, and then cupped her entire breast. "Her one vote alone is not gonna swing it because Jock and Fallon are rolling with me. That still leaves the rest of them one vote short. So we're good."

Pilar frowned and pushed his hand away. "I don't know, B. Mink is slick and Dane is greedy. We gotta keep stacking up ammunition, so let's stick to our original plan. I still think you should go to New York and see what that private investigator has on her."

Barron shrugged, then nodded. "A'ight, I'll probably go. But I gotta be back in time for Animal's birthday. The bruhs are throwing him a party at the frat house and I promised my dude I would be there."

Go to New York. Pilar thought. *Hell yeah, get your ass gone.* The last thing she wanted was for Mink to be up in the mansion flouncing her heart-shaped ass up in her man's face. No matter what Bump said out of his mouth, he had a case of the hots for that hood chick, and his drawers got rocked up every time he looked at her.

"Yeah," Pilar said softly. "Let's go ahead and stick to our plan. You'll be back in time for the frat party. Just get up there to New York and make sure you bring back all the dirt you can find. Yeah," she said again. Reaching through the bubbles for his hard black dick, Pilar let out a wicked little laugh. "I want you to bring back enough dirt to start us a cemetery."

★ ★ ★

Barron had dirt on the brain all right.

Some dirty, nasty thoughts about Mink.

Him and Pilar had messed around in the Jacuzzi for a little while, just feeling on each other and getting each other hot. He'd been chilling a lot with her lately, hanging out, fucking, and spending a lotta cash, and with Carla out of his life everybody in the family woulda had to be blind not to see who her replacement was.

Now, did he feel fucked up about banging Pilar? Barron asked himself as he eyed her swaying hips and followed her upstairs to her bedroom. The answer was an honest hell no. He'd always known he was adopted, and he'd always been attracted to Pilar, even while he was running around fucking as many white girls as he could find. Him and Pilar had no biological ties to each other, and for the past few weeks she'd been throwing major hints about wanting his last name and what it would be like to be his wife.

Barron followed her through the quiet house. It was much smaller than the Dominion spread, but it was still classy and upscale. Pilar would make a perfect Dominion woman, Barron knew. She had the right look, the right style, the right package, the right pedigree.

But did she have his jones thang on lock? Barron asked himself as they entered her bedroom and she stripped out of her bikini and stood booty-liciously naked in front of him.

She was fine as shit. Her caramel skin was fuckin' lickable. Her titties were full and juicy, like they were ready to squirt warm milk with just one suck. Her stomach was toned and her hips were sweet and round. He knew without looking that Pilar's ass was high and firm. She was the kind of woman you would make love to like a queen, but right about now Barron wanted a chick with the body of a stripper that he could fuck like a ho.

He stepped out of his boxers and his dick sprang free. Backing Pilar up, he laid her on the bed and lifted her leg over his shoulder. Without uttering a word, he put his face between her legs, closed his eyes, and let his fantasy begin.

Mink's twat was fat and hot as he licked at her swollen pussy lips. Her wide, ghetto hips grinded up to meet him, and she moaned and leaked on the bed as he inserted his tongue deep inside her and gulped down her juices, wanting—no *needing*—to swallow as much of her sharp-tasting honey as possible.

Pilar moaned, and Barron reached up and grabbed one of Mink's bold titties in his hand. They were so damn big, and her nipples were so damn long 'til they were almost obscene. He urged her to turn over onto her stomach and the sight of all that luscious ass almost choked him. It was an almighty ass. An ass that was as thick and ghetto as they came. It stood out from her body like a question mark, or like a camel's hump, but it was soft and perfectly shaped and oh so damn round.

Barron gripped Pilar's hips and urged Mink up on her knees. "I'ma fuck the shit outta you," he muttered in her ear, and then he slapped her butt and plunged up in her hard and raw. "Yeah," he growled as he banged Mink's wet pussy with a combination of lust and rage. He reached under her and pinched her nipple, then sighed and pressed his cheek to her naked back and licked at her soft skin. "I'm fuckin' you, you know," he told her as Pilar bucked back and threw that pussy down on him. He withdrew his dick until only the head was left inside her, and then he rammed it up in her guts and slammed it home over and over again.

"I'm fuckin' you, goddamn it!" Barron hollered as he pounded Mink's pussy with a passion he had never felt before. He was just about to cum when he snatched his dick outta her wetness and licked her hot pussy out from behind. He spread her ass cheeks wide with both hands, and his eyes rolled back in his head as he groaned and flicked his hot tongue around her hole, licking her back door out too.

"Yeah," he taunted that skank Mink as he straightened up

and drove home in Pilar's soggy pussy once again. This was the best fuck he had ever had. The absolute best one! With his eyes squeezed tight, he reached around and fingered Mink's clit, and then he grunted and dropped a load in her that was so big and hot that he lost his balance and they both fell flat on the bed. "Yeah, bitch!" Barron screamed in Pilar's ear. "I am *fuckin'* you!"

"So," Barron said the minute I scooted my chair up to the dinner table later that night. Selah had wanted to do a little welcome-back dinner for me with just the immediate family members. "What brings you back to Texas, Mink? Hold up, let me guess. You spent all your money, huh?"

Barron had me clocked at a thousand, but I didn't get mad and I damn sure didn't get loud. Instead, I cut my eyes at him and cracked a sweet, sexy little smile. "I thought I already told you. I came back to Texas to check on my father," I said softly. I leaned over and put my arm around Selah. "And to see my *mother* too."

That nigga almost choked on his dinner roll.

I giggled like hell and winked at Bunni and she winked back with her red-eyed self. Between her and Dane they smelled like a whole groove of good weed.

I turned my attention back to Barron. I loved to watch him squirm whenever I called Selah my mother. Seeing him get so shook was like sticking a hook in a fish's mouth and yanking it out of a body of water. Dane chuckled at what I had said, but Fallon had the nerve to look at me and roll her grown little eyes, and Jock stayed quiet and kept his face in his plate.

"Nah, for real, though," Barron said, getting back on his game real quick. "I'm sure that hundred grand was more money than you've ever seen in your whole life, Mink. So what did you do with it? Did you invest in any stocks and bonds?"

All eyes were on me now, but I gave not a damn.

"Yep," I lied. "I sure did."

"Oh really?" Barron smirked and nudged Dane, who was stuffing his face like he had the munchies. "Which ones?"

I laughed real loud because I didn't know shit about stocks *or* bonds. "Uh-uh, big brother," I wagged my finger at him and said mysteriously. "You know I can't tell you all that. You ever heard of trading insider secrets? That's what got Martha Stewart put under the jail."

My shit sounded real slick and clever, and Bunni and Dane laughed with me, but Barron wasn't done fucking with me yet.

"Okay, so how about metals? No portfolio is balanced without them. Did you buy yourself any precious metals, Mink?"

I thought about the grip I had dropped on diamond earrings, platinum necklaces, silver ankle bracelets, and glittering gold belly rings in places like Tiffany, Neiman Marcus, and Michael C. Fina.

"Oh, I got all that." I waved my hand and bragged, picturing my icy platinum jewels and all my gorgeous white gold. "Don't worry about me. I covered myself with precious metals, baby." I glanced at Bunni and giggled again. "From my head to my toes!"

"Mink," Selah cut in and tried to change the subject. "It's actually good that you came back when you did, baby. You're right on time for our annual Labor Day picnic. Viceroy hosts it every year in honor of his employees at Dominion Oil."

"Hold up, Mama," Barron said. "Don't tell me you still wanna have the picnic this year. That's a whole lot of work, and with Daddy being sick and all . . ." He shook his head. "I've gotta make a little run out of town soon, so it's a bad time for us to throw a party. I think we should just skip it."

"I disagree," Selah said, and frowned at her oldest son. "I think we should do just what we've always done. None of our employees stopped showing up for work when Viceroy got injured. They kept right on doing their jobs and doing them well. I think they should be rewarded for their loyalty and dedication the same way they've always been rewarded. By us giving them their annual bonuses, and providing them with a day filled with good food and good times." And then she added as an afterthought, "Where are you going anyway? I didn't know you had an out-of-town trip scheduled."

"New York," Barron said, and looked dead at me. "I'm going to New York. I gotta see a man about a snake."

While Barron was steady grillin' me, I was steady watching Selah. I busted the way her face crumpled when Barron said the words *New York*. She looked like somebody had stabbed her in the gut, and her hand shook as she reached for her glass of wine and tipped that baby way the hell back.

"Yo, what's poppin' off in New York?" Dane came up outta his haze and put his fork down. He poked me with his eyes, and then turned back to his brother. "If you lookin' for snakes, we got more belly crawlers right here in Texas than you could ever find in New York."

"Yeah, but New York snakes are slicker," Barron said as he looked at me and then chuckled. "And from what I can see, them belly bouncers crawl a whole lot closer to the ground."

Me, Dane, and Bunni stayed up half the night drinking gin and talking mad shit about Barron. "Ay, he's going to New York to try to get you, Mink," Dane said. "I heard him talking to somebody on the phone about tracking down fingerprints and arrest records. I sure hope your shit is clean."

I slept with that thought on my mind, and the next morning we boarded Selah's private jet called the *Diva Dominion*, so we could go see Viceroy at the hospital in Houston. The *Diva Dominion* was a dope little flying lounge that had every luxury that you could want while you was up in the air. I sat beside Selah feeling right raggedy from all the slut juice that I had guzzled the night before, and even though the flight was smooth, I had a hangover and my gut was tossed up pretty bad.

We touched down at the same airstrip that we had landed at the first time I visited Viceroy in Houston, and once again there were some bad-ass limos with big shiny rims waiting to whisk us away to the hospital. The whips were spotlessly clean and straight-up luxury on wheels, but that didn't stop me from leaning over and up-chucking all over the place before we could get to the hospital.

"Damn, girl!" Barron jumped and cursed and tried to scoot outta my splash range. No dice. I couldn't help but hit him. The bottom of his expensive pants was now dotted with pink and yellow goo, and his face was all frowned up as he stared at the nasty slime that had also hit his thirty-eight-thousand-dollar Amedeo Testoni shoe.

"Mink!" Selah patted my back and handed me her lace handkerchief to wipe my mouth. I had turned away from her when I felt the hot tide rising in my throat, so she was safe. "Are you okay, baby? You catching a stomach virus or something?"

As pissed as he was, even Barron had to laugh real loud at that one, and for once I didn't blame him because Selah woulda had to be stone dead not to smell all that nasty gin that came up outta my stomach.

We were escorted into the hospital by some administrative staff, and instead of going into the ICU with Selah, me and Bunni headed straight to the girls' bathroom so I could rinse out my mouth.

"What did you do?" Bunni got hyped when I told her I had thrown up on Barron. "Stick ya damn fingers down your throat just to piss that square off?"

"No, stupid." I ran some water in the sink and started rinsing out my mouth real good. "I think I just got car sick."

Bunni smirked. "Car sick my ass. Girl you just need more practice holding your liquor."

I shrugged Bunni off with the *whatever* look. My stomach felt like shit, and as much as I wanted to go crash out in one of

them big chairs in the visitors lounge, I needed that three hundred grand, so my ass had work to do.

I waited until Fallon came out of Viceroy's room, and then
I went inside. That nasty smell of hospital sickness hit me as
soon as I opened the door, and I almost gagged again as I
stepped up to Viceroy's bedside.

"It's okay." Selah rubbed my shoulder, mistaking my gag
for a muffled sob. She stared down at the empty-looking shell
on the bed that was her husband. "It's been a long, hard jour-
ney but he's in good hands now."

I got real hopeful.

"You mean in Jesus' hands?"

Barron shot me a shitty look.

"No, idiot. He's in his new neurologist's hands."

I stared down at Viceroy. "Them doctors ain't tryna tell
y'all he's gonna wake up, are they?" I asked with my voice full
of doubt.

"That's what we're paying them the big bucks for, Einstein.
To figure all that out."

"Well how long is all that gonna take?" I demanded, getting *waaay* too hasty with it. "I mean," I said, tryna clean it up,
"doctors like to do a whole lot of experimenting sometimes,
you know. If it's all gonna end up the same anyway, I just don't
think we should let him suffer like this forever, y'all feel me?"

"Mink, we got this," Barron barked, swelling up and shutting me out. I could tell he had peeped my hold card just by
the way he said it. "Nobody's pulling no plugs or making any
decisions yet. We don't know *how* this is gonna end up. You
feel *me?*"

Selah sighed and put her arm around me. She pulled me
close to her and I fought the urge to shrug her off. "I just wish
he could have gotten a chance to really see you, Mink. A
chance to get to know you like the rest of us have. You were
his little girl. His baby. The apple of his eye. I think it would
have meant the world to him."

Ain't gonna happen, I wanted to tell her as I stepped out of her embrace. I didn't care how many new head doctors they dragged through the door. Viceroy was gone. His whole vibe had been deaded. They might as well call the funeral home, dig the grave, and pry the lid off the trust fund, because papa-man was a wrap. Yep. That big old eyeball wasn't even giving me the heebie-jeebies no more because his ass just wasn't there. But hey, I was just a scheming little paper-chaser from Harlem. Who was I to pronounce the old man dead?

CHAPTER 12

I could tell shit was crucial the minute I heard Peaches' voice.

"Mink," he said. "Girl, when you and Bunni bringing y'all asses back home with that money, girl?"

"Why, what's wrong?" I asked, frowning. "Is it Mama, Peaches? Is something wrong with my mama?"

"No, your mama is doing okay. But it's that nigga!" Peaches said. He sounded scared, and fear wasn't something I was used to hearing from a dude like him. "It's Gutta. That fool is back on the streets and he's looking all over for your ass!"

"For real?" My voice was damn near a whisper.

"*Errrrm-herrrrm!* If he ain't bangin' on the damn door then he's blowing up my spot! That nigga is hunting for you, Mink. He wants his money and he ain't playing!"

I didn't know what the hell to tell Peaches, or what the hell to do.

"Umm . . . I ain't got it yet, P. I'm working on it though . . ." *Die, Viceroy, die!* "But I ain't got it yet."

"Well what the fuck you gotta do to get it, Mink, huh?" Peaches wanted to know.

"I gotta wait a little while," I told him, trying to calm him down. "Don't worry, I'ma have it soon. If Gutta comes back just tell him I moved and you don't know where I am. I'm sorry all this fell on your head, Peaches. I really am. But I'm trying. I swear, I'm trying."

"I know you are, Madame Mink," he said, and I was glad to hear some of the fear was gone from his voice and he was back to loving on me. "Just get that loot and get back here as fast as you can. I would hate to have to bust a cap in Gutta's ass, but I will stretch that muthafucka out if I have to, *okay*?"

Now that's the gay beast Peaches that I liked!

"Handle ya bizz, P," I told him. And then I added, "You said Mama was doing okay, right?"

"Yeah. I went up there the other day. Your aunt Bibby was sitting with her and I chased her ass right out the door."

"Good," I said. P knew I didn't want them trifling-ass LaRues nowhere near my mama. "Thank you, Peaches. I lub you, boo."

I was a New York City snake, just like Barron had said, and I didn't waste no time sticking my forked tongue deep inside Selah's ears. I had a hunch that Dane was dead right. Barron was going straight to Harlem to try to dig up some doo-doo on me and fuck my game up with the board. Uncle Suge had pulled up the company cell phone records, and damn if Barron didn't have about a million calls to some Harlem private eye named Frankie Gaines. Well, two could play the sneak-tip game, and when Barron left for New York he was barely out the door good when I hit Selah with a smooth little story that was sure to cushion my fall when Bump tried to flip my ass down to the mat.

But not everything I told Selah was a lie, though.

"Selah," I said softly as we held hands and took a walk around the large pond in the back of the mansion. The gardeners had planted all kinds of colorful flowers around the border, and every now and then she stopped to pick one, or just to stare down at them or gaze out at the water.

"I almost didn't get to come back down here, you know."

"Why?" she asked, looking at me with those soft eyes of hers.

I shrugged. "Not because I didn't wanna come back but," I lowered my gaze and whispered, "but because I had to go to court."

I bit my lower lip and kinda turned my upper body away from her, like I was so damned shamed of myself.

"You had to go to court? For what?"

I took a deep breath and glanced at her real fast. "For writing bad checks," I blurted out. I caught her quick frown, and I went deep into actress mode.

"But I didn't write them," I insisted, which was true. I *didn't* write the hot checks that I was telling her about, but I had damn sure written a whole bunch of other ones. "It wasn't me. They had the wrong girl. The checks didn't even come outta New York. They came from some other city when I could prove I was in New York, so they had to drop the charges and let me go."

"But why did they blame you in the first place?"

Now I damn sure wasn't about to tell her all that! The truth was, I had gotten busted for getting down on an insurance scam, and somehow when they arrested me and ran my fingerprints, they came back a match for some chick who had a warrant out on her ass for cashing stolen checks and failing to show up in court. Even though I had to sit in jail madder than a mutha for getting knocked for somebody else's scheme, the idea seemed like a damn good one to me, and as soon as they cleared shit up and let me loose, I got me my own check-cashing hustle going and I rode that baby until the wheels fell off.

But was I gonna explain all that to Selah? Hell to the naw!

"I was a victim of identity theft," I told her instead, and that was not a lie. "Somehow my fingerprints came back a match for a girl who did all kinds of illegal stuff while she was pretending to be me."

"Really?" She frowned. "Who was she? Did the police ever catch her?"

I shook my head and said truthfully, "I don't know who she was, or if she ever got caught, but she was good. Real good."

Matter fact that chick was *damn* good. I'd gotten busted more than once behind her bullshit. Just like me, she was a fraudster. A master thief. Any kind of scam you could think of that involved stealing somebody else's dollar, this grifter had pulled it off.

"That girl was into *everything*," I told Selah, and ran her down a list of stuff that I had been busted for in the past, as well as some shit that I didn't really do but had been charged with anyway. "And guess what? Right before I came down here the first time, this same girl got busted in some kinda credit-card scam, and *I* was the one who had to show up in court!"

I spit all that out like I was real offended by the fact that somebody was skunking up my good name, but the truth was, if it was this easy for me to take over Sable's identity, it had probably been way easier for some other chick to steal mine.

Selah pursed her lips and looked pissed off.

"It's such a shame," she said, shaking her head, "that nothing is sacred or safe these days. Sure, the Internet gives us great access to information and cultures and trends that we could have never reached before, but it also gives other people a lot of opportunities to exploit us. Really, your word and your good name is all you own in this world. I'm told it can take years to get your credit straightened out after your identity is stolen."

"Uh-huh," I agreed real fast, setting the stage for all my other denials later, "and it can take years to get your arrest record wiped clean of all those bogus charges too."

"Well, be careful, baby. Nothing is truly secure these days. Thieves are everywhere, and if they're trying hard enough to get you, they'll get you."

CHAPTER 13

Barron knew better than to roll up in Harlem looking like an oil mogul and smelling like cash, so instead of hiring a limo and a driver the way he usually did when he traveled out of town, he rented a nice little Acura at the airport and drove into Manhattan on his own.

New York was full of flossers, and even though he dug the city, especially Broadway and the financial districts, Barron wasn't feeling the kind of women that places like Brooklyn, Harlem, and the Bronx spit out.

He had driven across the bridge and toward the projects of Harlem, and everywhere he looked there were chicks like Mink who were living strictly for the city.

They walked around all glossed and glammed up in the city heat, with more ass and titties popping out of their skimpy clothes than a little bit. Their quick, hungry eyes checked him out as he drove by, and he eyed them right back. Yeah, some of them were fine and packing big bombs, but a whole lot of them were also rough and grimy. Tough chickens that the streets had dried out and used up. With their crazy four-color curved nails and matching wigs, tatted-up tits, swap-meet Gucci purses, and over-the-top gear, they were colorful products of the gutters they were trying so damn hard to claw their way out of.

Barron had hit up the PI dude named Frankie Gaines as soon as he touched down at the airport. Frankie was an ex-parole officer who came from a big family in Harlem. Although most of the men in his family were in law enforcement, Frankie had ditched his monkey suit so he could be his own boss. They were planning to meet at T. C.'s Place, a renovated pool hall that one of Frankie's boyz ran, and Barron wanted to make sure he was there right on time.

"Yo, ya girl Mink LaRue been bizzy as hell. Bizzy, bizzy, bizzy!" Frankie said as he dapped Barron out and greeted him at the front door of the old pool hall that was now a youth nightclub. He had a folder in his hand, and Barron followed the young, street-tested dude to a small office down a hall. "So how much did this fine-ass thief hit you for?"

"A hundred grand."

Frankie's eyes got big as he shook his head. "*Damn*, fool! Where you from, my brotha? That trick *stole* you! You shoulda called a nigga up a long time ago and I coulda saved you some cash!"

"Lemme see what you got," Barron said. His hands shook with greedy excitement as he reached for the report Frankie was holding.

Frankie waved him off and started reading. "Pick pocketing, drug distribution, credit-card fraud, shakedowns, blackmail schemes, wire fraud, identity theft, grand larceny, breaking and entering, prescription scams, bad-check writing . . ." He held up a glossy head shot photo of Mink and then tossed it on the table. "And I'm not talking about just here in Harlem neither. This chick done hit everywhere," Frankie said, shaking his head. "Jersey, Connecticut, Philly, Baltimore, DC . . . believe it. If Mink LaRue ran across something that wasn't nailed down— her ass stole it."

Frankie let out a bitter chuckle and passed Barron the report. "The only thing I didn't find on her is dead bodies. I ain't saying she don't have none, it's just that ain't none of them started stinking yet."

"God*damn*," Barron muttered under his breath, and then whistled out loud as his eyes continued to scan the report. "This is worse than I thought."

"Word, bruh. The more shit I dug up on her the more shit came pouring in. This little chicken's been criminal minded ever since she hatched out the egg! For real, and her moms is the one who got her started pulling scams in the first place."

"Her mother?"

Frankie nodded. He searched through the stack of paper in the folder and pulled out two sheets.

"I got a report right here that says she was just a toddler when her and her mother were on a city-owned bus and it crashed into a parked car. Her moms faked a bunch of injuries for both of them and she used Mink to get a big fat settlement from the city's insurance company. I guess pulling ganks got good to them because they've been pulling them ever since."

Barron thought about his own mother who was back at the mansion with the felonious Mink right now. Dane was there with her too, but he couldn't be counted on to protect Selah because if it wasn't about getting high then that pussy nigga wasn't shit. Barron shook his head. "Yo, I'ma have to get back home and toss that lil bandit up outta my crib, man."

Frankie laughed. "Nigga you better hope you still *got* a crib when you get back. The way this chick's been running through other people's paper you might go back and find all your shit transferred into her name!"

Barron took that shit in stride. He knew this hood dick was sitting there laughing at him, but it was cool because Mink really did have him looking just like a clown.

"I found one more thing for you," Frankie said as his laughter faded away and he got real serious.

Barron frowned. "Yeah, what's that?"

"I found Mink's nigga. Her ex-convict boyfriend. A cut-throat street slanga they call Gutta who just hit the bricks. He rolls with a killer click, and word on the streets is that Mink dipped out with a whole grip of young dude's paper. And now that nigga wants it back. Every goddamn dime of it."

Barron's ears perked right up. Now this was the type of shit he liked to hear!

"So, Mink beat a drug dealer out of some money? And now he's on her ass?"

"Yep. That's the story. I dug up a heap of dirt on dude too. He ain't no petty thief like ya girl Mink is, but he *is* a killer."

Barron wanted to jump up and down.

"Yo, I wanna meet this dude. Put me on to him."

Frankie nodded. "A'ight. I might can do that. That nigga's on probation, so lemme holla at a few of my brothers and see if we can work something out."

Barron grinned and rubbed his hands together. He loved a good fight, and he was willing to trick off mad money to watch this cat Gutta fly Mink's head upside a wall. Hell yeah. If he could sic a dog like Gutta on Mink and get those two to go at it hard, then he'd gladly sit back and watch the show and buy everybody in the room some damn popcorn.

Frankie Gaines was good to his word. He had mad family who worked in New York law enforcement, and his little brother Dutchy was actually Gutta's probation officer.

"Yo, you sure we're gonna be good running up on him in here?" Barron asked as they walked into the probation building and slid past damn near a hundred convicted criminals. They were scattered everywhere in the large room. Some were lounging on the chairs, and others were leaning up against the walls, and a few were even laid out on the grimy floor.

"Yeah, we straight," Frankie said over his shoulder. "He's in there with my brother Dutchy right now. You know they gotta make sure his shit is straight and he ain't violating nothing."

They walked down a long hallway that had small offices lining both sides. Hard-looking ex-cons were flowing in and out of doorways looking pissed off at the world. Frankie led Barron into an office on the right side of the hall. A brown-skinned brother sat behind a desk, and another dude, muscle-bound and huge as shit, sat in a folding chair with his back to the door.

He was a hard nigga, Barron could tell that even before dude turned around and grilled him. Young, but dangerous. He was dressed like the streets and a cold look of disdain lurked in his eyes. He shifted his massive shoulders slightly to the right so he could see Barron better, and everything about his chiseled posture and the vibe he was giving off labeled him a predator.

Barron waited while Frankie went over to the desk and dapped his brother out, and then he introduced Barron to Dutchy, and Dutchy introduced them both to Gutta.

"Sup," Barron said and reached out to Gutta for some dap.

That nigga never even blinked. The look in his cold eyes said Barron was just a sweet lil bitch who didn't deserve no love.

"Check it out," Frankie explained to Gutta as he closed the office door and got ready to play power broker and fit all the puzzle pieces together. "This here is my boy, Bump. He's from Texas. He's cool with ya girl, Mink. Matter fact, she's his sister."

Leaning against the wall, Barron felt the chill go up in Gutta's eye when Mink's name was mentioned. Dude had a jaw that looked like it could stand up to a sledgehammer and he clenched it hard when he heard her name, like he was ready to chew something up.

Frankie spent the next few minutes running Mink's latest game down to Gutta, who got more and more swole by the minute. Barron got his two cents in too, and dropped big dimes on Mink and blew her shit up without an ounce of brotherly love. He told Gutta about the hundred grand that Mink had scammed his family for, and about the rest of the cash she was down in Texas trying to get her hands on right as they were speaking.

"Yo!" Gutta growled, opening his mouth for the first time. "You tellin' me that bitch tricked off all my fuckin' money and then she stole a hunnerd grand off you and dipped with that shit too? Wit'out paying me minez?"

Barron shook his head. "Nah, man. I'm telling you she spent the hundred grand she got from me too. And *then* she dipped. Her ass is broke again right now, but unless I can come up with something concrete on her, she's probably gonna clean us out again. And this time she's gonna get even more than she got the first time."

Gutta shrugged. He was a solo gorilla. Barron could see it all in his face. He was gonna take Mink down in his own vicious way, and he didn't need no pack of wolves to help him hunt neither. "So what y'all pussy niggas need me for?"

"I need you as my proof of what she's been out here doing, man," Barron said. "Proof in the flesh. Come with me back to Texas, man, and I'll make sure you get back five times what Mink owes you. Plus a whole lot more."

CHAPTER 14

Two nights later Barron was ready to get back to Texas and be about the bizz of blowing Mink's shit up. Gutta had agreed to roll with him to Dallas, and Frankie Gaines drove him to the projects to scoop dude up so they could head to LaGuardia Airport and catch a red-eye flight going south.

"You think he's really gonna fly?" Barron asked as they got outta Frankie's whip and strode up the walkway to the fourteen-story project building in St. Nick projects.

Frankie shrugged. "I guess so. Shit, the nigga said he would."

A group of rowdy young slangas stood loitering outside the entrance to the building wearing huge white tees and loose jeans sagging low on their asses. Barron wasn't no bitch by any stretch of the imagination, but he wasn't no banga neither. He rode the fence between the worlds of the haves and the have nots, but he damn sure liked chillin' on the money side better.

He had left his expensive business suits and thirty-thousand-dollar shoes back in Texas where they belonged. He had left his 9mm behind too, and even though he was dressed in decent shit, it was still the gear of the streets. His ensemble might have been understated, but it was still fresh as hell. It didn't come off a rack on 125th Street, but it hadn't come outta Brooks Brothers neither.

He followed Frankie toward the trap boys with a tight feeling burrowing in his stomach that he recognized as unease. Whether it was Houston or Harlem, the hood was still the hood, and dudes from the projects could smell a nigga who wasn't from around their way. Even though he wasn't strapped, Barron manned up and made sure he wasn't giving off even the slightest whiff of fear or concern, and when Frankie dapped out the young'uns and they showed him love by parting to let him through, Barron walked easily through the crowd right behind him.

They took the elevator up to the twelfth floor and got off and walked around the corner to the last apartment on the left. Frankie knocked on the door, then stood back a little bit so whoever looked out the peephole could see who he was before they opened the door.

"Who is it?"

"It's Frankie. I'm looking for Gutta."

Locks turned and the door swung open. The two men stepped inside the small apartment. The old lady who had let them in smelled like Newports and fried eggs. She motioned for them to wait in the living room. Barron looked around the small area. There were statues of Jesus on the cross all over the walls, and it smelled like a pot of beans and fatback was cooking on the stove in the kitchen.

Barron wondered again about Gutta. He had his doubts about that nigga. As hardbody as he was, the thought of getting on an airplane scared the shit outta him.

"Yo, I fucks with whips, trains, and buses, nah'm sayin?" Gutta had told him. "I don't fuck with no airplanes and all that kinda aerodynamic bullshit right there."

Gutta had tried to play him by telling him he needed half the money up front, but Barron wasn't no sucka and he had let that big nigga know it. His offer was non-negotiable. Wasn't no transactions going down until they got to Texas, and if

Gutta wanted to get paid and get his hands around Mink's throat, then his ass had to get on an airplane and roll with it.

Gutta came outta the back of the apartment looking mean and tight. The odor of hard liquor surrounded him in a cloud. He glanced at the men standing in the living room, then brushed right past the old lady and walked straight out the door.

"What the fuck?" Barron muttered as the door slammed shut. He scrambled behind Frankie, who snatched the door open and followed Gutta out into the narrow hallway.

"Yo," Barron hollered as Gutta pushed through the stairway door and bounded down the pissy, garbage-strewn stairs. "You still going, right? Where's your bags and shit, man?"

Gutta led them all the way down to the first floor, through the crowded project lobby, and outside into the warm night air. Barron didn't know if this nigga was gonna get in the whip and ride out to the airport or not, but to his surprise Gutta paused and followed Frankie down the walkway and got in on the passenger side of the car.

Barron squeezed into the backseat with his long legs crunched up, and they rode a short distance away to Frankie's crib, where Barron had left his rented Acura. He had already dished off the dollars he owed the private investigator, so him and Gutta switched cars and left Frankie standing on the curb outside of his building.

As soon as they pulled off Gutta turned the radio to a rap station and cranked the volume up loud. They rode down the streets of Harlem with their windows vibrating from the bass, and Gutta tryna stomp a hole in the floorboard as he kept up with the song's beat. Barron had just turned onto Lenox Avenue when Gutta threw him a stiff bow and told him to stop the car.

"Yo! Pull this shit over!" he barked over the music. They were just about to pass Club Lick 'Em, an elite titty bar and strip joint where the streets were packed and a big crowd of people were coming and going. "I need to make a quick stop in that joint. My manz supposed to be up in there tonight."

Barron cut his wheels to the right and got out of traffic, then shook his head in mad exasperation. He knew Gutta wasn't trying to get inside no strip club to get up with no nigga. This fool had the fear of flying and a thirst for liquor on the brain.

"C'mon, my dude!" Barron tried to reason with him. "There's some drinks waiting for us at a lounge in the airport. This ain't the time to be hollering at no freaks in the club."

But Gutta had already opened his door and hopped out.

"Shit!" Barron cursed and turned the radio down as he watched Gutta bounce through the club's front door. It was crowded as hell out there. Every parking spot was taken, and the streets were lined with double-parked whips. All kinds of pimp-type nigs were rolling out of limos with half-naked working girls hanging off their arms. Barron doubled-parked his rental car a block away and started walking briskly toward the club.

Selling pussy wasn't what it used to be, he noticed as a giggling pair of young hookers brushed past him and he caught a whiff of their scent and frowned. A lot of chicks on the stroll these days looked tapped out. Instead of fixing themselves up so they could turn a dude on, some of the shit they slapped on was a straight turn off. If Barron was gonna lay out good money for some used pussy then the chick better smell like honey and perfume, not like a whole jar of sour pickles and some flaming-hot Cheetos.

Outside the club, fliers were taped to the door and plastered on the windows that said Club Lick 'Em was hosting its fourth annual Tri-City Playa's Ball for the Labor Day weekend. Hustlers and chicks from New York, New Jersey, Baltimore, DC, and Philly were ballin' and partying together and drumming up money so a portion could be donated to a children's outreach foundation.

Barron pulled the door open and the thick smell of funky carpets and sweaty ass washed over him. He stepped inside and immediately his eyes were drawn to the stage on the far side of the room. The overhead lights were dim, and colorful spot-

lights shone down on the strippers as they snaked their bangin'
bodies around the shiny golden poles.

Barron walked in deeper, and his eyes scanned the tables as
he searched for Gutta. He spotted him sitting with a bunch of
hood nigs, right up front where the action was. Picking up an
empty chair, Barron joined them at the round table that had
been pushed off slightly to the side.

Gutta was chilling with his set and getting even more lit.
Him and all his boyz fronted Barron off with killer glares
when he sat down, but the hostility disappeared when a long-
legged waitress in a short skirt and high heels came over to
take Barron's drink order and he told her to bring him some
yak and to give Gutta and his friends another round of whatever the fuck they was already drinking.

"Goddamn!" Gutta hollered real loud as a new round of
strippers came up on the stage. It looked like a bunch of fine-
ass working girls were out in full force tonight. A lot of them
had come from out of town with their pimps, and they seemed
hot and hyped to participate in all the sexy contests that Club
Lick 'Em was hosting for the weekend. With his eyes glued to
the chicks on the stage, Gutta tossed back his drink and
pointed at the one in the middle and yelled, "That bitch right
there got some nice big titties!"

Gutta's crew laughed in agreement as Barron checked the
girl out. Her chest *was* puffed out real tight, but it didn't look
half as good as Mink's did. All of a sudden he felt something
like jealousy jump up in his chest as he cut his eyes at Gutta.
This drunk fool had been all up in Mink's guts. He'd sucked
those pretty titties with the nice thick nipples, and he'd banged
that plump ass of hers and tasted that juicy slit too.

"I gotta piss." Gutta got up from the table and disappeared
into the darkness of the crowd. Barron couldn't help plastering
his eyes back on the stage. The combination of thinking about
Mink and watching the sexy stripper grind her ass on the stage
pole made a knot rise in his drawers. He scooted his chair fur-

ther under the table and tossed back his Hen dog, then signaled to the waitress to bring him another round.

But before she could come over to the table, the lights changed on the stage and a slamming cut blasted from the speakers. All the little tester-strippers ran toward the background, and a whole new slew of fine big-booty girls, about six of them, busted out from the darkness strutting their thick thighs and round hips on center stage, and started twerkin' and grinding and mopping up the floor as they dipped their sexy chips.

Every man at the table sat there with his mouth wide open, mesmerized and damn-near sucked into a coma by the spectacular thighs on one particular shawty who was rocking a frilly yellow thong. Her legs were thick and shapely and she was shaking her ass like she was trying to make both cheeks fall off.

Just about every chick up in this set could make the average nigga cum in his drawers, but none of them had shit on the explosion of red feathers that suddenly burst out from deep in the back of the crowd. She wore a mask over her face, but her luscious body was high yellow and exotic. Sicker than sick. A small halo of red feathers circled her head and two tiny ones were stuck to each of her nipples. Her hips looked like sweet lemon perfection. Her waist was tighter than tight, and her redbone ass was hunked out in the back like it shoulda had its own zip code. She coiled and winded her body at the waist just like a snake, and every eye in the house was molesting the hell outta her stunning bottom half.

Barron couldn't believe what he was seeing. Mami was twerkin' her thick butt so hard her flesh jiggled and made his eyes go gaga. She shimmied across the stage with her magnificent body drawing whistles, big bank, and resounding applause. Barron's dick swelled up in his pants to twice its normal size, and he was just about to holler out loud when Gutta came back to the table. He stared at the gorgeous stripper for a quick second, and then that drunk gangsta nig wilded straight the fuck out!

"Yo, *Mink!*" he hollered at the top of his lungs.

The chick on the stage ignored him as she spread her stunning legs for all the men to see. She ran her tongue around the edge of her lips and massaged her slick pearl with one slim finger. Greenbacks rained down on her like a tropical shower as dudes tossed their entire pocket stash at her feet. She bit down on her lower lip, then grinded her hips in a sexy circle and humped her hand at the same time, and a puddle of drool leaked from almost every mouth up in the joint.

Gutta lost his head. He snatched up his chair and held it over his head, and then he launched that shit up on the stage like it was a missile. Strippers came up off their poles screaming and ducking. The girl pulled her finger outta her pussy, snatched off her mask, and bent down and started scooping her money up off the floor as fast as she could.

Two bouncers in white tees rushed over to get at Gutta, but he was a big muthafucka. He swung on the tall one with the bald head and crashed dude flush in the grill. Before the other bouncer could get him some, Gutta leaped up on the stage and grabbed the girl around her ankles as she tried to run away, yanking her down to the floor.

"Mink!"

The other strippers screamed in terror as the girl slammed down on the stage ass–first. Red feathers flew everywhere. Fighting like a true soldier, she kicked out viciously at Gutta, digging her pointy high heels all in his face. Screaming at the top of her lungs, she threw a flurry of man-blows at his head that had that drunk nigga covering up instead of fighting back.

"Get the fuck offa me, you psycho bitch!" she hollered as Gutta got her in a bear hug and laid her out flat. He was all over her ass, and he flipped her into a headlock and started choking her lights out right in front of Barron's eyes.

About five bouncers attacked outta nowhere. They rushed up on the stage and swallowed Gutta up as the music came to a screeching halt and the overhead lights were flicked on.

Gutta's crew started wildin' out too. They jumped up on the stage swinging and tossing mad dudes off of their manz.

"*Mink!*" Barron could hear Gutta bellowing drunkenly from somewhere near the bottom of the fighting pile. "Bitch I'ma kill your ass! I'ma kill your ass, Mink!"

More security dudes jumped up on the stage and Barron caught a glimpse of Gutta being pinned down with his hands roped behind his back.

"Mink!" he hollered. "Mink! What the fuck is you doin' up in here, Mink?"

Yeah, Mink, Barron raged inside as he stared at the girl and thought about the two empty seats that were about to be on that red-eye flight to Dallas. *Just what the fuck is your ass doing up in here?*

It took a good minute to get everything calmed down, but shit was always jumping off at a strip club and the management at Club Lick 'Em was quick to restore order and get their clients back to pinching titties, buying drinks, and shooting off during lap dances.

"Yo, I coulda sworn you was her! I swear to God you look *just like* her," Gutta muttered over and over to the stripper he had assaulted up on the stage. He had a big bruise from getting busted upside his head in the fight, but he'd sent three bouncers crawling off the stage covered in blood too. If it hadn't been for Barron sliding the club's owner some big loot to cover the damage that had been caused, wasn't no telling how the night would have ended.

"You really do look like her," Barron told the girl who sat across from him in the red-feathered thong. They were drinking in a back room with the chick and one of her funny-looking girlfriends, and both of them said they worked at a strip club in Philly. "I mean, *just* like her."

It was true, but even though the girl, who told them her name was Dy-Nasty, had the same pretty face and stacked body as Mink's, there was something a little different about her too. Barron checked her out while she talked to Gutta. This girl looked harder than Mink. Tougher. Her fingernails were broken off and every one of her toes had either a bunion, a corn, or a callus sitting on top of it. Mink was definitely a rat from the projects, but this beautiful chick right here was a 'rilla from the zoo. She had some crust on her that wasn't on Mink, Barron had to admit. Some kind of hard-knock grime that looked like it would never wash off.

"Hey, lemme ask you something," Barron said as he stared at Dy-Nasty. He'd been steady looking her up, down, and side-ways, with his mind racing crazily a million miles a minute, and when the light bulb finally went off in his head the glass shards rocked him like an explosion. *Nah, it couldn't be,* Barron told himself. *Hell fuckin' no! It just couldn't be!*

"Yo, you ever been to Texas?" he blurted out.

Dy-Nasty turned away from Gutta, then frowned and gave him the dumb-ass look. "No. Why?"

Barron shook his head quickly. "Nah, no reason. I'm just asking." He paused for a few seconds, then went in at her again. "You ever heard of a girl named Sable Dominion?"

Dy-Nasty's hand trembled and her drink spilled over the edge of her glass. She glanced at her funny-looking girlfriend real quick, then stared hard at Barron.

"Yo, who the hell is you? You got a badge up under that Polo or what?"

"Nah," Barron said, "I ain't got no badge, but I do have some DNA results back at my crib. What you know about that?"

Barron had asked a loaded question and he damn sure got a booming answer. He couldn't believe what the fuck came out of Dy-Nasty's mouth.

"I just took me a DNA test not too long ago!"

Barron nodded at her. The Gods must have been smiling down on him, because for once in his life it seemed like all his little ducks had just snapped to attention and lined up in a row.

"I'm Barron Dominion. I got your test results."

"For real?" Dy-Nasty exclaimed when Barron told her exactly who he was, and then ran a plan down her so sweet and made her an offer so scrumptious there was no way her broke, trifling ass could refuse.

"So you tellin' me you're Sable's brother and you want me to come with you to Texas so I can get all that rich girl's money?"

"Yep," Barron lied as he eyeballed her. This chick was even worse than Mink. Much worse. He didn't know how the hell both of them had managed to pull one on the DNA lab, but neither one of them was Sable. He knew that for a fact. Especially Dy-Nasty. This chick had *lockup* written all over her, and she probably had Mink's rap sheet beat up and down, coming and going. And that was exactly what he was counting on. He had the perfect opportunity to catch two hoodrats with one fat hunk of cheese. With Dy-Nasty's DNA match in his pocket, it was gonna be real easy to prove Mink was a fraudster, and even easier to have Dy-Nasty's crusty, criminal ass disqualified from the trust account.

"All you have to do is come to Texas," Barron told the raunchy stripper with the dollar signs flashing in her eyes, "and with your results in my hand, I'll present them to our board of directors and you'll get your money. It's just as simple as that."

"Yo," Gutta barked. His bottom lip was busted and the noogie on his head was fucking up his whole flow. "So when I'ma get my money, nigga? Yo, son, you owe me! I'm telling you, you better not try to fuck me outta minez!"

Barron half chuckled. "I got you, man. You gonna get paid in full. I'll wire it to Frankie tomorrow and he'll slide it to you."

"Wire it to Frankie? I thought me and you was flying out tonight, slime?"

"Nope." Barron waved him off and reached out for Dy-Nasty's hand. "You missed your flight, my man. I gots me a new rider now."

CHAPTER 15

Me and Bunni had only been at the mansion for about a week when some Texas-sized shit-balls hit the Dominion family fan. I was sitting at the kitchen counter eating some grits and eggs that Miss Katie had fixed for me, when a crazy-loud scream cut through the air.

It sounded just like Selah. Me and Miss Katie both froze.

There was a big commotion coming from the front of the house, and I heard Barron's voice above everybody else's. He was back in town and he sounded straight-up shook.

"What in the world . . ." Miss Katie gripped the neck of her dress as both of us looked toward the front room. Instead of answering her, I jumped off my stool and hauled ass outta the kitchen and sprinted down the long hallway. I met up with a servant they called Big Grownie, who was waddling toward the kitchen as fast as she could.

"What in the world happened?" I asked her.

"It's Mrs. Dominion!" she blurted out. Her flat nose was sweating like crazy and her stockings swish-swished as her fat legs moved. "I gotta get some ice. She done passed plum out!"

I went dashing down the hallway and into the big living room, and what I saw made me skid right in my tracks. Selah was down, all right. She was stretched out in the middle of the floor with Barron crouched down beside her, slapping her cheeks and tryna bring her back.

It looked like everybody in the whole damn house had come running, but it was the person I saw standing right beside Barron that had my full attention. I struggled to figure out what kinda bullshit I was seeing in my brain, and I got smashed with a lightning bolt to the eyes as I looked past first Barron, then Dane, and then Bunni and one of the housekeepers, and to my shock and surprise . . . damned if I wasn't looking straight at . . . *me!*

Oh yeah, the shit had hit the fan and sprayed all over the Dominion Estate! Barron had came back from New York with some chick who looked just like me! And just like me, she was claiming to be Sable Dominion and now everybody in the mansion was going straight-up fuckin' bananas!

It felt like a bomb had gone off in the damn house as Barron stood in the middle of the room and announced that he'd found the real Sable, and then held her DNA test up in the air to prove it.

Gasps went up and suddenly everybody turned and looked at me like I was a liar *and* a goddamn thief! Jock had the nerve to smirk and shake his nuts in my direction, while the rest of the family got hyped and started talking real loud all at the same time.

I stood there feeling like a sho'nuff convicted criminal. I could see why Selah had passed the hell out. My knees were wobbly too as I stared at the bodacious new chick who was now striking a pose on Barron's arm.

"So, who's really who?" Fallon demanded over all the noise. "Are y'all related or what? 'Cause y'all look just alike."

"*Ooooh*, Mink!" Bunni pushed her way in between me and Fallon and whispered all up in my ear. She was so amped she pinched the shit outta the underside of my arm, and if all eyes wasn't on me I woulda knocked her ass to the moon. "That bitch *do* look like you!" she whispered. "She really do!"

"Well she *ain't* me!" I snapped as me and the rough-looking chick stood across the room from each other doing the Harlem stare-down. Mami was in the *life*, I could tell just by looking at her. She was hardcore with her shit, too. She probably stripped, danced, turned tricks, and did whatever else she could do to press a nickel into a quarter.

"Mink!" Barron called my name out real loud. This nigga had a suspiciously slick grin on his face as he pulled the girl over to me and introduced us. "Mink, this is my little sister Sable, also known as Dy-Nasty. Dy-Nasty this is Mink. Say hello to each other ladies."

I stared into her hazel eyes and I couldn't deny the truth of my lie. I was caught out there. Busted in my hustle. Straight thrown off my game. I peeped the hostile smirk that flashed on mami's face, and right away I knew I wasn't gonna open my mouth and speak unless this bitch spoke to me first!

The element of surprise mighta had me shook, but Miss Thang was all up on her toes. Bobbing and weaving and ready to knock me right out. She grinned at me, then bust out laughing.

"Mink, you say?" She glanced at Barron and nodded. "Oh, so this the chick you was telling me about, huh? Well, hey, Mink! I'm Dy-Nasty. Capital *d*, capital *n*, with a dash between the *n* and the *y*."

I blinked my eyes at her like she was crazy, and she moved up on me and gave me a quick wink and whispered, "But you can call me Sable."

Stepping back, she took a deep breath and looked around the room with a real big smile. "Wooo-hooo! Damn this joint is *laid*! Hey ere'body!" She waved her arm and then pumped her fist high air. "It feels *good* to be home!"

That stupid-fuck Barron musta told the whole damn family to come over to the mansion so he could show Dy-Nasty off. Pilar had shown up with her fat-head fiancé Ray, and Uncle Digger even came over too. Barron went around introducing Dy-Nasty to everybody as the long-lost Sable, and the whole time he was busy showing her off he kept grinning at me over his shoulder and shooting me some real slick looks.

"It's Dy-Nasty," I heard the girl tell Pilar. "Capital *d*, capital *n*, with a dash between the *n* and the *y*."

Pilar's whole face frowned up when she asked, "Sweetie, are you dyslexic or something?"

"Listen everybody," Barron said as he pulled her into the center of the room and got everybody's attention. The spotlight was shining real bright on Dy-Nasty, and she started primping and posing like a camera crew was standing off to the side snapping glamour shots.

"I know this looks crazy, and *somebody* is gonna have a whole lot of explaining to do to the police later on, but I've found our Sable," Barron said and pointed at Dy-Nasty. You could tell his ass was a lawyer just by the way he tried to get in everybody's head. "I got a tip from a private investigator that she was living in Philadelphia, so I found out where she was and went to talk to her for myself. Trust me," he said, and gave everybody the honest-john face like he was in the courtroom about to close a case, "I've done my homework and everything she's told me about her past lines up perfectly. And best of all, her DNA test came back a perfect match for Sable's."

All I could do was look down at my feet. The truth was out. The game was over. My scam had been exposed. I knew damn well I was the one who'd been lying, but I didn't know how to walk that shit back or how to get my ass up out the door without getting arrested and thrown under a hot Texas jail.

"But hold up." Dane got in it, shaking his head. "Wasn't Mink's DNA test a match for Sable's first? And everything she told us was solid too. Plus, Mink is from New York where

Sable was kidnapped. You said you found this girl somewhere in Philly, right, Bump? So how does *that* line up?"

"We *moved*!" Dy-Nasty blasted all over Dane, drenching him in about twenty gallons of ghetto juice. "We *used* to live in New York when I was little," she said with a nasty dip to her bottom lip, "but then we moved! Can't people move around? Damn!"

"Yeah, people can do a whole lot of shit," Dane beefed back at her. "Especially when they're tryna to get their hands on somebody else's *money*!"

I just sat there looking stupid as hell in the face. I was burning on a thousand inside, but Selah was the one who was really pissed. All this time she had been laid out moaning, rocking back and forth, and crying out stuff like, *Oh my God . . . Jesus have mercy, what is this world coming to? My baby . . . my child . . . how could anybody in their right mind be so damn cruel?*

But now she slung that ice pack off her head and stood up and got on her Brooklyn tip. "I don't know what the hell is going on here," she shrieked and put her hands on her hips. She was mad as hell and tears were running down her face as she locked me and Dy-Nasty together in a real icy glare. "But somebody is *lying*. This is no kind of joke to be playing on people! It's a serious situation and the police call it identity fraud!" Her face crumpled in as she fought to hold back her tears. "You just don't *play* like this when it comes to people's children and their *hearts*! I don't know what's going on, but one of you is a *liar*!"

She grilled me like, *You better come clean with this shit!* and I felt my chest cave in a little bit as I got scorched by the heat shooting outta her eyes.

"What you looking at *me* like that for?" I blurted out. "Give *her* the look!" I pointed my thumb at Dy-Nasty. "Shoot, I was here first!"

Selah's lips were real tight as she cried silently and stared back and forth at both of us. "Barron," she said quietly, "you'd better go check out that goddamn DNA lab! Something flaky is going on in there and I want to know exactly what it is!" She pointed at me and Dy-Nasty. "As for you two, both of you will have to be retested, and we'll find an independent lab to verify your results. Until that happens, I just don't know *what* to think or *who* to believe. But trust me, we're gonna get to the bottom of this. The truth is going to come out sooner or later, and when it does I'm going straight to the police so one of you better watch out."

"Don't worry, Mama. I'll take care of the lab," Barron said. "I tried to call them on my way in but they're closed for the Labor Day weekend. But like I said, don't worry. I plan to be there when they open for business first thing Tuesday morning."

"Oh, we *both* gonna be there," I assured his tight ass and blasted him with a heat round from my eyes.

"All three of us!" the Philly skank piped in, grilling me like she wanted some.

"Cool," I said, heating her ass up right back. "All three of us then!"

I walked over to Selah and reached out for a hug. She didn't even move. She just looked at me. "I'm sorry, Mama Selah. I don't know who this girl is or how any of this happened. But please believe me. I'm telling you the truth. Please don't be mad at me."

"Excuse me, Mrs. Dominion," one of the housekeepers spoke up and interrupted us before Selah could respond. "Which room should we put Miss Dy-Nasty in?"

Stick her ass out back in the pool house! I wanted to scream.

But instead, I got punched dead in the stomach when Selah glanced at the housekeeper, then turned and said with a big sigh, "Take her upstairs to the west wing. Put her in the guest suite right next to mine. That'll give us a chance to get to know each other a little better."

CHAPTER 16

"That bitch is really Sable!" I whispered to Bunni as we stood locked in my bathroom with the doors to our suites closed up tight. "That's *her!*"

Bunni nodded with her eyes all big and wide. "I know, girl. Ain't that some shit? But you and her look just alike. You think y'all might be related or something?"

"Hell no!" I shook my head. "Everybody got a twin somewhere in the world who looks just like them. Her people probably came up outta the same grimy Louisiana swamps as the LaRues."

"Well, mami got her a *real* DNA test!"

"I know. And ya fuckin' pain slut Kelvin at the lab better act like he know! I paid him good money and he better not bust us out!"

"Don't worry, I got his freaky ass in check. But how in the hell did that broad find out about the money?"

I shrugged and boosted myself up on the edge of the sink. "Probably the same way we found out about it. She saw Sable's picture somewhere and did a little digging around, and bam. She bumped into the same shit on the Internet that we did. Damn! Why that dusty bitch had to turn up right *now?*"

"I'on't know," Bunni said, frowning, "but did you see that critter's *feet*?"

"Crusty!" I blurted. "Straight crusty!"

"And the heels on them turned-over shoes?"

"Kickstands! Lean wit' it, rock wit' it!"

"So what we gonna do now? They ain't gonna give that money up to both of y'all, and we sure as hell can't take our asses back to Harlem broke!"

I thought about Gutta laying in a New York cut and ready to strangle me, and I shook my head. No, hell nah we couldn't go back broke. We just couldn't.

I slid down off the sink and started pacing the floor. They had put Dy-Nasty in a suite that was right off of Selah's, and it pissed me off that she might be up there sticking her dirty tongue all down in Selah's ear.

My mouth was dry as shit and my stomach was in knots as I tried to come up with a whammy. I didn't know how the hell I was gonna get outta this one but the look in Selah's eyes made me think my lil con number was definitely up.

Me and Bunni were deep in scheme-mode and burning up our brain cells when Dane hit me on my cell and told us to meet him in his crib. "I figured this shit out," he said as we got lit and smoked some hash in his bedroom. Dane's get-high was exactly what I needed right now because my ass was totally shook. Selah had called him and Barron upstairs to her suite and I couldn't wait to hear what he had to say.

"Bump is tryna fuck you up," Dane told me as he passed me a straight shot of gin. "He's tryna fuck both you *and* Dy-Nasty up."

I tossed the gin back real fast and almost peed on myself when all that pure alcohol burned a hot trail of fire down my throat. "What you mean?" I said, coughing hard with tears coming outta my eyes. "What the hell you talkin' about?"

"Bump's a strategist, Mink. He's a real slick lawyer. He's setting both of y'all up. Tryna play y'all both into a trap. That nigga don't care which one of y'all is really Sable. He don't give a damn about none of that. But what he does give a damn about is that trust fund and control of Dominion Oil."

I wiped my eyes and shook my head. "What does all that got to do with me and Dy-Nasty? Why would he bring that dusty trick all the way down here if he thought she was lying?"

"Because," Dane said, tryna break it down to me. "He's gonna try to take both of y'all down at one time. Check it out. If he can prove to the board that Dy-Nasty is really Sable, then two things happen. One, it knocks you outta the fight for the trust fund, because obviously if that chick is really Sable, then you ain't. And if she *is* Sable, well, c'mon. Y'all saw what she looked like. Like he snatched her up right outta Strip Clubs R Us. He's probably got pictures of her swinging off a pole and everything. Mama might not care about none of that, but the board damn sure will."

"That slick-ass dog," Bunni said, toking real hard on the stick of hash. "He's tryna catch y'all in a cross-con, Mink. You know how that shit goes. He's gonna use you and Dy-Nasty to cancel each other out!"

I sat there with my head spinning. I needed me another shot. And another joint too.

"So how the hell are we gonna get around him?" I asked Dane, praying he had some answers. I was way too pressed out to come up with anything. My scheme bag was bone dry.

"That's easy," Bunni said. "All you gotta do is make friends with Dy-Nasty. Be nice to the bitch."

I gave her a shitty look. "Make friends with her? Bunni put that hash down! That chickenhead got a major attitude problem. *Me* be nice to *her*? You must be trippin'."

"Damn," Bunni said, shooting me a look of disgust. "I gotta get you outta all this Texas heat, Mink, because your brain done got fried. It don't matter whether you like Dy-Nasty or not, you gotta make friends with her. At least for a little while."

"Why?" I demanded. I didn't see where Bunni was going and I wasn't feeling her logic at all.

"Because," Bunni said simply. "We might be able to use her ass one day. You know how that shit goes. You gotta keep your friends real close, but your enemies even closer."

Everybody was real excited at breakfast the next morning. Everybody except me. Bunni had started snoring like a truck driver the minute her head hit the pillow, but I had stayed up tossing and turning and worrying like hell for half the damn night. All I could think about was the three-hundred-grand pay day that was about to slip through my fingers. Dy-Nasty had come pissing in my territory at the worst possible time, and unless I came up with something to convince Selah and the rest of the family that she was the fraud and I was telling the truth, everything I had worked for was gonna go up in smoke.

I had started to go upstairs and climb in the bed with Selah and order in breakfast the way she liked me to, but I felt kinda funny inside, and the way she had fronted me off in front of everybody made me wonder.

Instead, I waited around for the cooks to start banging the pots and pans. Everybody in the family showed up for the grits, pancakes, sausage, and egg breakfast that Miss Katie had cooked, and the only person who was missing was Pilar's boyfriend, Ray. I had planned on getting a seat at the table right next to Selah's, but by the time I got downstairs Barron was already sitting on one side of her, and Dy-Nasty had stolen the seat on her other side. The seat that was supposed to be *mine*.

I ended up sitting between Bunni and Fallon, and when I glanced down the table at Selah she was so busy listening to Dy-Nasty run off at the mouth that she didn't even look at me.

"Let's go ahead and bless the food," Barron said as soon as the maids had set all the serving trays out. We all held hands and bowed our heads, but I was peeking outta one eye the whole time he prayed.

"Dear Heavenly Father, thank You for all the blessings You have bestowed upon this family. Thank You for our health, our wealth, and the many gifts that You have seen fit to allow into our lives. But most important, bless You for allowing me to meet Dy-Nasty so that our lost little sister could finally come home to her family. In Jesus' name, amen."

I coulda put my foot straight up Barron's ass! Instead, I sat there with a brick in my stomach and mad attitude steaming in my chest. I couldn't even move as everybody started reaching for the platters full of food and fixing their plates. I took two sausage links and a spoonful of grits. Bunni piled her plate up. She picked up her sausages with her hands and tore them in little chunks, then mixed everything together, the sausage, cheesy eggs, grits, and hash browns, all in one nasty-looking lump.

"Y'all got any hot sauce?" she asked one of the servers. The old lady nodded and went to get it, but when she came back holding out a bottle of Texas Pete's to Bunni, Dy-Nasty jumped her ass up and snatched it right outta the old lady's hand.

"Ooh! Hot sauce!" Dy-Nasty shrieked like it was a bottle of tequila and tomato juice. She shot Bunni a slick hater look and then opened it up and started shaking the sauce all over her food. That chick shook for a good minute too. By the time she was done her whole plate was swimming in that mess and half the bottle was empty.

"Yum," she said, setting the bottle down way on the other side of her plate. I frowned as she dug into her food like her fork was a snow shovel. This trick ate worse than Bunni did, who was sitting next to me burning on fire and still waiting on her hot sauce.

"Pass the damn hot sauce!" Bunni barked, and Barron had

the nerve to turn his nose up and look at her like, *Damn! Have some manners!*

Pilar was the first one to dig up Dy-Nasty's ass and she didn't treat her no better than she had treated me when I first came to Texas. "I don't know about you guys," she said, holding a piece of buttered toast in her hand, "but this just seems so crazy to me. You know, like it's déjà vu and we've all been in this situation before." She put her toast down and picked up a sausage link. She took a real tiny bite off the tip and then pointed it straight at Dy-Nasty.

"So, what's your story, Dy-Nasty? I mean, we've got two of you sitting here claiming to be Sable and no doubt going after her share of the trust fund, but at least we know a little bit about Mink. Who the hell are you?"

"I already told you," Dy-Nasty rolled her eyes and said all funky-like. "I'm Dy-Nasty. Capital *d*, capital *n*, with a dash between the *n* and the *y*."

"Yeah, yeah, yeah." Pilar waved her sausage around in aggravated little circles. "You've got your name down pat. We already got that part. But where did you come from?"

"From my mother's wound!" Dy-Nasty snapped. "Where the hell did *you* come from?"

"Ay," Dane said. He reached over and play-punched her on the shoulder and grinned with his mouth full of food. "It's all good, baby D. The fam is just curious, that's all. Ain't nobody jumping on you, they just asking a few questions, okay?"

Dy-Nasty took a quick peek at Barron. She did it so quick, and with such smooth slickness that nobody else mighta saw it. But I sure as hell did.

"Well what else do y'all need to know? I'm Dy-Nasty. I'm twenty-one, I grew up in Philly, and I'm an only child."

"So what made you decide to go after the money?" That was Bunni for you. Getting all in it when she wasn't even family herself!

I was surprised when Selah cut in real softly before Dy-Nasty could answer. "Are your parents still alive, Dy-Nasty? You took a DNA test, but what made you think you were Sable? Surely your mother never told you that she kidnapped you, did she?"

I wanted to toss my damn plate up in the air when that trick tried to bust my old move.

"No, she didn't never say nothing like that, but umm, I always knew I was different from the rest of my family."

"Hey! I already said that!" I reminded Selah. "I'm the one who said that first!"

"But did you ever think," Selah igged me and continued questioning Dy-Nasty, "that your mother wasn't your real mother? Did you ever get the feeling that you belonged with someone else?"

Barron had been coaching this chick. I could tell by the questioning little looks she kept sliding him on the sneak tip. His ass had already schooled her on exactly what she needed to say.

"Yeah," Pilar jumped back in. "If you *are* Sable, and if your mother really *did* steal you from that drugstore, then she needs to go to jail and answer for her crimes!"

I just knew this trick was gonna keep biting my flow and monkeying my moves, but she shocked me when she stared into her grits and got all emotional and shit.

"Look," she said, all of a sudden playing like she was soft. "This ain't fair! I don't even know y'all like that and everybody's tryna get all up in my head. I been through a lot in my life, okay? I wasn't raised with all this"—she looked around the huge, beautifully decorated dining room—"*fancy* shit."

Cursing in front of Selah? Slack-ass heathen! We all gave her the look. Even Barron.

"I remember one day when I was about five," Dy-Nasty went right on talking. "I was playing in my mother's closet and I found a little outfit balled up in a plastic bag that I thought would look good on my new doll baby. She was one of them real big dolls with blond hair and blue eyes, and the only clothes she had was a fake diaper and a dirty little undershirt."

She swallowed hard and made her bottom lip tremble like shit was about to get real emotional. *Old trick,* I wanted to scream at her ass. *That's a real old trick!*

"I took the clothes in my room and put 'em on my dolly, and when my mother came in and saw her she just went crazy. She slapped the shit outta me and then she snatched the doll and threw her in the bathtub and set her on fire."

That lip was really quivering now. She was sniffling too.

"My baby got burnt up! It was all because of them clothes and I could never figure out why until I saw this."

My mouth dropped open when she reached inside her bra and pulled out a small square of paper. She unfolded it and held it up high so everybody could see it. It was a faded color flyer of a missing child's poster. It showed a picture of a three-year-old girl wearing a lime green jumper and a bright pink shirt, and the words on the bottom read, SABLE DOMINION. KIDNAPPED CHILD.

A tear fell from Dy-Nasty's eye. "These are the same clothes my baby had on when she got burnt up! The only reason I even have this is 'cause my mother left it for me in an envelope when she died. There was a letter in there too. Mama's letter said she was sorry for all the things she had did wrong, and that she hoped one day I would find my real mother. The mother she stole me from all those years ago."

She passed the wrinkled piece of paper to Selah and started sniveling like a little kid. I watched Selah's eyes skim over the photocopied article, and then her head dropped to her chest and her hair fell into her grits as she started crying her eyes out.

"I'm sorry, Mama Selah." Dy-Nasty rubbed Selah's heaving back in wide circles. "I ain't mean to make you cry." That trick had the nerve to look around the table and pinch her lips together and give all of us the evil eye. "Now enough with all this sad stuff! I don't wanna talk no more about my other mother! She's dead and gone, and it ain't nothing I can do about whatever the hell she did or didn't do. Besides, I took the DNA test already. It said I'm Sable, so it don't really matter *what* Mama did all them years ago. A mama's love is something a child don't question, and I ain't about to sit here and start questioning it now!"

I almost wanted to clap and whistle. Barron had trained this little monkey real good. Instead of letting us go hard up her ass with no kinda Vaseline, Mami was shutting shit down. She had punked us with some real good defensive moves, and it sounded like everybody at the table had all of a sudden swallowed their forks and their damn tongues too.

"Well." Selah finally lifted her head and broke the silence. She pulled her napkin from her lap and used the end of it to wipe her eyes. "You're absolutely right about one thing. A mother's love is not to be questioned." She pressed her napkin to her face again and re-dabbed her eyes. "And, no, baby." She blessed Dy-Nasty with a warm smile. "That kind of love is nothing you should have to defend."

CHAPTER 17

The Fourth of July barbeque at the Dominion Estate didn't have shit on their Labor Day picnic. For one thing, there were a ton of clear people wearing Wrangler jeans and ten-gallon hats all over the place. There were shaded people and Latinos on the scene too, but they didn't work for the oil company. Most of them had been bused up from one of Viceroy's community centers in Houston where they ran a mentorship group called Dominion Diamonds, a nonprofit organization that took in young teenaged girls and taught them life skills.

It was a real pretty day. Huge, colorful blankets had been spread out in the grass surrounding the pond, and there were balloons, Frisbees, and Nerf balls flying around everywhere. A bunch of Viceroy's and Selah's hood relatives had shown up to party, but there were also a whole bunch of rich folks from the suburbs running around, and Dane told me most of them were longtime investors in Dominion Oil.

I finally dug what Bunni had said about me needing to make friends with Dy-Nasty so I could know what she was up to, but obviously Bunni hadn't given that slick chick the memo. Dy-Nasty strolled around in the grass stuck like glue to Barron, and he grinned all stupid with his arm draped around her shoulder as he introduced her to every damn body he passed.

I was burning up on fire as I watched Dy-Nasty sashay her big booty around in a pair of ugly yellow stripper shorts and a stank little push-up bra. It was hot outside, but it wasn't that damn hot! She looked real skankified from the back, and even though we were shaped a lot alike I knew my ass was firmer and looked way better than hers.

My lips were straight twisted as I checked out her flow. She was into wigs too, but hers wasn't the good Glama-Glo shit like mine was. She wore some tired-looking horsetail glued to the back of her head that was way longer than it needed to be, and even though her real hair was black and curly like mine, her edges were raggedy and damn near bald.

"Mink!" Bunni yeasted me up as we watched Dy-Nasty work the crowd. "Get up, girlfriend! Get out there and show your shit too!" I jumped on Bunni's advice, and me and that chick was out there grinning and kissing babies like hungry politicians as we both introduced ourselves to all those people as the Dominions' long-lost daughter Sable.

The problem was, we looked a whole lot alike, and a lotta people I went up to with my hand held out either thought they was seeing double, or they just smiled at me and said, "Oh, we met already. Don't you remember?"

The smell of grilling meat was in the air. Selah had catered all the food except for the chicken, ribs, and steak, and there were three Texas-sized barbeque grills sparked up and giving off sweet hickory smoke. Waiters and waitresses had been hired to serve the drinks and keep everybody's stomach full, but by the time I finished working the crowd, I was so wound up I couldn't even force a chicken wing down my throat.

"Barron is so damn stupid." I plopped down on the blanket and elbowed Bunni, who was leaning over a big plate of food tryna inhale that shit. I hated the way my homegirl ate. While I was busy worrying she sat beside me on the blanket smacking real loud and chewing with her mouth wide open. Her grill looked like a giant damn clothes dryer with a whole bunch of colored clothes tumbling around inside.

"Barron is stupid? Why you say that?" She swallowed hard, and then stuck two fingers deep in her mouth and sucked off some barbeque sauce.

"*Because*. Just look at him. Pushing that busted-looking bitch all up in these white people's faces. I know they can see how ghetto she is. The least he coulda did was told her to put on something decent before she brought her thievin' ass out here. I bet them fingers is sticky as hell. Them rich fools better check for their wallets as soon as she walks away."

"Oh, Barron ain't stupid," Bunni said. She picked a deviled egg up off her plate and pushed the whole thing in her mouth. "He's smart as hell," she smacked. "He knows exactly what he's doing."

"Oh yeah?" I smirked. "And what's that?"

"He's letting the board members get a real good look at Dy-Nasty," she said. "He wants them to see her. *Raw*. That way when he tells them her ass is a thief, a ho, and a low-crawling crook, they'll believe him."

The party didn't get hot until Uncle Suge got there, and it seemed like everybody in the world knew it. There was music blasting from the outdoor speaker system, and beer and liquor was flowing like a river. All the cowboy-looking types and their wives were either standing around drinking beer and eating, or splashing in the pond and having fun. Fallon and her little girlfriends had taken over the pavilion, and they were over there flossing their tight bodies around in their bikinis, while Jock and some of his cousins from Houston had walked up into the edge of the tree line to get buzzed and lifted.

Uncle Suge made a real big splash when he busted up on the scene, and I do mean a real big one. That fool took a flying leap off the end of the dock and jumped straight into the pond with all his clothes on, even his cowboy hat and his Cartier watch, and all the white people who were swimming and paddling around on floats laughed like that was the funniest shit they had ever seen.

He clowned around with the kids in the water and told crazy jokes that made all the men laugh and all the white girls blush, and as everybody's mood got a lot more crunk I could tell how much the people at Dominion Oil really liked Uncle Suge.

He socialized for a good little bit, and I couldn't help but lick my lips when that tall hunk of beef finally climbed outta the pond and walked up on the grass with water still streaming outta his clothes. His chocolate skin and lumped-up muscles was showing all through his wet shirt, and his massive build had a whole lotta female eyes checking him out.

He looked like a sexy male calendar model when he put his wet hat back on his head and grinned, and I almost melted as I stared at the natural bulge in his crotch. I stood up off my blanket and brushed a few wrinkles outta my miniskirt, and I was just about to go over there and put a lil sumthin in his ear, but Barron beat me to the spot when he rushed over with Dy-Nasty hanging all over his arm.

"Yo, Uncle Suge!" Barron said, sounding all phony like him and his uncle was the best of friends. "My dude! I got somebody here I think you're gonna wanna meet."

He turned to Dy-Nasty. "Dy-Nasty, this is our Uncle Suge, our father's baby brother. Uncle Suge, this is your niece, Dy-Nasty. She's visiting us from Philadelphia and her DNA test came back a positive match for Sable's."

I wanted to jam my toe up Dy-Nasty's stank ass when she tossed her horse mane over her shoulder and stepped up on Uncle Suge grinning all in his face. "Hey, Uncle," she cooed and pressed her hand to his wet, rocked-up chest. "Yum." She giggled and licked her lips. "It looks like fine runs all up *in* this family, now don't it?"

"She's a ho!" I hissed to Bunni. "That trick belongs out on the track!"

"Hold up now," I heard Uncle Suge say as his eyeballs jumped down in the split between her nasty titties. He was halfway lit and probably smoked out too, but he was still sober enough to realize that something real funky was going down. "Where in the world did you get this delicious young thing from, Lil Bump? And how is she gonna be Sable when Mink is already Sable?"

Barron laughed. "We don't know *who* the hell Mink is," he said. "But Dy-Nasty is family. She's my sister Sable and I'm willing to put a whole lotta money on it."

While Mink and Dy-Nasty tried to out-show their asses in front of company, Pilar stood off to the side with her eyes on rotate, taking notice of everything that moved. Especially the two chickenheads who had come clucking in from up north. They were going at it toe-to-toe, and it looked like Mink had finally met her match. If their little throw-down ghetto cat fight wasn't so damn disgusting Pilar would have laughed.

Instead, she sipped her chilled white wine and watched the drama unfold. *Mink is a real gold-digging bitch, but I don't like this other chick neither,* Pilar admitted to herself as she followed Dy-Nasty with her eyes. The girl was pure trash. She was even worse than Mink. Hell, if Mink was the sidewalk then this chick was the gutter. She looked real low-class, puffing on her Newport kings and walking up to every white man in sight and asking him, "So, who is you? What's your job? How much bank do you yank?"

This fool should have stayed her grimy ass in Philly some-where. The last thing Pilar needed was more competitive pussy camping out in the mansion and getting in Barron's head. And this girl was a real fabulous troll. She actually made *slish-glump* noises as she chugged her beer from the bottle, and right now she was out there laughing extra, extra loud over every little thing that was said. It was all a ploy to get some male attention, Pilar knew, and with Dy-Nasty's big titties and monster ass, she was getting it too. Every man at the estate—black, white, and orange—had their eyes glued to her lower body as she got up under the pavilion with Fallon and her friends and started showing them how to twerk it stripper-style. The girl had enough meat on her ass to make the cooks spark up another grill, and all the men were panting as she threw her head back, held her arms high in the air, and made her yellow booty vibrate back and forth from the left to the right.

But panting wasn't all some of the guys out there were doing. Pilar glanced over at her fiancé, Ray, who was sitting in a lawn chair beside the pavilion because he was too fat to get his ass down on a blanket. Ray was up close and mentally fucking the shit outta this chick. He had an expression on his face that Pilar knew very well, and she recognized that glazed look in his eyes as he nutted in his drawers just from watching Dy-Nasty's lady lumps rotate in a vicious, dizzying hump.

"Ray!" Pilar hissed, frowning in disapproval when he looked at her. "Get your ass over here!"

Ray licked the drool off his bottom lip and pushed his wide butt out of the chair and waddled her way.

Goddamn horny-ass bunch of fools, Pilar fumed as she drained the last of the wine from her glass. All it took was a stank display of jiggly tits and ass and most men would get to buzzing after some coochie like a hive of bees on some honey. She glanced at Dy-Nasty, who had dropped it down low and was squatting with her butt between her feet trying to twerk it to death. Nah, Pilar corrected herself as she smirked at the Philly chick in disgust. Not like bees on honey. More like flies on shit.

CHAPTER 18

When you crammed too many slick gutter chicks under one roof crazy shit was bound to pop off. Me and Bunni was about to go club bangin' with Dane, when Dirty Dy-Nasty ran her stank ass outside and tried to hop in the whip.

"Wait up!" she hollered and wobbled down the steps in a pair of cheap eight-inch Payless heels.

"Oh no this trick ain't!" I muttered from the backseat and reached over to slam the Hummer's door. I clipped the shit outta Dy-Nasty's big head and almost caught her nose in the crack. "Lock that shit!" I hollered at Dane, but he was moving way too slow and Dy-Nasty snatched the door open and damn near plopped down in my lap as she jumped inside.

"Watch it, goddammit!"

"Well scoot your ass over then!"

I inhaled a thick cloud of her cheap-ass perfume and started choking on the fumes. "Damn!" I coughed and sneezed as I scooted way over to the other side of the car. "What's that shit you done sprayed all over you? *Raid?*"

"Uh-uh." She laughed and dug her ass deeper into the seat. "It's called Bugs Be Gone. So be gone, bitch! Be gone!"

That's one, I thought quietly as she cracked herself up. This trick could laugh all she wanted to. Bunni said I needed to make friends with her but I wasn't gonna be but so many bitches for *nobody*. Matter fact, I was only gonna be three bitches for *any* damn body, and this chick right here had two more left.

She musta took my silence for weakness because she kept right on illin'.

"Dane! My *bruvvah*! I know you wasn't tryna sneak off nowhere with *these* jawns and leave *me*, Dane!" She scooted to the edge of her chair and leaned between the two front seats, crowding Bunni's shoulder. "That ain't how a bruvvah s'posed to do his lil sister now, boo-boo! Blood is thicker than water, ya heard? Now pass that weed back here, man! I'm tryna get lifted!"

I igged her raunchy ass and tried to get my head right on some chronic as we rode to the club. Dane cranked the music up real loud and drowned her loud ass right out, and by the time we pulled up outside the party I was feeling good again.

The club was in the middle of the hood, and it had run-down, abandoned buildings on both sides of it. All kinds of shady-looking hoodlums were chillin' on the block, and my New York radar went off as a few of their eyeballs slid sideways over us while we were hopping out the ride.

"Yo," I joked with Dane as he clicked the door locks and they beeped twice. The last time he took me and Bunni to a party he had lost his kicks *and* his pants, and all three of us ended up getting robbed. "Look at all these gangsta niggas standing around here with larceny in they eyes! You sure the whip is still gonna be here when we come back out? Lemme know if you need me to fold the Hummer up and stick it in my purse, 'kay?"

I knew shit was crucial when we got up to the door and saw there were two pat-down lines we had to go through before we could get inside the club. One line was for dudes, and the other one was strictly for the ladies.

Me and Bunni both had shitty looks on our faces when we saw who was in charge of our line. She was a stud female with mad tats up and down her muscled-up arms and a big-ass clit-tickler ring hanging from her bottom lip.

Dy-Nasty stepped up to her first, and she giggled like crazy as mister girl ran her hands down her back, over her ass, back up between her legs, and across her stomach. I coulda sworn mister girl slid her hand over Dy-Nasty's left titty, and the way her twisted ass grinned and squealed I could tell she liked it.

It was my turn next. Nope! I jumped smack over into the men's line and pushed myself in front of Dane. Mister girl wasn't getting none of me. "Ga'head!" I held my arms in the air and hollered at the Puerto Rican dude who had his hands out ready to put in work. "You can ga'head and feel me up, Papi! Feel all *over* me!"

We got up in that club and let our glow show. I had on a tight silver body-glove dress that made me look damn-near naked. It had sequins on the ass that shimmied from side to side when I switched my hips, and the top of it dipped low at the cleavage and left one of my shoulders bare. Bunni's shit was definitely on point too. She wore a pair of classy red polyester booty shorts that showcased her round hips and high booty, and outlined the deep split in her beloved venus mound. Bunni's stunning bowlegs were naked from the thighs down, and her calves looked sleek and shiny and her ankles were set off perfectly in her pointy-toed pumps.

Dy-Nasty was turning niggas' heads too, but it wasn't because she had her shit together though. Stink-a-Dink had on a too-tight money-green cat-suit, and it was made outta that kind of real cheap material that pulled every which'a way it wanted to. It had a zipper running from deep in her crotch all the way up to her neck, and there was a gold microphone dangling from the end. But Mizz Nasty had only zipped the shit up halfway though, and the tops of her big ol' titties was jumpin' out and smackin' the shit outta every nigga she walked past. I cracked up when Bunni pointed at her ass and giggled. Mami was struttin' around flossin' like she was the bizz, when little did she know the seam going up her big booty was crooked and running way over to the right, and the leather on her turned-over heels had peeled down to the cheap white plastic tubing underneath. This bitch was just plain ol' raggedy!

The three of us hit the dance floor and it wasn't long before mad niggas rushed out to get up on us. Everybody knew when you danced with a dude at a club that meant certain shit was already agreed on. It wasn't about getting in no kinda groove or showing off your dance skills, it was about how much dry fuckin' you was gonna allow a cat to perpetrate on you. Trust, he was gonna feel on that ass if you let him, and if he could rub his hard dick on you until he busted in his drawers, he would do that too.

While me and Bunni was out there handling our dance partners, Stink Dy-Nasty was out there handling her bizzness. Them horny mofos shoulda been paying her by the hump because she was straight-up tricking out there! Them niggas was about to fight tryna get next on her. I watched as she stood on one leg and cocked her other one real high in the air. A dude with long dreads stepped up on her and cupped her thick ass with both hands, and she wrapped her leg around his waist and let him mash her shit up right through her skimpy clothes.

Three songs later me and Bunni went looking for Dane and found him chillin' at a table with a fat dude he introduced as one of his boyz from college. I could tell big man was scoping on me right away, so I sat down right beside him. Dane stood up and pulled out a chair for Bunni to sit in, but Dy-Nasty came outta nowhere, bum-rushing the shit outta her as she stole Bunni's chair and plopped her ass down next to Dane.

Bunni laughed and shook her head. "A'ight now, Loosie-Goosie!" she sang out a warning as she moved one chair down. "You must not know 'bout me, you must not know 'bout me!"

Dane's friend was cute in the face but chubby.

"Wus good, wus good! Y'all ladies doin' okay tonight?" he said, staring all up in our mugs. "I'm A.T. and I got the next round of drinks, cool? So what's y'all names? Who we got here?"

Somebody just had to get stupid with it.

"Don't worry about who they is! I'm *Dy-Nasty*." She showed him all her teeth and flung her sweaty horsetail over her shoulder. "And when I'm on the scene don't none of these other bitches matter!"

Bitches? *That's two.*

A.T. laughed with her, but me and Bunni's faces was straight-up stone.

"Seriously though," he said and looked back and forth between me and Dy-Nasty. "Y'all two are sisters, right? Prolly twins, huh?"

"No!" we both blasted on him at the same damn time.

We looked at each other.

"I don't even know her!" we said together again.

"Shut your ass up." She frowned and rolled her eyes.

"No *you* shut the hell up!"

"C'mon, now," Dane cut in. "We came out to party, right? So y'all chill with all that hostility for a minute. Y'all fuckin' up my high."

A.T. bought me, Dy-Nasty, and Bunni round after round of drinks, and all three of us showed him how long our throats could get. I figured since somebody else was paying I might as well drink from the top shelf, and I chugged back Courvoisier and Coke while Bunni drank Cîroc and cranberry juice, and Dy-Nasty sucked down shots of Bacardi 151 straight.

We had sparked up a couple of blunts when a nice slow jam cut by Uncle Charlie Wilson came on. Dy-Nasty musta really been feeling her liq because outta nowhere she snatched Dane up and yanked him out on the dance floor. There wasn't nothing sisterly about the way she was out there grinding him down, and her wide ass moved like a rollercoaster as she grabbed his waist and worked those hips all over his dick.

"See, that right there ain't right," Bunni muttered, grilling Dy-Nasty's bomb booty with much 'tude. She started chewing her gum all reckless and poppin' it between her back teeth real loud. "That shit right there just ain't right."

"What a skank-ass skeezer," I said as I twisted my lips and stared at her too. Mami was puttin' it on Dane, going in on him like he was her boo, and I could see why Bunni was mad. Shit, she had been working Dane her damn self, and here this bitch was tryna throw damage in her game.

"I'ma fuck her up," Bunni said quietly when the song was finally over and Dy-Nasty and Dane started walking back to the table grinning and laughing together. "Yeah, I'ma straight fuck her up."

I heard the Harlem hoodrat in her about to slip out.

"Hey now, Dane ain't your man," I reminded Bunni. "Y'all might fuck around a lil bit, but he ain't your man."

"He ain't hers neither!"

"Whew!" Dy-Nasty said as she came back to the table and wiped some sweat off her face. She picked up her purse and laughed. "That shit felt good as *hell*! We gotta do it again when we get home tonight, Dane, okay?"

She tipped off toward the bathroom with her monster-booty catching mad eyeballs as she tossed it left and right.

Bunni was burning on fire. "That bitch needs her ass kicked!" She jumped up from her chair. "I'ma get her, Mink! I'ma split that ho's melon! I'ma take her top square off!"

I stared at my best homey and narrowed my eyes. I felt a ghetto battle royal coming on and I was ready to snatch out my earrings and kick off my heels. "Yo, is you thinkin' what I'm thinking?"

"Hell yeah!"

"Well c'mon, then, *babeee*!" I jumped up and cracked my neck from side to side. Fuck waiting for that Philly troll to call me bitch number three! "Let's get kick some ass then, Bunni Baines! Leggo!"

There were plenty of gutta chicks primping for the mirrors in the dirty little bathroom, but me and Bunni was about to roll up on one in particular. There was a long line waiting for just two stalls, and we stalked from the background until it was Dy-Nasty's turn to go inside the one on the right. As soon as that skank took two steps toward the stall, me and Bunni bum-rushed from the back of the line and busted through the swinging door right along with her.

"Yeah, bitch!" Bunni pony-rode Dy-Nasty into the stall and slammed her forehead against the wall over the toilet. "I'm *tired* of your stank ass!"

We got to fucking her ass up! Mad chicks started scream-ing and hollering like they had never seen a fight before. Dy-Nasty screamed out in surprise too, but only for a quick second. When she realized she was getting jumped she started throwing blows too, trying her best to get hers in before we took her down.

And don't get it twisted, we took that ass *down*! I snatched her by her ratty little ponytail and banged her in her nose, while Bunni went to work pile-drilling her with body shots, punt-kicks, and karate chops like she was bare-knuckle fight-ing in a cage.

The cubicle was too small for all three of us and we were swinging so hard and wild that we were banging our knees and elbows all up against the walls. Yanking her horsehair down and back, I yoked Dy-Nasty up and dragged her outta the stall with her crazy ass kicking and scratching the whole way.

Chicks scattered out of our path while they screamed and cheered. Some for us, and some for Dy-Nasty. That dirty rat scratched me on my arm and I scratched her right next to her ear. I slung her ass all over the place as I jerked her by her weave. It must have been sewn in or gummed up on her scalp with some superglue, because even though there were plenty of random strands sliding out and billowing down to the floor, why that whole raggedy shit just didn't snap off in my hand, I don't know.

We fought our way outta the door and into the narrow hallway, and the next thing I knew two security guards were grabbing at my wrist tryna separate us and force me to let go of Dy-Nasty's hair. One of them giant-sized nigs clenched his big hand around the back of my neck, and then he clamped down on Dy-Nasty's neck the same damn way. We squealed and almost dropped to our knees as that nigga dug his fingers sharply into our throats and made us choke and see stars. We scratched his hands bloody as he hurled us through the crowd and toward the front door. The other bouncer manhandled Bunni and tried to push her ass outta there too.

We were almost out the door when the big bouncer got stupid and banged me and Dy-Nasty's heads together, clapping our domes until they vibrated like a pair of cymbals. Without a word, we spun around and ate his ass up, swinging wild hay-makers and tryna claw his eyeballs outta the sockets with our nail tips. The dude who was handling Bunni let her go so he could come help his boy, and what did he do that for because Bunni jumped in it too. We rat-packed his ass! We fought like a trio of men, punching, biting, and scratching until they tossed us out the door and all three of us landed outside on our asses.

Dane came busting out the door right behind us, and he helped us stand up and hustled us across the street.

"Damn *Three the Hard Way*! What the hell happened in there?"

Our shit was hit. Dy-Nasty's zipper had ripped and her jumpsuit was hanging wide open, the strap over my shoulder was torn and my dress was flapping free at the top, and Bunni was limping on one foot because she had lost one of her shoes.

"What the hell happened in there?" Dane repeated. "Why y'all had to get so ill?"

"Ask her," Bunni pointed at Dy-Nasty and rolled her eyes. "That dirty bitch started it."

That Philly trick had the nerve to throw it all on me.

"Nah, don't be asking me shit! *She* fuckin' started it!"

"*Uh-uh* baby," I said, looking down at the strands of horsehair that were still tangled between my fingers. "Mizz Mink didn't start it, *mamacita*, but I damn sure finished it!"

CHAPTER 19

I got up with the chickens the next morning so I could get an early start on my grind. Even though my head was still bangin' I was gonna go upstairs and snuggle in that big bed with Selah and let her hold me the way she liked to. I figured we could call down to the kitchen again and have the cook bring us up some French toast, and this time I would even eat a lil bit of that dog food-lookin' corned beef hash just to make Selah happy.

My morning breath was still kickin' hot from last night's yak, and I ran in the bathroom to brush my teeth real quick. Bunni was snoring in her room next door, and after I brushed my brights and gargled with some cinnamon Scope, I slipped on my cute mint green Baby Phat bathrobe and slid my feet into the sweet little slippers that matched.

The sun was just coming up and the mansion was creepy quiet as I ran up the circular staircase and headed toward the far wing of the house. My feet were silent as they sank into the plush carpet, and the smell of lemon air freshener greeted me in the halls.

Even though it was real early I knew Selah would be up. And even if she wasn't up yet, I knew she would be glad to see me. Yeah, she had kinda fronted me off and played me a little chilly in front of everybody, but how could you expect some-body to act when they had just had the shit shocked outta them?

Probably the same way I acted when I knocked on her bedroom door and got the shit shocked outta me!

I knocked twice real soft. My mouth was kinda dry as I pressed my ear to the door, and I coulda sworn I heard voices coming from inside. I bit my bottom lip and frowned. *Chill your ass out, girl. It's prolly just the TV.* I knocked again, a little bit harder, and Selah's voice rang out real loud and clear.

"Come on in."

I pushed the door open and took three steps inside, and then I straight-up froze.

"Oh!" My eyes bucked open and my heart jumped way down into the pit of my stomach.

That *bitch*. That dirty, rotten, grimy *bitch*!

Dy-Nasty was laid up in Selah's big old bed. On *my* side. In *my* spot! And with that stringy, nasty, ghetto horsehair of hers spread out all over *my* pillow!

I swallowed my shock and surprise. A re-run of *Survivor* was playing on the DVR. "Oh, sorry. My bad. I didn't know you already had company."

"Yes," Selah said coolly as she walked over to where Dy-Nasty was laying, "but come on in, Mink. What gets you up so early this morning?"

My eyes swept over the room and landed on the half-eaten plate of food on Dy-Nasty's end table. There was a piece of crust leftover from some French toast and the smell of maple syrup was in the air.

"Nothing," I said, tryna play it off.

"Okay, hold still," Selah said like she didn't even hear me. She leaned over Dy-Nasty and I saw she had a Q-tip in her hand. "That's a real nasty scratch on your pretty face, baby. Don't worry," she said as she dabbed some kinda ointment on Dy-Nasty's jaw where my nails had raked her. "This is the good stuff so it won't even sting."

That goddamn *faker*! She had the nerve to close her eyes and wince in pain like somebody had sliced her damn throat open or something! "Thank you, Mommy," Dy-Nasty cooed like a sweet little girl, and as soon as Selah turned around to throw the Q-tip away, Dy-Nasty flashed me a grin and shot me the finger too.

"I guess I better go back downstairs," I said, feeling some kinda way inside. And it wasn't just because I was all of a sudden having to go head-up and compete with Dy-Nasty neither. That part was easy. Nah, this thing kinda felt like jealousy. 'Cause ever since this trick right here showed up it seemed like Selah had forgotten all about me!

"Okay, baby. We're leaving for Houston in a few hours," Selah reminded me offhandedly. "I'll see you then."

That heffah didn't try to stop me from leaving or say nothing else, so with pain in my heart and my ass dragging down to the floor, I dipped.

"Never let 'em see you sweat," Bunni advised me later that morning when it was time for us to leave for Houston. "Stop whining and fix your damn face, Mink. Your ass gots'ta be fly and flouncy today. Get on up outta that bed and throw on something real slutty. I want you to show your tits *and* your teeth today, ya heard?"

I shrugged and rolled over in the bed and punched my pillow. "I ain't getting up. I don't feel like going."

Bunni broke. "You don't feel like going? What in the hell wrong wit'chu? Don't tell me you lettin' that raggedy hood chick punk you out! We came down here to *work*, baby. To stack some paper and get some *cheese*, girl! Since when Mizz LaRue don't feel like making her no money?"

I understood where Bunni was coming from but after seeing Dy-Nasty all up in Selah's bed like that I had come downstairs and got straight up under my covers, and now I didn't wanna move.

"On the real tip, I don't see what the damn problem is *anyway*," Bunni hollered as she turned around and stomped toward her bathroom. "So *what* Selah likes Da-Nasty's ugly ass better than she likes you? You came down here to *gank* yo play-mama, remember? Not marry her ass! The only thing you need to be worrying about is passing that damn DNA test again. We still ain't found out which lab they're gonna use."

I groaned into my pillow. The DNA test was another big problem I was facing. Uncle Suge and Dane were supposed to find the new lab and work out a big-money deal with the management to make sure I was a match, but if that shit fell through then me and Bunni could just bend over and kiss our black asses good-bye because Dy-Nasty was gonna be rollin' around all in our dough.

I got up and started putting my clothes on. Bunni had said I should go slutty, but I decided to put on a cute pair of jeans that were dark navy and dressy, but fit the humps of my ass like a real thin glove. I topped up with a cherry-red spandex shirt that had a deep V-dip in the front and in the back, and the word *DIVA* centered in diamond studs. I styled my bright red Glama-Glo with the thick spiral curls, and put on an elegant diamond necklace that I had boosted and a pair of earrings that matched.

I didn't feel like putting no whole lot of makeup on my face, so I just slapped on the basics. A little mascara and some pretty red lip gloss. I slipped on my navy-blue Cha-Cha sandals with the cute diamond-studded buckles on the sides, and I was ready to dip.

I had never been one for hospitals and I didn't see why we had to go back to see Viceroy all the damn time, but Selah said the doctors wanted to discuss giving him some kind of experimental drug from China that was used as a brain stimulator for people who were in deep comas. "And besides," Selah also said, "I'd like Viceroy to have a chance to meet Dy-Nasty. This could be his last opportunity."

Trust me, I was all about exploiting opportunities when we got on the *Diva Dominion* and went to take our seats. Any other time my ass woulda flew straight to the back to try to sit with Bunni and Dane, but this time I made sure to get the seat next to Selah. She gave me a big smile that made me feel a little better, but my mood got sho'nuff busted again when she patted the seat on the other side of her and waved Dy-Nasty over, and then told Barron to go sit in the back with his brother.

It was a real short ride, but for some reason it seemed like we was up in the air forever and ever and ever. The whole time we were flying I sat there with my arms folded and my lip poked out as Selah and Dy-Nasty igged me and went on and on and on talking about those damn reality shows just like I wasn't even there.

That lil Philly heffa thought she was slick when we landed and we went to get in the limos too. We did the bump tryna be first to get inside the car with Selah, and when Dy-Nasty tried to step in front of me I shot her an elbow to the kidney that shoulda dropped her to her knees. Instead, mami yelped like a mutha as her ankle twisted and turned over in her cheap shoes.

"*Owwww!*" she hollered all loud like somebody had shot her in the damn foot. She started limping around in stiff circles like she was tryna walk it off, making all kinds of crazy pain noises so she could draw everybody's attention.

That shit worked too.

"What happened?" Selah yelled from inside the limo. Her voice was full of concern as she peered right past me and searched for Dy-Nasty with her eyes. "Are you hurt?"

"My ankle!" Da-Liar gasped. "She made me sprain my ankle!"

"Come!" Selah patted the spot beside her. "Move over, Mink and let her in. Get up in here and sit next to me so you can put your foot up, baby. There's plenty of ice in the champagne bucket. The last thing you want that ankle to do is swell."

Smoke was coming outta my ears as Da-Faker hopped her

ass into the limo and slid across the seat and snuggled right up under Selah. I cut my eyes at her and I was just about to roll 'em real hard too, but before I could make my move that silly trick stuck her tongue out and winked at me, then lowered her head down tenderly on Selah's motherly shoulder.

Outta all the times I had come to see Viceroy in the hospital, this time was the worst. I was walking around with my ass on my shoulders while Dy-Nasty was busy milking her fake ankle injury and playing up to every dude in sight.

"What kinda work you into, Big Daddy?" she said to Digger Ducane as we sat in the waiting room. The Houston aunts had met us up at the hospital, and they'd followed Selah, Barron, Dane, and Uncle Suge into a meeting with Viceroy's doctors. I figured they were tryna decide whether that Chinese medicine was gonna kill him or make him get better.

"I'm in the logistics business," Uncle Digger said, puffing out his flabby chest. He looked real excited to be getting some attention from a young chick, which was cool, because my fast ass had never given him the time of day. "I work with trucks. I make stuff move."

"Well, *move* me, Daddy!" Dy-Nasty giggled and threw her hands over her head and did a little wiggle in her chair. *Lap dancer!* I flashed her a hater look. She was sitting with her foot up and a plastic bag full of ice wrapped around her ankle, and the way she was stuntin' you woulda thought she was a queen on a throne.

"C'mon, *Daddy.*" Pilar walked up behind her father and looped her arm through his and pulled him toward the other side of the room. She turned her nose up at Dy-Nasty. "Something over here stinks big-time, so let's *move* it somewhere else."

Uh-huh, I thought, twisting my lips as I watched Pilar snatch her daddy up and switch her ass on outta there. She wasn't feeling this trick neither. Stank Dy-Nasty was like a goddamn bedbug and getting up under everybody's skin.

When Selah and them came outta their meeting everybody looked kinda down. "What happened, Ma?" Jock asked
her. "What did the doctors say?"

Selah sighed and looked around at all of us. She shrugged.
"They said even with the experimental drug your father's odds
are very slim. They don't have enough data to say for sure what
might or might not happen, but they don't want us to get our
hopes up too high. So we're just going to do what we usually
do. Hope and pray."

As much as I hated going in Viceroy's hospital room, I
damn sure didn't want Dy-Nasty going up in there without
me. I had a feeling this trick was gonna perform like she was
on a Broadway stage, and that's exactly what the hell she did.

"Wh-wh-why?" she moaned and bent over at the waist as
she stared down at Viceroy's still body and dripped fake tears
all over his sheets. "Lawd, *whyyyy?*" she screeched and cried
like she was at a funeral. You shoulda seen how that slick little
actress put on a show. She was clutching her heart and sagging
all at the knees like she could barely stand up. Barron had her
up under one arm and Selah had her under the other one. The
nurses came running and started fanning her face like they
were church ushers and she had caught the Holy Ghost.

"Daddeeee!" she wailed, reaching out for Viceroy like he
was being lowered into his grave. They damn near had to drag
that fool outta the room. "Daddeeee, *nooo!*"

"You sure can tell that's Viceroy's chile 'cause she took it
hard," some of the Houston aunts was saying when I went
back in the waiting room. "Yeah, that there baby really took it
hard."

I bucked my eyes. Traitors! These was the same chicks that
I had partied with at the Fourth of July barbeque! We had
drank and danced and wilded our asses off, and now they
barely even glanced at me as they poured out all that sympathy
for Dy-Nasty!

"I can't stand that bitch!" I fumed to Bunni when we went

into the bathroom together and sparked up some yay. "I mean, I know she's prolly Sable, okay, but she ain't gotta turn everybody against me!"

Bunni gave me the bizz. "Hell, ain't that exactly what she's s'posed to do? Look a'here, Mink! I'ma need you to get your shit together, okay? Da-Funky didn't come down here to make no friends, she came down here to make her *money*! Now, Miss Thang is on her grind and she's on it hard. I hate I gotta say it, but you kinda got too comfortable with these rich marks, Mink. You forgot about the grift and got thrown off your hustle. It ain't about who Da-Nasty really is, or whether or not she has a better con game than you, it's about you needing to step your game up! So get after it, baby! The fight ain't over yet. Get back out there and kick, scratch, bite, and punch! *Sheeiit*. Play dirty! Fuck her shit up! That's how you win a fight."

While I was busy tryna win the fight Bunni was busy putting some serious wrestling moves on Dane. Somehow she got it in her head that since Dane was a Dominion and they were fuckin' like rabbits, that she could hook up with him and be set for life.

"Girl what you mean you wanna marry Dane?" I asked her as she stood in the mirror twisting her locs. I'd had a funny feeling that she was scheming ever since we came back from seeing Viceroy in Houston, and now I knew what it was.

Bunni sucked her teeth. "Why you gotta say it like that? You ain't the only one who got money to make, Mink! What about me? I want me some cars, and clothes, and a whole lotta weed just like everybody else! Hell, you's a Domino, ain't you? And you got Uncle Suge on lock and he's a Domino, right? Well, shit! I'm tryna be a Domino too!"

"How? By marrying Dane? That nigga ain't looking to wife no damn body! Remember, Dane already got his inheritance and he smoked that shit up! He's sweatin' that trust fund money so he can take his dick back to college and finish fuckin' every chicken with a twat. Bunita Baines, I'ma need you to *recognize!*"

"Recognize what?" Her lips got all twisted and she leaned back on her bowlegs and put her hands on her hips. Her camel toe jumped out at me. "Recognize that you *selfish*, Mink? That you's a undercover *hater*? Why is that Domino dick and Domino cash good for *you*, but it ain't good for *me*?"

I took a deep breath and sighed. "It's Dominion, and that ain't what I'm saying, Bunni. Damn right these people's money is good for you too. I want you to have it too! I just don't wanna see you chasin' all behind Dane tryna have no relationship when that nigga is just runnin' around chasin' after the booty, okay?"

Rolling her eyes, Bunni grabbed her Gucci purse and slung it over her shoulder with much 'tude.

"Yeah, well, I guess he's about to catch him summa this booty today because he said he wanna take me out. Somewhere in Dallas. I'll holla at you later Miss Diva fuckin' *Domino!*"

I was looking in the mirror tryna fix the glue on my fake eyelashes when I heard a familiar horn blow outside. Running through our connecting doors, I jetted into Bunni's suite and looked out the window.

"Yeah, *babeee!*" I shrieked when I saw Uncle Suge's silver bullet monster truck in the driveway. He had come to get me! Next time I was gonna make his ass call first, but I was gonna have to give him a pass right now because with Bunni gone I was dying to get outta the mansion for a little while too.

I ran back in my room and held my eye open wide as I peered in the mirror and scraped the leftover glue off with my fingernail. Wiping my hand on my bathrobe, I got on my shoes, grabbed my purse, took one more quick peek in the mirror, and I was out the door.

I had a big-ass grin on my face as my hand skimmed the polished banister and I jogged down those long, winding stairs. I hit the bottom step at full speed, and my heels clacked loud and fast as I rushed through the house and beat feet toward the front door. With my hand on the doorknob, I squared my back and stuck my chest out so my titties would look nice and fat, and then I snatched the door open and stood there posted up and grinning like a mutha!

For about two seconds.

'Cause that's about how long it took for me to see that *some* damn body was already sitting in the front seat of Uncle Suge's truck! Matter fact, that shiesty bitch was sitting there with her hot shredded beaver-tail weave hanging halfway out the window, and right before my eyes the truck pulled off toward the open gates with her in it!

Our eyes met in the side-view mirror, and that raggedy beast had the nerve to wink at me and wiggle four of her damn fingers good-bye. I stood there with my mouth wide open and sucking up exhaust fumes. Here I was thinking that nigga had come over to surprise me, when his ass had only swung by to scoop Dy-Nasty up!

Uncle Suge! Really, muthafucka? *Really?*

I couldn't even cop to what I was feeling all up in my heart. I just *knew* he was taking her ass to lunch and to a horse race, and then back to his bangin' crib to feed her some dick for dessert. A hammer called *betrayal* had cracked me dead in the forehead, and I got dizzy as hell as I turned around to go back inside. But I got mad as hell too!

Fuckin' with my man? Uh-uh. I didn't think so! Uncle Suge was *mine.* We had us a real good thang going on, and right after I whipped up on Dy-Nasty's ugly, indecent ass, I was gonna beat his ass too!

Thirty minutes after Uncle Suge and Dy-Nasty rode off I was still fuming and mad as hell. I had decided that slum-bum

definitely needed her grill banged up again, and I was upstairs
in my suite about to cake some Vaseline on my face and wait
for her to come back when Uncle Suge blew my spot up.

"What?" I bitched as soon as I snatched up the phone.
"Oh, so *now* you wanna call me, huh?"

"Hey, Mink," he said quietly.

"Nah, nah, *nah!*" I wilded. "Don't *Mink* me! You wasn't
saying my damn name when you rolled outta the gates with
that hit bitch Dy-Nasty, now was you? Ga'head, Suge. Do ya
little horse-racey thing! Take that troll to ya office and to that
nice hotel where you took me too. You can take her to your
crib if you want to! I don't care. Matter fact, wherever you and
that trick is at y'all can stay there!"

"I'm downstairs, Mink. Right out front. Waiting on you."
Click.

"Downstairs?" I looked at the phone and frowned, and then
ran back in Bunni's room and looked out the window again.
Yep, he was right there. "Damn!" I said under my breath. "That
shit was quick!"

I was feeling kinda embarrassed but my face was straight
twisted as I stomped down the stairs and walked outside. I
stopped right before I got to the passenger door, and crossed
my arms over my chest.

"Get in," he said, staring at me from the window.

"No, you get *out!*" I snapped. "I ain't sitting my prime ass
where that funky trick just sat!"

I thought I heard him laughing. He got outta the truck,
then fumbled around and took something outta a box in the
back. He walked around on my side and opened the passenger
door, then sprayed leather cleaner on the seat and wiped it
down with a small white rag.

He turned and looked at me. "You happy?"

I smirked. "Get the door handle too!"

He sprayed the rag and then wiped down the inside door

handle and the outside handle too. "She wasn't in here but a minute, but I'll vacuum it out if you want me to, baby."

He held the door open, waiting for me to get inside. I rolled my eyes and climbed right in. He grinned at me as he walked around to the other side and got behind the wheel.

"I bought you something," he said, and reached behind his seat and came out with a bunch of real pretty flowers wrapped in bright pink tissue paper.

I couldn't believe it. I bucked my eyes at him. Nigga's didn't buy a chick like me flowers every day!

"I came by to see if you wanted to go hang out for a little while, but when I pulled up Dy-Nasty came running outside." He shrugged. "She asked me for a ride to Western Union. She said she had to send some money to her mama real quick so I took her."

"Her mama?" I poked out my lip. "That trick said her mama was *dead*!"

Suge shrugged, and I felt my lil heart melt as he handed me the colorful bouquet of flowers. He had the nerve to have some roses stuck all up in the bunch too!

"I went and picked up these while I waited for her."

I took a deep breath. "Do you like her?" I asked him as I pressed my nose to the flowers.

He shook his head. "Nah. Not the same way I like you."

I cut my eyes at him. "But do you think she's pretty?"

He frowned for a second, and then nodded. "Yeah. She's pretty. But she ain't gorgeous like you."

I pressed my nose to the petals and sniffed them again, and then I looked up at him feeling real stupid about myself.

"See, when I came out here and saw y'all leaving I had thought—"

"Shhh . . ." His voice was real deep as he pressed his big finger to my lips. "I know what you thought, lil mama, but you was wrong. I'm a grown man, Mink. Remember that. A grown man. I know exactly what I want, and it ain't that girl."

His finger trailed from my lip and down to my thigh. He leaned over and kissed me with something real powerful on his lips. "Hell." His chuckle was deep but his eyes was speaking mad truth when he looked at me and said, "The way your fine ass got me going I don't think I want nobody else, Mink. I just want you."

And on the real tip, I wanted Uncle Suge's ass too.

He said he wanted to cook dinner for me so I was all smiles as we rode down the highway toward his crib. He had a big house that had all the little bells and whistles you would expect to find where a rich dude rested. Everything in the joint screamed money and power. He was high tech'd out, and I could tell he had poured mad cash into his domain. Suge liked to hunt and fish too, and there were animal heads hung up on the wall, and stuffed fish with googly eyes were posted up on the damn fireplace mantel.

He poured us both a double shot of Rémy as soon as we got in the door, and I gulped mine down and enjoyed the way it felt heating up my stomach. I had been up in Uncle Suge's space a few times before, and I felt real comfortable chilling up in there now. Peaches was the only dude who had ever cooked for me in my whole entire life, and I couldn't believe the way Suge was handling his shit in the kitchen. He freaked me out the way he chef-chopped onions, green peppers, and tomatoes. He looked like one of them professionals you see on TV, dicing and slicing all fast and furious, with every piece of vegetable coming out the same size and in the same shape.

He put a bunch of seasonings and stuff on two big steaks and set them in the fridge, and then he poured us another double shot of that yakkety-yak, and we carried our glasses up to his bedroom.

It was a real big room for a real big man. He let me go in first, and I walked over to an extra-long leather sofa and sat down while he turned on some R & B music. That sexy-ass

Lloyd started crooning "Lay it Down" through the speakers and I felt my body melting and getting loose.

"Why are you all the way over there?" Suge asked me. I grinned as he kicked off his boots, then gulped down his yak and lay back on his bed with his hands behind his head.

Shiiit . . . that was all I needed to hear and see.

I tossed my shot of poison back in one gulp too, just to remind him that I wasn't no punk and I could handle minez, and then I stood up and walked toward his bed stripping all the way. By the time I got over to him I was butt-ass naked and had left a trail of my clothes on the floor.

I stood by the bed and let him look at me. I knew my body was ripe and flawless, and I was used to being appreciated by men, but not like this. Suge wasn't even looking at my big ol' titties, and he wasn't drooling over my hips neither. He was staring into my eyes, like he was tryna find something I had inside me, and I didn't know how the hell to take that so I did that thing I do best.

I reached over and unbuckled his big old belt. It was one of them cowboy joints that you would never catch a thug playin' on the streets of New York, but Suge wasn't no regular nigga from the streets, and this I already knew.

I lifted the tab on his zipper and slid it down. My fingers crept inside his drawers and I heard him suck in his breath.

"You know what you doing, lil mama?" His deep voice boomed in the darkness.

I grinned and licked my lips. "Hell yeah." I took his dick out. "And if I don't know I can damn sure figure it out."

His wood felt nice and warm as it throbbed in my hand. I stroked it up a lil bit, but I wasn't tryna play no games. I opened my mouth wide and hovered above the head, and he groaned when the heat and moisture from my mouth hit him.

"Ahhh, shit!" he cursed as I sucked his mushroom into my mouth and slid my lips down his shaft. I slobbed all over that thang, topping him off like a real pro. He touched my shoulder and we got us a nice lil rhythm going. Only the two of us could hear this beat. I reached deep inside his drawers and cupped his balls. And then I came up off his dick and pressed my face down to his crotch and sucked one of his nuts gently between my lips. He loved it. So I went in for the other one and sucked that one in my mouth too. I actually gargled on those big babies. A trail of slobber slipped from my lower lip as I rolled his nut sack around and stroked it with my tongue.

A few moments later I released his balls gently, one by one, and then I climbed up on the bed as he pulled his pants off and tossed them on the floor.

"I wanna ride," I whispered as I straddled his groin. I giggled. "Bronco style."

Suge grabbed me by one hip and cupped my other ass cheek. His gigantic hands were strong and steady as he lifted me in the air and let me hover over the tip of his dick.

"You ready?" he asked me.

I nodded in the darkness. I could feel the muscles in his forearms tightening up as he held me. "Yeah," I said sexily. "I was born ready."

I trembled as I felt the head of his pole tapping at the gate of my pussy. I placed my hands on his rocked-up stomach and gapped my legs open, then braced myself as he lowered me down onto his throbbing pole.

His meat was thick, and for a second I felt like I was gonna split, but then my juices came raining down and coated his path. I plunged down on that dick with a nice sweet plop. Leaning forward until I was on my knees, I rotated my ass around in circles for a few seconds, and then I got to riding.

We just happened to be in a real good position for me to throw my patented double-hump move on Suge, and I bore down with my pussy muscles and let him have it like I was back home in Club Wood. His big hands massaged my ass as I twerked it on him, humping twice and then vibrating my booty like it had double-D batteries in it.

My coochie was nice and slippery and we was both moaning as the friction we created started a real big blaze. Suge gripped my hips and thrust upward and I yelped. He was in too deep but he wasn't about to back out. He held me in place and pumped up with his hips, banging my shit up as my cream slid down his shaft and drenched his pubic hair.

"T-T-Too much d-d-dick!" I stuttered as he pounded all up in my stomach. I grabbed my titties and rubbed my nipples, and then I bounced on his dick three times real hard and nutted, taking a wild ride on an internal roller coaster and screaming the whole way.

Suge was right behind me too. He pulled me down until I was laying flat on top of him, and then he gripped my ass and squeezed it real tight. The next thing I knew he had flipped me over and I was flat on my back. He beat my pussy up in a frenzy, slamming his dick deep inside me as his cup tipped over and he lost his seed.

"Ahhh." He collapsed on top of me as his dick jerked wildly inside my hot pussy until his balls were empty. I was trapped underneath him and it seemed like hours passed before he rolled off me. I felt him get outta the bed but my ass couldn't move. I was whipped, totally fucked out, and every muscle in my body was limp.

I musta dozed off because at some point Suge was standing beside the bed calling my name. I opened my eyes and he slid his strong arms under me and scooped me up and snuggled me against his chest. He carried me into the bathroom, and I didn't know how to feel when he lowered me gently into a huge tub filled with scented, soapy water.

"Damn." I grinned up at him as I lay back in the warm water with my eyes half closed. "A chick could get used to this type a' thang," I joked.

I heard him laugh as he stepped into the bathtub with me and eased himself down into the water. "You damn right. I bet she could."

CHAPTER 20

Seeing his father at the hospital again had really taken a toll on Barron. Pilar could tell he was hurting, and she knew just what she needed to do in order to comfort him. But Ray was over. He had shown up at the mansion wanting to sniff around her ass, but Pilar had fronted him off and left him stuffing his face in front of the television while she snuck down to Barron's suite anyway.

Her and Barron were laying in bed rubbing their feet together and talking, and Pilar was shocked when she started throwing around hints about getting married and having babies, and Barron actually listened.

"Yeah," he said after she started laying her fantasy rap down on him. "I could see that happening, P. I think you would be a real good wife, baby. And a good mother too."

"I would be," Pilar agreed as she lay with her head on his naked chest and traced the outline of his dark nipple with her finger. "I would be a damn good wife." And then she added slyly, "For the right man."

Barron pulled her close. He was naked beneath the covers but Pilar was still wearing a bright orange bra and a matching thong. "It's gonna happen, baby," he whispered, pulling her bra down over her right titty until it popped free of the cup. He kissed her nipple. "For both of us. At the right time."

Pilar moaned and pulled his head closer, pushing her nipple into his mouth. He sucked the stiff bud and rolled it around on his tongue until her body started to tremble. He swiped between her legs with two fingers and she pulled back, allowing cool air to slide between them.

"It's gonna happen, B?"

"Yeah," he whispered. He tapped her hip, urging her closer. "It sure is."

Pilar frowned and backed off a little bit further.

"But not until you find the right girl, huh?"

Barron sighed deeply and sat up. He reached out and smoothed her hair off her forehead, and then bent over and softly kissed her lips.

"I already found her, Pilar," he said quietly. "I've known her all my life."

That was all she needed to hear.

Scooting down in the bed, Pilar took his hard dick in her hand. Freeing her other breast, she rubbed his bone all over her titties, gently smacking the head against her nipples as sparks ignited in her pussy. Above her, Barron moaned and started pumping his hips. Pilar craned her neck and opened her mouth. She sucked the head of his chocolate pop into her wetness and slathered it with her tongue. His dick jerked and throbbed under her touch, and she reached down and cupped his balls, jacking, sucking, and squeezing him all at the same time.

Pilar blew Barron's bone with everything she had in her, trying her best to show him how good life was gonna be when she had his last name and his ring. Just thinking about hooking a rich nig like him turned Pilar on to heights unknown. She felt loose and freaky. Like she wanted to fuck Barron so good he'd want to marry her the next damn day.

Pilar urged him down in the bed, and then positioned herself until her pussy was dripping in his face and his dick was tapping against her lips. They sixty-nined like crazy, licking and sucking and moaning as they went all out to please each other.

Before long their bodies were covered in sweat and the sheets were soaked too. Pilar's jaw ached deliciously as she bobbed and slobbed all over Barron's knob, and as his probing tongue whipped her clit and he bit down gently on her pussy meat, she climaxed with a loud scream, shuddering as her orgasm tore through her body with the force of a speeding jet.

"I'm cumming!" Pilar shrieked as she clenched her ass cheeks and ground her wet pussy all over his face. "Oh yes, baby! I'm cumming . . . ooooh, I love you, baby. Yeah, I'm cumming . . ."

Barron was cumming too, and as he shot his load deep in her mouth and scalded her throat with his warm, thick semen, Pilar could have sworn she heard him mutter, "I love you too, P. I love you too."

Pilar had been exhausted after her lovely mash up with Barron, and she'd laid in his bed and fallen asleep with a smile on her face. It was dark outside when she woke up, and after taking a quick shower and brushing her teeth, she'd slipped her clothes back on and went looking to see what was going on in the mansion.

She was intending to go back to her suite and tell Ray a good lie about where she had been for so long, but instead something led her in the direction of Fallon's room. The two of them had always been real tight, and Fallon looked up to Pilar as a sister and as a diva. But for the last couple of days the girl had been acting kinda distant. Not funky, just quiet, which was definitely out of the norm for the wild young teen.

Pilar rounded the corner to Fallon's room, and the first thing that hit her was the distinct smell of weed wafting down the hall. The second thing that hit her was the faint sound of music she heard. It was a hot rap song by Reem Raw, spit over a funky stripper's beat, and Pilar couldn't believe it was coming from Fallon's room.

She hurried over to the door and knocked. She could hear

the voices rising over the music, and it sounded like somebody was saying, "Yeah, girl! Right there, mami. Work that shit!"

Pushing on the door, Pilar damn near fell into the room, and what she saw made her eyes pop open wide. A he-she was sitting on the sofa with her legs cocked open and her hand stuck down inside her baggy pants. She wore a white doo-rag and a diamond-studded earring, and she was moaning and massaging one of the real big titties that was popping out the top of her wife-beater undershirt.

"Look at all that sweet ass," the chick muttered, grinding her hips up into her hand as she fucked herself with her fingers. "You fine-ass sexy *bitch*, you! Roll that shit for daddy, baby. Roll it!"

Spread-legged and stretched out on the rug in front of the sofa was Fallon and Dy-Nasty. They were air fucking, gyrating their hips and making their backbones slip. Fallon's body looked young and luscious in a hot pink string bikini with the thong string splitting the middle of her birthday cake, and Dy-Nasty's fat banana booty was in a black stripper's get-up that showed off her bombastic shape and sexy curves.

"Wind it real slow," Dy-Nasty instructed Fallon. "Now twerk it hard like this!"

Pilar couldn't believe her lying-ass eyes. She watched as Dy-Nasty got down in the push-up position, and then bent one knee up to her chest and started bang-womping the floor like she was starring in a marathon fuck-fest. Her booty meat jiggled in lemon ripples and waves, and when Fallon got in position and started doing the same thing, only better, the stud getting off on the couch actually dug deeper into her pussy and moaned out loud as she busted her a big one.

"Fallon!" Pilar hollered. The young girl looked up and jumped a guilty mile, and the dyke on the sofa snatched her wet hand out of her baggy men's pants. "Get up off that damn floor! What the hell are you *doing*?" She glared at Dy-Nasty and blasted some heat at her. "Look at your raunchy ass! You're walking around claiming to be her sister, right? So what the hell are you *teaching* her?"

Smirking, Dy-Nasty rolled over onto her back and sat up. "I ain't teaching her shit." She bent her knees and let her legs fall open and Pilar caught a peek of her curly-haired pussy. "Hell, ain't no men up in here fuckin' with her. Besides, she already knows everything she needs to know."

"Let me explain something to your dumb, ghetto ass," Pilar exploded. "Fallon is a child, okay? A *child*. Not a stripper, not a freak, not a two-dollar ho, she's a child. A *young lady*. And if her mother knew you were giving her phantom-fuck lessons, and that *your* old ass"—she turned and blasted on Freddie with a look of pure disgust—"was jacking your imaginary dick like you were at a peep show, both of you twisted bitches would be out the door in two seconds flat!"

"Pilar!" Fallon finally spoke. She put on her bathrobe and tied the belt tightly around her waist. "It wasn't what it looked like," she said quietly. "We were just acting crazy and having fun. Nobody touched me. We were just playing. Nothing was going on."

Pilar looked around the room. A half-empty bottle of Bacardi Light was on the coffee table, two bottles of Schlitz Malt Liquor Bull were on the end table, and a big fat blunt was still smoldering in the ashtray next to Freddie.

"Hell," Pilar said, shaking her head and waving her hand around the room. As much conniving shit as she did on a daily basis, she had never once corrupted Fallon. The girl was still young, and she was the only sister that Pilar had ever had. She was protective over her and felt responsible for what happened to her. "If you think all this is nothing, Fallon, then I'm really worried about you because you're just as stupid as these two bitches are."

Pilar smirked at the two guilty-looking chicks in the room and pointed her finger in both of their faces. "Y'all bitches are some bad-ass influences, you hear? Horrible influences! Fallon." She looked at her cousin. "Do yourself a big favor and stick to hanging out with your little high school friends. Freddie, you do yourself a favor and stay away from my cousin before I call the cops on your pedophile ass, you got me? And Dy-Nasty?" Pilar shook her head as a sick, disgusted look came over her face. "What the hell was Barron thinking when he dragged you up out of some clogged-up drain? You better hurry up and get that DNA test done, baby. And when the results come back and everybody finds out that you've got a little bit of dog in you mixed with a whole lot of skunk, you're gonna have to pack your shit and get your nasty ass up outta here!"

Tears fell from Fallon's eyes as she threw her clothes into a suitcase. She was done with the bullshit! Done with all her fucked-up family! Everybody got to do whatever the hell they wanted to do except her. Dane ran a drug den over the damn garage, Jock snuck underage honeys in and out of the pool house every weekend, Selah was steady sipping in the closet, and Barron was banging his own damn cousin!

"And they got the nerve to worry about *me*?" Fallon screamed into her empty room. Everything had happened so damn fast. One minute she was ballin' and partying with Freddie and Dy-Nasty, and the next thing she knew Pilar was blasting on her and running off at the mouth to Barron.

Barron. She had never seen her brother so mad before. Fallon had wanted to fight his ass when he busted up in her suite and told Freddie to get the fuck out before he tossed her out. *Hold the damn phone!* she had screamed. Barron wasn't her daddy! He didn't pay her damn bills! Fallon had shocked the hell out of him when she jumped in front of her girlfriend and cursed him out real good. She let that nigga know! She told Barron that if Freddie wasn't welcome in the house, then she wasn't staying there neither!

Which was why she was about to get gone right now, Fallon thought as she crept down the steps and out the side door. Pulling her suitcase behind her, she walked around to the front of the mansion and waited for the cab she had called. While she was waiting, she pulled out her cell phone and called Freddie.

"Hey," the older woman said when she answered the phone. "Are you okay, baby? I'm sorry I had to dip out on you like that."

Fallon thought about the way Barron had slung Freddie by her wife beater and banged her head against the wall. Freddie had screamed and jetted. She jumped straight over the coffee table and hit the door like she was running for her life. Fallon fumed. That kinda shit was violence against women! Hell, Freddie wasn't no *real* man!

"I'm leaving," Fallon told her girlfriend. "I'm moving out. I just can't live with these people no more. It's time for me to go." She swallowed hard. "I just called a taxi. Can I come over there and stay with you?"

A big empty pause flooded the phone line. And then Freddie coughed and said, "Um, sorry, baby girl. I'm bunking with my son's father right now, you know? Sorry, but we ain't got no room for you over here."

Fallon sniffed. "I guess I gotta go to that shelter we talked about then."

"Nah," Freddie warned her. "Don't do that shit. Don't go there, okay? Stay at the crib with your family, Fallon. Ain't nothing out there on the streets for you, girl."

Fallon hung up. Being young was no damn fun! Fresh tears were falling from her eyes when her taxi pulled up to the closed gates. Rushing down the walkway, she climbed in the back of the cab and dialed a number she has saved in her phone. The line rang three times before somebody picked up, and when they did, an upbeat voice flooded her ears and said, "You've reached The Dallas House of Joy for LGBT youths. How can I help you?"

CHAPTER 21

"I don't give a damn if that girl really *is* Sable," Pilar bitched as her and Barron zipped down the wet streets of Dallas. She had found him reading in his father's study and spilled the whole pot of beans on Fallon. "You need to keep her slimy Philly ass away from Fallon! And the same thing goes for that old-ass child molester Freddie too! I'm telling you, B. Those two chicks had your sister in there doing some unspeakable shit. They were turning her out. Both of them."

Barron's face was set in a grim mask as he drove. He had wanted to kill that bitch Freddie, but Dy-Nasty *was* Sable. He was convinced of that. But he didn't put nothing past her and he couldn't wait until the vote was over so he could send her grimy ass packing and get her the hell up out of their lives.

"At least Freddie told you where to find Fallon," Pilar went on, even though Freddie really hadn't had a choice. Barron had practically kicked the girl's door down and told her he was gonna set her building on fire if she didn't bring her ass outside. "Who in the world would have thought to look for her at a shelter for gay teenagers anyway?"

Not me, Barron thought as he clenched his jaw tight and stomped down on the gas. He didn't know what the fuck was going on with his family, but every last one of them needed to get their shit together, and fast too.

He sped down the highway toward the shelter, feeling the weight of his father's inheritance on his shoulders. All he wanted to do was find Fallon and get her back home before any of this got back to Selah. Barron was a mama's boy down to the bone, and the last thing he wanted to do was give his moms any extra shit to worry about.

Thirty minutes later him and Pilar were back on the road and heading home. And with a pissed-off Fallon in the back-seat. She had bitched and cried and refused to leave the shelter with him, but Barron had illed so hard that she had ended up in his backseat anyway.

Even though Barron drove fast and mad, he was filled with relief. He wasn't a helpless seven-year-old no goddamn more. There was no way in hell he was gonna lose another baby sister when it was his job to watch her. He didn't have no other choice but to get Fallon and bring her back home. His heart couldn't have taken it any other way.

Bunni was mad as hell and she was hungry too. She'd gone out to a wing joint with Dane, and when she hinted and beat around the bush that they should prolly be a couple, that fool had bust out laughing.

Well, Bunni had ended up laughing like a muthafucka too! And her laugh had been the loudest! She'd thrown every fuckin' wing on her plate at his ass, and then she cracked him in the forehead with her dish too! She had stormed outta the joint and taken a taxi back to the mansion, and when she couldn't find Mink nowhere around she had headed straight to the kitchen.

"Ooh," she marveled as she rummaged through the freezer and then looked in the cook's pantry. These fools had so much bougie-ass food in the joint 'til it made her head spin. This mug didn't look shit like her cabinet back at home, where all she had was some crumbled Ritz crackers, a couple of cans of Spam, and some potted meat. Nah, the Dominos had the real fancy shit up in here, like gourmet water crackers and some chopped tomato-looking stuff called bruschetta, red Salmon and foie gras, and some crispy gourmet cookies with coffee-flavored whip cream falling out the sides. Bunni had gotten used to eating that good stuff since she'd been in the mansion, and she knew she coulda told one of the cooks to bring her up a little midnight snacky-snack, but she was mad and she had a taste for something real greasy and real ghetto.

There was a big tray of seasoned-up catfish in the fridge that Miss Katie was planning on cooking for dinner the next day, and Bunni slid three nice-sized pieces off the top of the heap and set them on a plate. She dug around in the pantry and came out with a box of grits, and got busy fixing herself a little midnight snack and a big jug of sweet red Kool-Aid.

She was steady singing "Girls Like You" by Miguel and shaking the pieces of fish around in a paper bag full of corn-meal when Fallon walked into the kitchen. She looked mad as hell too, and Bunni paused with a hunk of catfish halfway out the bag and frowned.

"Hey, now! What's up? Why you looking all bent?"

Fallon shrugged, and her eyes went to the cast iron black skillet full of hot grease that was just starting to pop.

"You want some?" Bunni offered, holding up the fish be-fore lowering it carefully into the sizzling grease. "I had a taste for some scrimps myself, but these just gonna have to do. I got some grits on the stove too if you want some."

"Yeah," Fallon said as the delicious smell of frying fish drifted up her nose. She kicked off her sandals and hopped up on a breakfast stool. "I'll take a little bit."

A few minutes later the food was done and Bunni hooked up their grits with salt, butter, and a whole lotta black pepper. Fallon swirled a crispy piece of fish around in her bowl of grits and got her grub on. All that running away shit was hard on a girl, and she had been too amped to think about eating before she left. They had offered her a stale turkey sandwich at the shelter, but Barron had tracked her ass down so fast and snatched her up so quick that even if she wanted to eat it, she didn't have a chance to.

Fallon had been too pissed off when she saw her brother walk calmly through the shelter's front door, and she'd had no choice but to leave with him when he told her if she didn't march her little ass outside and be sitting in the backseat of his whip before he got there, then he was gonna call his friends at the police station and have Freddie locked up as a child molester. Barron had brought her straight back home, and she was just about to stomp up the stairs to her room when she smelled something cooking in the kitchen. Still mad, but with her stomach talking loud, Fallon had followed her nose.

"So where you was hanging out at tonight?" Bunni asked her as they chowed down together at the breakfast counter.

Fallon watched as the New York chick picked up the pepper shaker and shook it until her grits turn almost completely black.

"Why you roll up in here with your lips all balled up like that, Fallon?"

"Because I was mad." Fallon smirked. "Bump was trippin'. Pilar told him I was getting smutted out in my room, and he came up in there swinging on people and going the hell off."

"Smutted? You? By who?"

Fallon sighed. "It wasn't even like that. Pilar lied and said I was stripping."

Bunni shrugged and slurped some hot grits off her spoon. "You was stripping? What's wrong with that?"

"But I wasn't even stripping. I was just dancing in my room. Barron went off about nothing. Hey," Fallon said, changing the subject. "I like your hair. I want mine twisted. Do you go to a salon or do it yourself?"

Bunni picked up her cup of red Kool-Aid with one hand

and touched her red hair with the other one. "Sometimes," she finally said, out of breath after taking about ten long gulps. "There's a lotta braid shops and whatnot around my way, but I do my own shit 'cause I'm a native New Yorker and I know how it's supposed to be done!"

Fallon nodded. "I wanna go to New York one day. Bad. As soon as I graduate, I'm there."

"Haaaaa!" Bunni stuck her tongue out and laughed. It was red and dotted with little balls of white grits. "Awright nah! There's a lotta freaky-deakies in New York! Be ready to party when you get there, okay?"

Fallon laughed and nodded. "I'm gonna be ready. I'm already ready." She reached over and took one of Bunni's spirally red dreadlocks between her fingers.

"I really like the color of your hair," she said. "The texture too. I want mine done 'cause yours is way cool."

"I know," Bunni said, grinning. "It's the shit, ain't it? C'mon, let's go upstairs to your room and play beauty parlor. I'll put some conditioner in your hair and twist you up a few locs too."

Pilar was finally heading back to her suite. Ray's car was still parked in the driveway, and she couldn't believe that after all this time his dumb behind was still sitting up in her room waiting for her to come back. He had been begging her to let him lick her out, but Barron had already eaten her pussy real good and it was still a little tender. The last thing she needed was for Ray to come stabbing his five-inch tongue up inside her coochie trying to get him a little taste too. Yeah, his tongue was thick and long and he knew how to use it just like a little dick, but then what? After she nutted she would still have to look at his fat belly and his hairy man tits. *No thank you,* Pilar thought and shuddered. She would really rather not.

Her sore pussy was still throbbing as Pilar walked up the stairs and headed toward the custom-designed suite that her aunt Selah had built specially for her. She had stepped off the top stair and turned to her left when she heard something coming from the opposite direction that stopped her right in her tracks.

Here we go again, Pilar thought as she looked over her right shoulder, but it wasn't stripper music that assaulted her ears this time. She listened closely. She heard faint noises. Fuck noises. Soft moans and sighs, and then somebody grunting and gasping and then groaning. The sound of a headboard striking the wall rang out a few times, and then a female voice growled real loud, "Yeah! Suck my clit! Eat this pussy, goddammit! Fuck me with that long-ass tongue and lick up *all* my cum!"

Pilar frowned, alarmed. The voice was so damn guttural she didn't recognize it, but on that hallway it could only be coming from one or two rooms: Fallon's or Dy-Nasty's.

Pilar turned around and headed down the other hall with her ear cocked and anxious to hear more, but now there was only silence. She got up close to Dy-Nasty's door and held her breath, listening. Nothing. A few moments later she ran down to Fallon's door and listened too. Nothing. She didn't hear a damn thing.

Until she walked past Dy-Nasty's door again. And that's when she could have sworn she heard somebody say *Shhh . . .* and then giggle. But maybe she didn't. She stood quietly, listening. Nothing.

Pilar had given up and had walked almost down to the end of the hallway when she heard a door open behind her. She slowed her pace until she was barely moving.

"That was so much fun," she heard Fallon say. "It felt so squishy and wet. I think you should leave it in there a little longer next time, okay? I like it to be nice and soft."

Squishy and wet? Pilar froze, then looked over her shoulder as somebody walked out of Fallon's bedroom. Her lip curled down in disgust when she saw who it was.

Bunni!

You nasty bitch! Pilar thought. Poor Fallon couldn't catch a break. She was like a sweet little sheep surrounded by a bunch of hungry ass wolves! Pilar cursed under her breath as she headed to her suite. From Mink to Freddie, to Bunni, to Dy-Nasty, all these twisted, perverted bitches needed to get up out of her aunt's mansion! She stormed down the hall and snatched her door open and stepped inside.

To Pilar's surprise, her man's glasses were still on the end table and the television was still playing real loud. But big fat Ray, with his five-inch tongue, was gone.

CHAPTER 22

The big day had come. It was finally time for us to retake our DNA tests. We were going to the lab as a family because nobody trusted no damn body. Selah and Dy-Nasty were already sitting in the shiny Rolls-Royce when I got outside, but when I went to get in the whip with them Barron checked me kinda hard.

"Nah, don't get in there," he barked, stiff-arming me and blocking the door handle. "This ain't your ride this morning. Go ahead and slide up in Dane's Hummer. He's gonna drive you where you need to go."

I looked him up and down in his Valentino suit and European Zanotti leather shoes, and rolled my damn eyes. That nigga had something up his sleeve. I could feel it along with the butterflies that were fluttering in my stomach. It was like he knew I was lying so he was throwing all his weight behind Dy-Nasty. As trifling and ghetto as she was, he seemed to want her to get up in that trust fund money, but he flipped out and acted the fool if he thought even a penny of it might come to me.

Barron got in the front of the Rolls beside the driver, and it seemed like he slammed his door a little extra hard. The car headed toward the driveway, and Dy-Nasty had the nerve to stick her tongue out and wiggle her fingers at me as they drove past.

I stood out there all alone. I felt ass-out, just like I was gonna be when those DNA results came back. Right now the only way I was gonna come outta this caper with a dime in my pockets was if the test results didn't come back until after the board meeting. If those babies could just be delayed until them white people at Dominion Oil got together and met, then I might still have a chance.

All this was heavy on my mind as I stood waiting in the heat beside the Hummer for Dane and Bunni to come outside. "They told you the name of the new lab?" I asked Dane when they showed up a few minutes later. The whip was hot as hell on the inside, so he cut on the air-conditioner and blasted it on high so the leather seats could cool off.

"Yeah, he told me five minutes ago," he said. "But Bump knew where y'all was gonna be tested all along. That nigga just didn't want nobody else to know."

"I know he didn't!" Bunni said. " 'Cause we woulda got up in that lab and worked them fuckers over!"

"We still gonna work them over," Dane said. "Trust me, every business has a weakness. A soft spot. Uncle Suge is the type of cat who knows how to find those spots and poke 'em until they bleed. Don't worry about your test, Mink. Let Bump and Dy-Nasty worry about hers."

"I can't *stand* your stingy-ass brother." I was feeling real evil after standing out there under all that hot sun. "Y'all got enough money to give me and Dy-Nasty *both* a little bit of change. It ain't fair that some people get to have a whole lot when other people got next to nothing."

"That's the way of the world, baby girl," Dane said, laughing as he held the back door open for me. I hopped up in the whip in my cute little lime green skirt and I had to sit on my hands because the seats were still kinda hot. "The big fish always eat the little fish. It ain't personal. That's just what big fish do."

Jock had learned his lesson about that group-home shit. He didn't care how many times his boy Dre begged him to ride out to Fort Worth and wait for some easy pussy to climb outta a group home window, he wasn't going for it.

Instead, after smoking some nice yay and popping a tab, Jock unbuckled his belt and let his baggy jeans fall around his ankles. Grabbing a jar of cocoa-butter scented Vaseline, he sat back on his couch as the Latina porn flick he had downloaded to his laptop started to play.

It was the weed and not the intro fuck music that was putting Jock in the mood. He dug his hand into the jar of grease and scooped out just enough to thoroughly wax his pole. Two hot Puerto Rican chicks with long curly hair appeared on the screen. One had light skin and the other one was dark. Both had massive titties and wide asses, and Jock stared at the screen as he stroked his shit up and watched them go at each other.

First they kissed passionately, showing a whole lot of darting, curling tongue. They gripped their breasts and rubbed their nipples on each other, with the camera zooming in to get a good shot of the stiff little stones.

"Wow," Jock panted as the light-skinned one reached down and inserted two fingers inside the darker one's pussy. She fingered her until her hand was soaked, and then she pushed the girl back on the bed and lowered her face to the girl's snatch.

The camera caught her from an angle that showed her pink tongue slithering in and out, stabbing both the pussy and the ass crack, and Jock's mouth started watering as he imagined his face all up in that good na-na.

The tempo of the fuck music suddenly picked up as a white dude with a real long dick walked in the room outta nowhere. He positioned himself behind the chick who was bent over licking out that pretty brown pussy, and then he slid his meat up in her and started pounding away.

The girl getting her shit ate out musta forgot her role because she started squealing like she was the one being fucked.

"Oy! Oowie, Papi! Fuck my cho-cha! Ay-ya-yiii! You beautiful fuggin' chulo!"

It was a cheap flick, but it still did the trick. When the white boy pulled his dick outta old girl and spurted a ton of slow-motion cum all over her back, Jock let his nut go too, and with the two girls screaming all kinds of nasty shit in Spanish, everybody in the room came at the same time.

Less than five minutes later Jock walked into his bathroom wide-legged and with his pants and drawers still around his ankles. He wiped his softening dick off with a hot soapy rag, and then he checked his text messages, got his shit together, and got out the door.

Jock was pumping up the sounds of Meek Mill in his 2012 Lincoln MKT as he sparked up his last fat blunt and took a nice long pull. He felt good. His nuts was empty and his head was right, and he was heading to Fort Worth to pick up his manz Glenn so they could cop some more 'dro and replenish their supply. The beat was sick, and pounding his hand on the steering wheel, he was almost down the driveway when his uncle Suge's Ford F-450 King Ranch pulled through the gates and blocked his exit.

He watched as the driver's door swung open and one big booted-up foot hit the pavement, followed by another one. Suge slammed the door, then nodded in Jock's direction and tipped his cowboy hat further down on his head.

"Shit!" Jock cursed. Dude was coming his way. Tossing the get-high out the window was outta the question. Instead, he snatched the weed out his mouth and fumbled to mash it out in the ashtray before sliding it closed. Uncle Suge was almost up on him and he was motioning for him to roll down his window. Cranking the air-conditioner up on high, Jock pushed a button and lowered all four windows at once, just in time for a big cloud of smoke to shoot out of the window and hit his uncle right in the face.

"W'sup, Unc?" Jock grinned, trying to play it off. Uncle Suge was like a legend to him. A big, strong-fisted gangsta-nigga who had lived his life down in the trenches and had conquered them too. Jock knew exactly what kind of gutter work Suge did for his father, and recently he'd had to call on Suge as his savior when he found himself in some trouble that could have fucked up the rest of his life.

"Where's the smoke?" Suge asked quietly.

Sighing, Jock fished the bent-up blunt out of the ashtray. He straightened it out and held it out to his uncle.

"Spark it up," Suge said and nodded, and Jock took his lighter from the tray and fired up the rough end.

They passed the blunt between them for a few minutes, with Jock feeling more and more like a man each time it was his turn to toke. And that's exactly how Suge wanted him to feel too.

"You growing up, Grayson," Uncle Suge said, calling Jock by his real name. "You done been through some shit now and you ain't a little boy no more."

Jock nodded. "Yeah," he said, reaching down to his nuts to make his voice sound deeper. "Yeah, that's right."

Suge's jaw was tight as he stared hard into Jock's eyes. "You know, when men are called upon to do man shit they don't hesitate. They do it."

Jock felt a surge in his chest and it wasn't from the 'dro neither.

He nodded again. "That's right."

"And," Suge went on, pinning Jock in his killer glare, "sometimes a man's gotta make a choice just like"—he snapped his big fingers in the air—"that."

Jock swallowed hard and nodded again.

"There ain't always time to sit down and think about shit, you know. Sometimes a man's gotta decide right on the spot where his loyalty is. He's gotta decide if he's gonna roll or if he's gonna ride. Quick! Just like that! You know the kinda decision I'm talking about, right?"

Suge kept Jock's eyes on lock as he pressed the blunt to his lips and pulled hard, paused, and then slowly exhaled. "The kinda decision I made for you that night you called me."

Jock was young and wild, but he was also Viceroy's son so he knew the drill. One hand always washed the other one in powerful families. Paying dues was part of being a man. And Jock had some big-time dues to pay.

He took the blunt Suge was offering him and took a deep pull and then exhaled. "A'ight. What the fuck I gotta do, Uncle Suge?"

His uncle grinned and grabbed the outside door handle of the Lincoln and yanked it open wide.

"Scoot over, lil dude, and I'll tell you."

CHAPTER 23

The lab Dane took me to was nothing like Exclusively DNA. For one thing, there were a bunch of clear females running the joint, and for two, it was big as shit and everything they did seemed like it was part of a long-ass process.

Me and Bunni cased the joint with our eyes and ears, and we both agreed that there was no way we coulda got in good with enough of these white chicks to pull off a successful gank. And as one nurse rubbed a Q-tip around inside my mouth, and then another nurse stuck me with a needle and filled up a big vial of blood from my arm, I knew my lil con game had been fried up extra crispy.

They couldn't give me an exact date on when my results would be back, but when we got back to the mansion I started packing my gear so I could be ready whenever Selah and Barron decided to toss my ass out the gates.

"Uh-uh!" Bunni protested as I pulled my suitcase outta the closet. "Girl put that shit back! We ain't going *nowhere!*"

"I don't see why not," I told her miserably. "They gonna throw us out in a minute anyway."

"Uh-huh." Bunni nodded. "Oh, they damn sure gonna throw us out. But they ain't gonna do it today. Don't be stupid,

Mink, be *greedy*. Just pretend like we at one of them real fancy resorts and somebody else is picking up the damn tab. Let's run that baby up! Let's get as much as we can of every fuckin' thing they got until they asses get hip. And *then* we'll leave. Plus, how you know for sure what's gonna happen? You got you one of them crystal balls stuck up in ya coochie or something? Hell, don't count us out yet, girl. It's gonna be a minute before your results come back. Who knows. We might think us up a good one by then."

We had decided to put on our bikinis and go hang out by the pool, and me and Bunni had one of the young servants runnin' back and forth bringing us mad drinks on the regular. Bunni had borrowed Fallon's iPod and hooked it up to the outside speakers, and we were rolling our hips and shaking our tipsy asses to a cut called "Spend It" by 2 Chainz, and a brand-new track called "Strugglin' Man" by Reem Raw that was laid over a nice beat by that hot producer dude named Ken Will.

I looked up and what I saw damn near blew my buzz. I didn't even know Dy-Nasty was back at the crib, and I damn sure didn't know who told her to bring her ass outside fuckin' with me and Bunni, but she did.

"Aw, y'all ain't doin' *shit*," she said, busting up on the scene in a pair of stank yellow boy shorts and a bright green ribbon tied over her nipples. "This how we do it on the norf side a' Philly, baby!"

She started working her hips and doing some simple Stripper 101 shit.

Bunni wasn't impressed. "That's how y'all do it?" She shimmied her booty and rolled her stomach at the same time. "Well this how we get it in Harlem, baby!" Bunni made her butt quiver. "What you know about that, huh? What you know about that?"

Dy-Nasty rolled her eyes. She gapped her legs open and squatted halfway down to the ground and started swinging her hips like she was riding a horse. She swept them shits back and forth in long, nasty strokes, and the whole time she was cupping her titties and licking her lips too.

"Y'all bitches ain't got shit," she bragged as she clenched and unclenched her ass cheeks. I knew that move she was doing and I had to admit it was a damn good one. I used to do it too, only I got down a whole lot lower to the ground and I had even picked up a bottle and swung it back and forth using just the muscles in my ass.

When Dy-Nasty got through showing her shit, she picked up my drink off the ground and tipped that shit back, killing it. "Now! Fuck with that, you New York hoes! Fuck with *that!*"

I was gonna fuck with her ass, all right! I was damn sure gonna fuck with her!

"Now, watch carefully, bitch!" I told her. "And take some notes."

I strutted over to the speaker pole and posted up on that shit. Grabbing it up high, I slid down to the ground and arched my back until it looked like a C, and then I reversed the move and twerked it all the way back up the pole. I wrapped my leg around it and bounced up and down real slow, like I was waxing it with my pussy. And then I lowered my leg and turned around. I leaned back until wasn't nothing touching the pole except my head and my rump. I pushed a little and let the pole split my thick ass cheeks, and then I made 'em jump. Up and down, one cheek at a time, causing the kind of visual banga and physical friction that would made any man's dick shoot off a big load of steam.

But it wasn't any man's voice I heard booming from the side door of the house as I showed off my stage skills and performed my extra-nasty booty dance up against that pole.

It was Uncle Suge's.

"*Mink! Dy-Nasty!* Cut that shit out! Get your asses in the pool house *right now*, goddamn it! Both of y'all! *Now!*"

★ ★ ★

Uncle Suge was on one as he tossed me and Dy-Nasty in the pool house together. He chastised us and said he was gonna kick both our yellow asses off the estate unless we got smart enough to work together and help him and Dane come up with a plan to outsmart Barron.

"I don't know which one of y'all is really Sable and trust me, I don't give a damn," he told us. "But I can tell you right now, Bump is gonna make sure neither one of ya'll get a dime of that money, you hear me?"

I nodded 'cause I believed him, but Dy-Nasty twisted up her lips like she already knew she was paid and in there.

"Uh-huh," Suge told her. "That goes for you too, Dy-Nasty. Bump mighta told you he was gonna make sure you got paid, but believe me, that's a lie. He's using you, baby. And you just about greedy enough and stupid enough to let him."

Dy-Nasty looked like she wanted to snap off with the mouth, but Uncle Suge grilled her like a killer for a few long seconds, and when she backed down and looked away he continued.

"Selah saw what y'all was out there doing just now, you know. She stood right in the kitchen window and saw every damn move y'all made."

"But I wasn't—" both us tried to lie, but he gave us a look that straight killed our noise.

"Come off that bullshit!" He shook his head with disappointment, and all me and Da-Stripper could do was stare down at our hands as he chewed us out. "I don't get it. How can two chicks so slick be so goddamn stupid? Both of y'all are about to miss out on a guaranteed fortune, and for what? Because y'all can't stop scratching at each other's faces long enough to think straight. Now I'ma need both of y'all to reach down and pluck ya brains out ya asses! Ain't *nobody* getting paid if Bump can help it. *Nobody!* Now let's go to work and get on top of this money, you got it?"

Me and Dy-Nasty cut our eyes at each other. I waited for a few seconds until I saw her nod, and then I nodded too.

"Here," he said, dropping a thick beige folder down on the coffee table. Dy-Nasty's name was written on it real big in black magic marker. "This is a copy of what Barron is planning on showing to the board right after the vote. It don't matter what the hell your DNA test says, Dy-Nasty. If them white folks get a look at all this criminal shit you been doing you ain't getting a dime of that money, you understand?"

Good for her stank ass! I thought as my eyes shot over to that thick-ass folder. I couldn't wait to see what was in it!

"Where'd you get that?" I asked Suge.

"From Jock. He stole it from Barron and made a copy. Don't worry. He stole a thick one on you too."

Damn!

"Here's the deal," Uncle Suge continued. "Everybody with half a brain knows if Sable is really still alive, then one of you is lying."

I gasped and opened my mouth to protest, and Dy-Nasty did too.

"Swallow that shit!" Uncle Suge raised his big hand up and shut both of us down. "I don't care which one of y'all is the liar and which one is the thief. All I know is you two can fuck it up for each other, and even worse, you can fuck it up for the rest of us too, you get me?"

We nodded again.

"So this is what y'all are gonna have to do." He gave us both a real hard no-bullshit look. "Y'all are gonna have to split the damn money."

Me and Dy-Nasty started bitching before the words were outta his mouth good, but he wasn't tryna hear none of it.

"A hundred and fifty grand a year is more than either one of y'all is ever gonna pull in from stripping, and it's free money too! I done already told y'all and I meant that shit. Either you come together on this right now or get thrown off the goddamn property. Both of y'all! Tonight. With nothing but the rags you wore up in here."

As it turned out, me and Dy-Nasty had a lot more in common than just our good looks. Yeah, we was both hustlers and con artists from the hood, and hell yeah, we were both real big liars who spoke the language of the streets, but we were both smart enough to recognize a once-in-a-lifetime opportunity when it was about to slip away too.

"Cool." I went ahead and said it first. Hell, I knew damn well I wasn't Sable so all this shit was just another hustle to me. If I walked outta here with a yard in my pocket it would be way more than I walked in with. Besides, Dy-Nasty mighta been a liar, but I was definitely a thief. I knew my mama's name and it damn sure wasn't Selah Dominion. I thought about losing all three hundred grand, and splitting the money in half every year became a real no-brainer. "Yeah, I'm cool with that," I said. "I'll do it if she do it."

Dy-Nasty looked greedy as shit as her head bobbed up and down and she nodded real fast. "Me too. I'll do it if she do it too."

Sometimes there had to be honor and cooperation between thieves, and twenty-four hours later me and Dy-Nasty had clicked up enough to form us a lil temporary hood partnership.

"A'ight, listen up, everybody. Here's how all this shit is gonna go down."

We were having a meeting at Uncle Suge's place and he was laying out the plan. We'd all come to an agreement that the best way to fight grime was by flinging back even more grime, and since Barron was tryna shit on me and Dy-Nasty and chop both of us off the family tree, then we were gonna have to dig up some deep roots and shit on him too.

Dane was sitting in an armchair, while me, Dy-Nasty, and Bunni were sitting on the sofa. Uncle Suge had our attention from the middle of the floor. The only person who was missing was Jock. He had already promised to throw his vote in with ours, but we was about to do some seriously shitty arm-twisting, and Uncle Suge didn't think Jock had the stomach for it.

"We all know Lil Bump is gonna try to cut all of us off from the family trust fund," Uncle Suge said. "He ain't even trying to hide that. Since Mink was already declared Sable and she got that inheritance money, we need Mink's vote to keep Bump from fucking us in the ass, and he's gonna do everything he can to make sure we don't get it."

Everybody nodded their understanding.

"Now, Mink, you already know that boy done went to New York and got himself a file on you, and a thick one too. The bad thing is, he's got one on Dy-Nasty too, and hers is even thicker. I know power players like Bump and I know how they think. That boy is betting a thousand that your second DNA test is gonna come back negative and that Dy-Nasty's is gonna come back positive. That way, he gets to get rid of two Sables with just one stone. Mink, you'll be eliminated based on your second DNA test, and Dy-Nasty, if your second test comes back positive, then Barron still wins. Because once he gets you to vote for him he's gonna pull out your folder and flick you off like a booger too. Now there ain't much we can do about that, but here's what we *can* do. We can put our feet on his neck and make him do what we want him to do. We gotta force him to hold that board meeting *before* the new DNA results have a chance to come in."

"And how we gonna do that?" Dane asked.

"By getting us a nice pile of dirt on him too. And if he don't wanna act right then we'll just take *that* shit to the board!"

Dane shook his head. "You looking for some dirt on Mr. Clean?" He chuckled. "Good luck, Unc. I been living with B my whole life, man. That nigga is the cleanest cat I know."

"Oh yeah? Well I found me a girl," Uncle Suge said slickly. "A young white chick I know from Houston. She used to be mentored by the Dominion Diamonds, but she dropped outta the program when she got pregnant and then she never came back."

"And?" Dane asked. "What's she got to do with Barron?"

"Nothing yet," Uncle Suge said, grinning. "But she will, Nephew. She will."

Dane shook his head. "Bump is clean, I'm telling you. That boy is squeaky clean."

"Yeah, that nigga might drink bleach for breakfast, but Mink and Dy-Nasty done already came up with a plan of their own," Uncle Suge said, looking at us. "Y'all ladies wanna run it down?"

Me and Dy-Nasty opened our mouths, and out slithered our identical forked tongues. We gave them all the details that we had schemed and connived and collaborated on, and our shit flowed so smooth that heads kept swinging left and right as we laid out our cross-con like it had come from one brain. We were so in sync with our hustle that before it was all over we were actually finishing each other's sentences. Our plan was so fuckin' sugary sweet that I felt cavities popping up in all my teeth. Uh-uh. Uncle Suge was right. Jock's young ass didn't need to be up in the bizz like that. His wimpy lil dro-head ass woulda straight-up collapsed in the ring tryna fuck with us heavyweights.

"I really think this could work, but we're gonna need you to get up with ya boy Kelvin Merchant again," I told Bunni. "Tell ya little pain slut we'll pay him triple if he hooks us up this go 'round."

"So," Bunni said, smiling proudly at me and Dy-Nasty like we were two brilliantly beautiful geniuses. "Y'all gonna get the white chick to go on television and say Viceroy was diggin' her out when she was a sixteen-year-old honey at his little tutoring academy? She's gonna stand up in front of a camera and lie and say she had a baby by him and she's got the DNA results to prove her son is a Domino?"

"Yeah." Uncle Suge nodded. "You got that shit right. That's exactly what she's gonna say."

"Well, damn!" Bunni hollered. "Y'all really gonna run up hard and dry in Viceroy *and* Barron's ass-cracks like that?"

"Whoa, hold the fuck up," Dane protested, shaking his head. Forget about Jock. From where I was sitting Dane was looking kinda weak in the chin too. "Y'all wanna throw some shit on *Pop's* name too? And y'all think Bump is gonna go for *that*?"

"Hell naw he ain't gonna go for it," Uncle Suge said. "That's the whole point. That nigga's gonna buck. And when he does, that's when we stick his ass. Hard. *Deep.* Right in the heart. With a fuckin' ice pick."

"Goddamn!" Bunni hollered. "You don't fuck around, do you, Uncle Suge? You sure know how to kick a muh'fucka around when he's down!"

Suge didn't blink. "Damn right. I'll stomp him out. Stomp his muthafuckin' ass *out!*"

Bunni rolled! "*Shiiit* . . . remind me not to get caught on your dirty side, *okayyy?*"

Suge winked at her and tongued his toothpick sexily in his mouth.

"I'm a gully muh'fucka, baby. This is what I do."

CHAPTER 24

If all the recent craziness with Mink and Dy-Nasty wasn't enough to frazzle her nerves and bring back old memories, now there was this. Selah's heart pounded as she studied the words and the picture that had just been texted to her cell phone.

I STILL HAVE IT.

The object on the screen glittered and sparkled, and back in the day it had been worth over a million dollars. Eighteen years had passed since the last time she'd seen it, and the memory of how and where she'd lost it was still fresh in her mind. She glanced down at the wedding ring she wore on her finger now. This one was nothing compared to the one in the picture. It didn't mean half as much to her as the original one had meant, but then again she wasn't half the wife today that she was back then either.

She sighed as she replied to the text message with a few short words.

I WANT IT BACK.

That fucker. That short, fat, gruesome troll. After all these years she could still feel his pudgy hands on her. Feel the way the sweaty sheets had been wrenched off the mattress by their pounding, desperate bodies. It was a weakness of hers, this knack powerful men had for turning her on.

He texted her back almost right away.

MEET ME. WEDNESDAY AT NOON. AT OUR OLD PLACE. I'LL GIVE IT TO YOU THEN.

Just reading the words on the screen sent shivers running down Selah's spine. She was excited and disgusted at the same time. And there was an element of shame in there too. But shame mixed with the sweet satisfaction of revenge.

I'm gonna pay him back with his worst fucking enemy.

The words she'd muttered all those years ago came back as a burning echo in her mind as she deleted the cryptic messages from her iPhone. She thought about her husband laying co-matose in his hospital bed. She'd paid his ass back, all right. She had damn sure done that. And on Wednesday at twelve she'd find out exactly what that payback was going to cost her.

"Them fools up at the college are trying to act like they don't wanna let me back in class," Dane told us as we chilled in his little crib over the garage. Me and Bunni had gone up there looking to get lifted, but for once Dane was stone sober when he opened the door.

"Classes start in a minute and I shoulda been gone by now. Back in the dorm. But I can't even reserve a room until I get some money and they lift the charges off me."

"When are they gonna do that?" Bunni asked.

Dane shrugged. "When they get good and fuckin' ready. I gotta go before a disciplinary board. They'll examine my case and decide if they're gonna let me back in my classes or kick me out and send everything over to the prosecutor's office. It's all up to them."

"Can't you get one of your father's lawyers to make all that shit go away? I mean, damn. I thought all rich people had to do was flash a couple of dollars and pay somebody off when they got in trouble with the cops."

"Yeah," Dane said and nodded. "Sometimes it works like that, but sometimes it don't. My case is all fucked up because it went too far for too long. I got caught out there with the wrong dorm chicken and niggas got jealous and set me up. I couldn't pay nobody off because I had already blown through all my money. The only thing I got going for me now is that trust fund. I need that safe to pop open real wide so I can get what's minez and get on with the rest of my life. Word."

"I can see why you don't wanna go to your moms and ask her for nothing, but you and Barron seem kinda close sometimes. You can't talk him into hooking you up with a couple of ends?"

He shook his head. "I don't trust B like that. If I showed him this brick I'm carrying around he might snatch it and bust me in the grill with it. I can't take no chances on him. He could post me up in front of the board and make me fight for my share of the trust fund too, and if somebody even whispered the words *sexual assault* they'd cut me off right at the nuts. I love Bump and all, but the boy is strange. My pops taught him how to squeeze the hell out of a dime, and when it comes to taking care of the family cash, he's got his foot on every penny."

Right now Barron had his eyes on the time as he checked his six-thousand-dollar Cartier Ballon Bleu and sped toward the local frat house. Him and his boy Animal Bates had gone to college together, and a bunch of his Omega brothers and dorm rats were throwing Animal a bash to celebrate his birthday.

Barron had agreed to show his face for a few minutes, but

he damn sure wasn't in the partying mood. The board was meeting in just a few days and he was seriously on edge. Never before in the history of Dominion Oil had a single vote been the deciding factor on such an important financial decision. Barron had been wheeling and dealing and sweating the board members twenty-four-seven, and it was looking like everything was going to work out just the way he wanted it to.

He'd gotten a call from one of the oldest board members, who just happened to be one of Viceroy's closest friends. He said he was pretty close to getting the other members to agree to delay the board's vote for seven days, but he needed the request in writing. Barron had damn near jumped up and down because that meant the DNA labs would have a chance to get their reports generated, and then everybody would find out that con-mami Mink, with her fine sexy ass was a fraud and that Dy-Nasty, even though she probably *was* his long-lost sister Sable, was a stank, foul, guttersnipe criminal.

Once the DNA results were in all Barron had to do was produce those results at the board meeting and let Dy-Nasty cast her vote with his team. Twenty-four hours later he would be instated as the new CEO of Dominion Oil, and then BOOM! He'd *smizzack* the board with a copy of Dy-Nasty's arrest record that stripped her naked and showed her in all her corrupted glory, and Little Miss Hoodrat would immediately be disqualified from the trust fund.

Barron was whistling as he pulled his bone-white Maybach into a parking space in front of the frat house. From the outside the place looked like a dump. Them niggas was probably still wildin' and cutting up like they were back in college. He looked around at the other parked cars and wished he had picked something else to drive. His shit would probably be sitting up on four milk crates when he came back out.

The inside of the small, one-story house looked a lot better than the outside, and Barron started tossing back shots as soon as he got with Animal and his crew. A lot of dorm chicks had been on his dick back in college, but there was this one girl who had hated his ass and used to diss him on the regular. Epiphany James. She was there, at the party, and with her slim waist, power-butt, and long fine legs, she was even sexier than she had been in college.

But Epiphany was one of them chicks who was all cultural and shit. She wore her hair in a wild Afro and talked all that Ungawa Black Power ethnic talk, and just the sight of Barron, a star football player with his skinny white cheerleader girl-friend on his arm, used to piss her off.

"Long time no see." Barron dropped his voice into Barry White land as he rolled up on Epiphany. "It's good to see you again."

"Barron," she said and nodded. Her slanted cat eyes and smooth, cocoa-colored skin sent heat flashing through his groin. "Yeah, long time no see."

Barron noticed she didn't say it was good to see him too, but he hadn't really expected her to. Ever since Carla had left him he'd been paying closer attention to beautiful black chicks like Epiphany, and he had Pilar to thank for that. White girls didn't even do nothing for him no more.

Barron made the rounds at the party and went in the huddle with a few older Ques and their girlfriends. He drank like a fish and smoked a little weed too, but when them niggas started talking about poppin' E and smoking meth and all that kinda bullshit he backed off and drew the line.

"Look at this fool," his boy Dopeman, a showboating wanna-be Omega bitched. "This nigga's asshole is still tight as hell!"

Bruhs laughed and Barron tried to play it off. Dopeman wasn't frat, but he had been around for a real long time, and all the young come-up bruhs idolized his ass.

"Yo, why you biting all on my nuts, Mr. Dopeman? Don't worry about what I do, nigga! Just do you!"

Barron chilled with the homeys for a few more minutes so

it wouldn't look like Dopeman was running him off, and then he dipped outta the huddle and went across the room and mingled with some of his old honeys. A butt-ugly chick named Maleeka Jones was hanging around with a bunch of other friends of theirs, and one of the girls had brought some line-backer-looking transvestite with her. The dude's name was Ben, and he was chewing gum and flapping off at the mouth like he was a girl for real. All that weed had Barron cracking the fuck up at the sight of such a big dude posted up on the couch in a halter and heels, with his thick legs crossed at the knees.

"Here, nigga!" Dopeman came up behind Barron and passed him a drink over his shoulder. "What you run out for? We was just about to break out the special shit. Don't say I never gave your ass nothing, dig?"

Surrounded by a bunch of giggling women, Barron tossed his drink back real quick and took a few hits off the blueberry sticky that was being passed around. Maleeka came over and sat up under him, and as he listened to her run her mouth he tried to remember why he had never hit that shit in college. Her titties were nice and round, and she had some pretty legs on her that would feel real good wrapped around his waist.

But she's ugly, Barron thought as Maleeka giggled and put her tiny hand on his thigh. *This bitch is ugly,* he thought again, and that was the last damn thing he thought too.

Giggles.

"Is he out?"

"Yep, his ass is gone! Slumped."

"What the hell did you give him, D?"

"I gave that nigga what he needed! Something to loosen his tight ass up!"

"Yeah, he's still the same old Barron. Stiff as hell. Always acting like he's better than everybody else."

"His family always did have money."

"Having money and having fun is two different things."

"Ay, we oughtta have some fun with his ass!"

Laughter.

"Yeah, let's fuck with this fool. Put some lipstick on him. Some mascara too."

"Ohhh, wait! Let's shave off his eyebrows! Here!"

Rummaging in the purse.

"Use my razor."

"Hold up, I know what we can do! Switch clothes with him, Ben! Let's put him in your skirt and a push-up bra!"

"Uh, hell no! Do you know how much I paid for this skirt?"

"Not as much as this nigga got in his wallet! Switch clothes with him, fool! Once you put on his pants whatever you find in the pockets is yours."

"Hold up, take some pictures, girl. This dude looks hilarious!"

"Yeah, take some pictures! Wait! Put your dick in his mouth first, Ben! Not all the way in, stupid! Just slap the head on his lips. Yeah."

Giggles.

"Just like that. Good. Now take the pictures."

Flash. Flash. Flash. Flash. Flash.

"Yo, nigga! Make sure you hit me with them joints so I can post them on Facebook!"

Barron was cruising. On a cloud far up in the sky. His bladder was full and he had to pee. Struggling to his feet, he staggered across the room and pulled open the door. The cool night breeze washed over his face as he leaned against a parked car and pissed all over the tire.

With his dick still hanging out, he opened the car door and climbed behind the wheel. He felt like he was inside a pinball machine full of swiping silver gates. Lights flashing, bells ringing. Just a' bouncing offa shit.

His vision blurred and he lurched hard in his seat. He hit a pinball gate. People screamed, others cheered. He was beating the shit out of the game, and he moved faster and faster through the colorful maze. Suddenly it was dark and he had to pee again. With the engine still running he flung open the car door and stepped out, then turned around and pissed directly on his front seat.

He didn't even put his meat away. Instead, a doorway loomed ahead and he made his way to it. He fumbled with the latch until it opened. Inside, he was feeling almost fine for a moment, but then he crashed into a large potted plant, stumbled to his right, and passed out again as the sofa broke his fall.

Selah woke up out of a deep sleep. She'd been tossing and turning with her body burning up. She'd been dreaming about her missing ring and how she had lost it. Her sheets were sweaty and she couldn't go back to sleep. Leaving her suite, she padded through the expansive mansion in the darkness. She knew every inch of this house because it had been specially built and designed just for her.

Downstairs, she entered the kitchen and turned on the lights. Pushing a button on the coffeepot she set it to brew, and then she stared out the back window and waited for it to be ready. It was almost dawn and the sun was trying to peek out from the early-morning clouds. Someone had left a light on in the pool house, and a child's rubber raft was still floating in the large swimming pool.

Selah thought about the two girls who were sleeping upstairs, both claiming to be Sable. One of them was surely lying, and the pain of that lie had stirred up some long-dead emotions that she had tried to bury a long time ago. But the past never stayed buried.

She thought about her ring again, and then about her missing daughter.

She pictured the flash of guilt on her baby sister's face as Viceroy's pearl-colored cum dripped from her lips.

It didn't mean anything. I swear. I was just helping him, that's all. He needed it. He needed it.

Selah sighed and shook her head. It was all such a dizzying loop. If she hadn't gone to his job that day she wouldn't have caught her husband mouth-fucking her sister. And if she hadn't caught Viceroy with her sister, she wouldn't have lost Sable. And if she hadn't lost Sable, then she wouldn't have lost her ring. And if she hadn't lost her ring, she wouldn't be driving herself to Dallas at noon on Wednesday to see the funny-looking man who had given her the very best dick she had ever had in her life.

It was funny the way so many things got tied together in life. How no action was really independent of the next one. Selah watched the sky as she waited for the coffeepot to give her its signal, but when a sound finally came it didn't come from the kitchen, it came from the front door.

Frowning, she glanced at the clock. Five ten a.m. The doorbell rang again, and gathering her bathrobe tighter, she headed across the house to answer it.

"Yes?" she called out nervously. She clicked on the parlor lights and looked outside. A police car was in her driveway with its flashing red and blue strobe lights on.

"Can I help you?" she asked as she opened the door.

Two uniformed policemen stood there.

"We're sorry to bother you at this hour, Mrs. Dominion, but we need to speak to your son, Barron. Is he at home?"

"Why, yes," Selah answered. She peered past them. "His car is here so he must be upstairs in his suite. What's the problem?"

"There's been an accident, ma'am," the older officer informed her. "And we need to speak to Barron. May we come in?"

"Of course," Selah said as she stepped back to let them

enter. "But I'm telling you, Barron is upstairs," she said as she closed the door and turned around. "He's upstairs aslee—" The word got stuck in her throat as her and the two officers stared at the thing that was stretched out cold on the sofa, a rose-colored miniskirt hiked up his thighs and his business hanging down low on his leg. One hand was flung over the top of the couch, and the other hand was resting on his stomach. Bright lipstick circled his lips like somebody had colored it on a clown. His eyebrows had been shaved off and dramatically drawn on and arched with a pencil, his cheeks were colored in deep red rouge, and the prettiest shades of eye shadow had been blended in above his lids.

"Barron!" Selah shrieked and ran to her son. She tossed a pillow over his crotch and slapped him on his painted-up cheeks. "*Barron!* What happened, baby? Wake up, son. Tell me what the hell happened?"

Barron opened his eyes and looked around slowly. He blinked a few times like he was trying to focus.

"What in the world happened to you?" Selah wailed. "Baby what is going *on?*"

Barron licked his lips. They felt crusty and sore. He opened his mouth to answer his mother, but when it became obvious that he couldn't speak, one of the police officers moved forward and spoke for him instead.

"Mr. Dominion, you have the right to remain silent. Anything you say, can and will be used against you in a court of law . . ."

CHAPTER 25

Barron spent seven whole hours wearing a rose miniskirt in a downtown Dallas bullpen before one of his lawyer friends came to get him out. By then he had slept his drugged-up high off and was ready to kill some fuckin' body.

"Here you go," said Jeff Rivera, a Hispanic dude he'd gone to law school with as he passed Barron a clean handkerchief. As with every DUI and suspected hit-and-run case, those fools at the courthouse had suspended his driver's license so Jeff was giving him a ride home. "Try to clean up a little bit before we get there. You got mascara all over your nose, man."

Barron snatched the cloth and dry-scrubbed his face until it burned. Whoever had painted him up had done a damn good job and he didn't even wanna think about what his mug shot looked like.

But the embarrassment he was feeling right now wasn't shit compared to what the public humiliation was gonna be when this drama got out, and it was gonna take some deep cash and an entire public relations cleanup team to make this kind of shit stain go away.

Jeff had brought Barron some clothes to ride home in, and the thought that his moms had seen him wearing makeup and a bra straight fucked up his heart. He was gonna have a lot of explaining to do, and while he was busy feeling sorry for himself, there was a ten-year-old little Mexican boy sitting up in the hospital with a broken ankle and it was all Barron's fault.

"So that kid I hit is gonna be okay, right?" Barron cut his eyes at Jeff and asked. "It was just his foot, right? The rest of him is cool, huh?"

Jeff nodded. "Oh, yeah. He's gonna be good. He's a little day laborer. He was crossing the street with his father to catch a job when you hit him. Yeah, you fucked up his ankle, but it coulda been a whole lot worse, you know? I already arranged to pay his hospital bill, and later on today I'm gonna go see his father and offer him a few dollars to compensate for the boy's lost wages. Don't worry. As long as we can keep this out of the media then everything should be okay."

Barron squeezed his eyes shut tight. He had never been in trouble a day in his life, and he wasn't sure if anything would ever be okay again. He had no memory of hitting the boy, or of crashing into any of the three parked cars the cops claimed he had smashed up either. All he remembered was getting nice at a party, and then driving through a fucking video game. It was one of those pinball machines with bumpers and bells. He was riding in the big silver ball, and people had been screaming and cheering as he bounced off the swinging gates. Everything else was a big long blur . . .

He glanced out the window as the car sped toward the Dominion Estate, where all kinds of problems were waiting for him. Fallon, Mink, Dy-Nasty, Pilar. His shit was getting raggedy. It was falling apart. He was trying to do too much, and he couldn't have gotten arrested at a worse time.

Damn! Barron slammed his hand down hard on Jeff's dashboard. Damn! Damn! Damn!

Selah was highly pissed off as she walked out of the Omni Hotel in downtown Dallas the next afternoon, which was also happened to be the headquarters of a prestigious oil firm called Ruddman Energy. Her stride was quick as she crossed the large lobby, and dressed in a hip-hugging Dolce & Gabbana dress she looked a whole lot younger than forty-eight.

She smoothed her hair back as she pushed through the revolving front doors and waved impatiently for the valet to bring her Mercedes around. She had driven herself into the city, and it had been a big waste of time because the old-ass fool she came to see was still playing childish games.

"Selah! *Selah!*"

She heard him calling her, but she damn sure wasn't about to answer him. This fool had brought out the New Yorker in her, and no matter what had gone down between them in the past, she wasn't the same woman she was back then, and she wasn't burning on fire for vengeance anymore either.

"Selah!"

She walked off a few paces and suddenly he grabbed her arm from behind.

"I'm sorry, Selah. I didn't mean to upset you. Come back upstairs and let's talk about it, okay?"

"There's nothing for us to talk about, Rodney! Not a damn thing. Why are you trying to come back in my life? Why now? First you steal my brother Digger away from my husband, and now this! I didn't come here to *fuck* you, Rodney! I came for my ring and you said you'd give it to me!"

He pulled her close and stuck his nose right under her ear. She heard his sharp intake of breath and then he whispered, "After all these years I can still remember how good you smelled. How sweet your pussy tasted. I remember how you sounded . . . the noises you made when I put my—" He sucked his breath in between his teeth and moaned, ". . . *ssss ahhh . . . oooh yes . . . go deeper, baby . . . ahhh, baby, yes . . .*"

Selah hauled off and slapped the shit out of him.

It was a Brooklyn move, and it happened so fast that almost nobody saw it. Almost.

"Stay the hell away from me, Rodney. You hear? Just stay the hell away from me!"

Fat, greasy, frog-looking Rodney Ruddman, CEO and president of Ruddman Energy and arch-enemy of Viceroy Dominion, touched his face where Selah had slapped him, and then he blew her a kiss and laughed.

"Now that hurt a little bit, but it's okay. Come back and see me sometime, Selah. Let me take care of you. Even on his best day Viceroy could never make you feel it the way I do. Remember, you can still get this if you want it, baby. You can get it anytime you want it."

Life was about to get a whole lot worse for Barron before it got any better. The mansion was pretty quiet when Jeff picked him up for his court date on Wednesday. Dane had taken all three ghetto trolls on a shopping trip at NorthPark Center, and Selah had taken the Mercedes and driven herself into Dallas to have lunch with an old friend.

Barron had an appointment to meet with the judge presiding over his case, and Jeff had assured him that everybody involved was interested in making this thing go away.

"Even the boy's father?" Barron had asked him as they got off the elevator and headed toward the judge's private chambers.

"*Especially* the boy's father," Jeff told him. "For two hundred thousand dollars."

Barron looked at him. How many fuckin' grapes were those people planning to pick that day?

Forty-five minutes later the two men had met with the judge and they were in the elevator riding back downstairs. Jeff had been good to his word, and after giving Barron a strong talking to about the dangers of irresponsible drinking and driving, Judge Halley, who was a personal friend of Viceroy's, and whose campaign for office had been heavily funded by Dominion Oil, poured the young attorneys a drink as they sat around and discussed local business and politics.

"Look, the chief of police is gonna try to bury this, but keep your head down and stay out of trouble," the judge warned Barron as he was leaving. "We should be able to keep this away from the media too, but make sure you don't give them anything else to throw at you. No more scandals, you understand?"

No more scandals.

Barron breathed a sigh of relief as Jeff pulled out of the private parking garage. They'd gone two blocks and stopped at a traffic light when Barron saw something that kicked him straight in the nuts.

It was Selah. His mother. She was coming out of the Omni Hotel with a man, and it damn sure wasn't his father Viceroy. Hell no. It was Rodney Ruddman, CEO of Ruddman Energy. Rodney was Viceroy's main competitor and sworn enemy. Barron watched in silence as Ruddman grabbed Selah's arm and his mother stormed away from the man. She looked angry in a way that he had never seen her look before. In a womanly way. And when Rodney reached out and grabbed her again and pulled her close to him, bending to whisper something in her ear, Barron exploded inside. *What the fuck?* His blood started boiling and he was itching to jump outta the ride and fuck that old bastard up.

But the light had changed and the car was on the move again. Barron turned around and put a crook in his neck as he tried to keep his eyes on them. He coulda sworn he saw Selah swing on Rodney and slap the shit outta him, but they were too far away now and he had blinked too, so he couldn't be sure.

Barron yanked his cell phone off his belt as Jeff turned the corner. He hit Selah on speed dial and cursed as her phone went straight to voice mail. He stuck his finger in his left ear and turned slightly away from Jeff as he spoke in a low tone. "Hey, Ma, it's me. Um, I just wanted to make sure you were okay. I thought I just um, saw something . . . um, I thought . . . Call me back. I'm just checking to see if you need me, okay?"

He hung up and tried to process what the fuck he had just seen. His mother and his father's business competitor coming out of an upscale hotel in the middle of the day. That nigga had put his hands on Selah. And not like he was trying to handle her neither. Nah, the way Rodney had pulled her close and stuck his nose in her neck said a whole lot about their relationship. There had been an understanding in that move. Some familiarity. Like dude had yoked Selah up before. Mama had hauled off and slapped the shit outta that old man! What the hell was up with *that*?

Barron's heart pounded as rage circulated through him.

He didn't wanna believe what his logical mind was telling him, but what else was he supposed to think? His father was laying up in the hospital about to fade out on the world, and his mother was out here fucking around with his enemies? And in broad daylight? He closed his eyes and tried to calm his breathing. *No more scandals.* Ya got that shit right! He thought about his mug shot. The last thing his family needed was another goddamn scandal. With all the drama going on in their lives they couldn't take not one more thing. Barron knew what he had to do. He was gonna have to shut *everybody* down. Make everybody crawl around on a real low profile. Because lately, every last one of the Dominions had been on some brand-new kinda shit, and if the board found out what *he* had just been through . . . well, the board just better not find the fuck out!

CHAPTER 26

Barron's shit was all fucked up. Nothing was going down the way it was supposed to. First he got a call from Judge Halley's secretary. She said her boss needed to speak to Barron and Jeff on a three-way call immediately.

"That kid," Judge Halley said quietly. "The kid you hit is going to be a problem."

"Why is that?" Jeff asked.

"Because his grape-picking father just reneged on the deal, that's why!"

"But he took the money!" Barron said. "He took two hundred fuckin' grand!"

"Oh yeah? You got a receipt? His side of the story is that you *offered* him two hundred grand to go away and keep his mouth closed. He said he turned it down."

Barron couldn't believe this shit! His throat got clogged with fear as he shook his head, trying to understand where the judge was coming from. "He's a liar! He's a lying muthafucka! But two days ago you told me not to worry, that this thing was gonna blow over. You said the chief of police was gonna bury it!"

"He tried," the judge said. "But after those narcotics officers got caught beating a suspect on camera, and with the big investigation on the ticket-fixing scam, the public has their eyes on every damn thing and the media has been merciless. Sorry, Barron, but you're on your own. The chief said he tried his best to bury this thing, but Internal Affairs just dug it right back up."

Barron was desperate. If this shit got out on the news he could kiss his law license and his whole fuckin' life good-bye!

"C'mon, Judge," he begged. "There's gotta be something you can do! Is there any way at all to fix this? Any way at all?"

Judge Halley cleared his throat.

"Maybe. But it's gonna cost you."

A few days later Barron pulled into his reserved parking spot outside of Dominion Oil's headquarters. Chest-high gold-crusted nameplates reading, VICEROY DOMINION, SUPERIOR DOMINION, and BARRON DOMINION identified the top-three parking spots in their pecking order of importance. Right now Barron's spot was last. His uncle Suge's truck was parked in the second spot, the one right next to Viceroy's, but once Barron took over for his father all that shit was gonna change.

He walked inside the sleek building with mirrored glass. A big oil painting of Viceroy loomed large on the far wall. Barron headed toward the elevators and nodded at the receptionist and the security staff. He'd known these people from the time he was just a tyke, but they all respected him as a man and called him *sir* whenever they spoke.

He used his key to call for the private elevator that would take him directly into the hub of business on the building's fifteenth floor. When the doors opened, he rode upstairs with a determined expression on his face. He tapped his foot impatiently. The board was waiting for his written request for a vote delay, and as soon as he took care of this other business he would deliver it to them by hand. The elevator stopped and the doors slid open soundlessly. He exited and stepped into a very large and busy room that held the cubicles for DO's most important staff members.

"Mr. Barron!" the receptionist at the desk called out to him. "The papers you need to sign are in Mr. Superior's office, sir. He has them waiting for you."

Since there were three Dominion men running the company, most of the employees addressed them as Mr. Viceroy, Mr. Superior, and Mr. Barron. That shit was gonna change too, Barron thought. With his father off the rolls, the only Dominion man who mattered would be him, and that's what everybody was gonna have to call him too. Mr. Dominion.

Barron headed for his uncle's corner office and pushed through the double doors without knocking. Suge was standing next to his desk and talking on the phone. He looked like big-time money dressed in his snakeskin boots and three-piece suit, but no matter what the fuck this dude wore he would always be a two-bit hustler in Barron's eyes.

"Let me call you back." Suge's voice was deep as he fixed Barron coldly in his sights and spoke into the phone. He hung up, then walked over and stood behind his huge desk.

"What it do, Bump?" he asked. His voice was even and casual, although Barron thought he saw something crafty shift into the older man's eyes.

"It do what it never did before," Barron barked, then waved his hand impatiently. "You need a signature on those requisition orders, right? Well hand them over."

Suge placed one thick finger on top of a small pile of papers on the center of the desk. Grilling Barron, he pushed the stack in his direction.

"Here you go," Suge said and shot his nephew a warning look. "And Bump, do us all a favor. Make sure you sign *all* of 'em, okay?"

Barron frowned and picked up the stack. After skimming the top sheet, he sat the papers back down on Suge's desk and pulled his father's Conway Stewart fountain pen out of his suit pocket. The room was silent as Barron quickly read and signed the first three pages of paper, but as soon as his eyes ran over the last sheet he cursed under his breath and then started laughing.

"Ay, what the fuck is this?" he blurted as he eyed his uncle and grinned. "You're kidding me, right? Yo, you must be fuckin' joking if you think I'ma sign some bullshit like this!"

"Nah." Suge shook his head and said quietly, "I ain't joking man. I ain't *even* fuckin' joking. Yeah, I'ma need you to go 'head and sign that, and I'ma need you to give up them files you got on Mink and Dy-Nasty too. The originals *and* the copies."

"Nigga you better come the fuck up off that purple *syz-zurp*!" Barron's lips curled down with mad disrespect. He snatched the paper off the desk and tossed that shit to the floor and stomped on it. "Why would I give up my files and sign some shit like this? C'mon, now. You play too much, dude. You play way too fuckin' much."

Suge came from behind his desk. He walked up on Barron with a stone-cold killer look on his grill, and then he turned around and walked toward his office door.

"Oh, you gonna sign it," he said, closing the door and flipping the lock. He flipped the overhead lights off too, and the natural light from his floor-to-ceiling windows was the only thing flooding in. "Believe that, son. You gonna sign it."

Suge picked up a remote control from his desk and pushed a button, and at the far wall, a movie screen slid down from the ceiling. He pushed another button and an overhead projector hummed and then cast a light beam on the white screen. He pushed a third button and a video of a young white girl appeared on the screen. She was standing in front of Viceroy's community center for underprivileged kids in Houston, and she held a squirming brown-skinned toddler in her arms.

"Dear Channel Seven News. My name is Ellen," she said softly, "and I have a 'Keeping Them Honest' complaint for you. I used to come to the Dominion Diamonds center to get free lunch, tutoring, and free health care." She walked over to the door and yanked on the handle a few times, and when it didn't open she scrunched up her face angrily. "And now when I come here to get milk and diapers for my son don't nobody wanna let me in! Channel Seven, *Viceroy Dominion* got me pregnant and now his family has shut me out and they won't even talk to me! I'm sending you this video so you can keep Viceroy Dominion and his entire family honest!"

The screen went blank and Barron bust out laughing real loud. He laughed his ass off, and pointed at his uncle. "Is that the best you can do, you slimy bastard? You tryna smear my father's good name in the gutter just so you can get your hands on his money? They call that shit *extortion*, homeboy! You can go to jail for that. But it's all good, because you ain't never been shit anyway!"

"Is that right?"

"Hell yeah, it is! Daddy mighta trusted ya ass, but I *never* did! Ever since that time I caught my girl sucking ya dick—"

"Nope!" Suge protested. "Uh-uh. Take that back, dawg. She didn't suck my dick, homey. She was *about* to suck it, but she never even got one lick in."

Barron exploded. "It don't matter, man! You still ain't shit! You ready to toss grime on your own brother in the name of *money*, man. Ga'head! Send that shit to Channel Seven! Who gives a fuck? Who's gonna believe you anyway? My father kept his hands clean his whole fuckin' life. Everybody knows he's solid. His rep can stand up to this. Besides." Barron swept his arm around the office. "He had dumb-fuck goonies like you to get down in the dirt for him, remember? That's the only reason you pulling in a paycheck as it is, nigga! Did you forget that?"

Suge shook his head quietly. "Nah, man. I ain't forget."

He pressed another button on the remote and the young white teenager popped up on the screen again. Her blue eyes were now red rimmed and her face was streaked with tears. She was still holding her little chocolate baby, but this time she was holding something else in her hands. It was a sheet of paper, and when the camera zoomed in on it the words, *Exclusively DNA* came clearly into view.

"Channel Seven 'Keeping Them Honest'? This is Ellen again." She brushed her long blond hair back and sniffed. "I just want to say I'm sorry and to tell you I made a big mistake. I thought Viceroy Dominion was my baby's daddy, but I was wrong. He's not. I got my son's paternity results in the mail today, and Viceroy Dominion didn't get me pregnant after all. He's not my son's father." Her voice snagged in her throat and a wave of tears spilled from her china blue eyes. "He's my son's *grandfather!*" She pointed her finger and stared angrily into the camera and blurted out, "*Barron* Dominion is my baby's daddy! Please, Channel Seven 'Keeping Them Honest'! I'm only seventeen and DNA doesn't lie! Can you make Barron Dominion take care of his son and pay me my child support? Can you help me? *Please?*"

The screen went white and there was nothing but stark silence in the big, plush office. Barron felt a wave of rage rushing up from his feet, through his chest, and straight into his brain. But that's where it stopped. Because even though he had never met this scrawny white girl in his life, and he damn sure had never fucked her, Viceroy and Selah didn't raise no fool. It was all about appearance and perception. Between the hit-and-run accident involving a child, being accused of paying hush money to the kid's father, and the half-dozen pictures circulating on the Internet that showed him in a skirt with his painted lips all over some nigga's dick, he might already be fucked. Whether this chick was lying or not, if a tape like this got leaked to the media, let alone to the board, his shit would most *definitely* be fucked.

Without a word, Suge picked the piece of paper up from

the floor and placed it back on his desk. Using just one finger, he slid it toward Barron again.

"Sign the paper, son. I love you, Lil Bump, but I will straight fuck you up. Now sign the goddamn paper."

Squinting in the semi-darkness, Barron bent over and re-read the last line on the full-page document that his uncle had drawn up for him to sign.

> *And in inclusion, I hereby request that the board's vote not be delayed, but held on the original date as scheduled. Lastly I swear and affirm that all parties to the Dominion Family Trust have been properly investigated and deemed qualified to receive their proper annual disbursements.*

Taking a deep breath and using his father's favorite fountain pen, Barron bit the bullet and signed that shit.

CHAPTER 27

"**M**ink."

I was having a dope-ass dream about the money I was gonna get and I was grinning all in my pillow. We had shut Barron's ass down, and I was locked in a big room with stacks and stacks of green piled damn near to the ceiling.

"Mink, wake up."

The dough was banded in stacks of hundred-dollar bills and wrapped in clear plastic. I grabbed a big shopping bag and started tossing brick after brick into the bag. And when that one was full, I grabbed another shopping bag and filled it up, and then another shopping bag, and then another one and another one and another one . . .

"C'mon now, Mink. I'ma need you to wake up, boo."

Bunni was patting the side of my face real gentle-like, and for once she wasn't yelling and screaming and waking me up bad.

"Mink."

Move, dammit! I wanted to tell her. Couldn't she see all my shopping bags? All my damn money? I started dragging the bags over to the door. There were so, so many of them but I had mad energy and I was nowhere near tired. When I got them all lined up at the door I grabbed two bags in each hand. I wrapped the twine handles around my wrists and twisted the doorknob and pulled. But it didn't open. I pulled again and again and again. It was locked. I knew I coulda banged on the door or kicked that bad boy with my feet, but I was scared. What if somebody came to open it and tried to take some of my money?

"Mink!" A sharp pain shot through my earlobe. My eyes flew open and I looked dead at Bunni. That bitch had *pinched* me!

"Mink, please wake up," she said softly. "Peaches is on the phone. He needs to talk to you."

I sat up in the bed and rubbed my ear. Traces of my money dream and how good I had been feeling swirled in my head. I licked my lips and took the phone that Bunni was pushing toward me. Any other time she would be wildin' and bouncing off the damn walls this early in the morning, and for a quick second I wondered why her eyes looked so sad.

"Hello?" I blinked a few times tryna make myself focus.

"Madame Mink?"

It was Peaches.

"Uh-huh."

"I think you need to come home now, baby."

"Wh-wh-what?" I frowned and my eyes searched Bunni's. She sat down on the edge of my bed and put her hand on my arm. "Why, wassup?" I swallowed hard. "Don't tell me that fool Punchie is still trippin. And oh lordy. Please don't tell me nothing about Gutta! I thought you said that fool was over me and on to the next bitch?"

"It's your mama," Peaches said quietly. "The nursing home called me. They think she had a stroke. The ambulance just took her to the hospital. I'm on my way up there, Mink, but it's looking kinda bad and they think you need to be there too." His voice broke. "I'm sorry, sweetie, but they don't think she's gonna make it."

"I'm coming," I whispered as I pushed Bunni out the way and swung my legs over the bed. Tears rushed to my eyes as I ran over to the closet to get my gear. "Please. Tell mama to hold on 'til I get there, Peaches. Please. I'm coming."

CHAPTER 28

It was a hurting-ass feeling when your lies came back to haunt you.

I had *been* told everybody in Texas that my mother was dead and gone, so there was no way I could 'fess up and explain why I needed to get back to New York so fast right now.

So, I lied again.

"It's my boss at work," I told everybody as the servants brought me and Bunni's bags to the front door. "She was closing the shop up last night when somebody pushed her back inside and robbed her. She got shot and the doctors don't know if she's gonna make it."

It was the fastest lie I could think of and it had actually happened to somebody I knew so the details were easy to cough up. But to my surprise, coughing up some money had been pretty easy too. As soon as I hung up from Peaches I had hit Uncle Suge on speed dial. He was at the house before I could finish packing my gear, and he tore me off ten g's in cash.

"I've got an emergency and I need some money so I can get to New York. I'll pay you back," I had told him, hoping like hell I wasn't gonna have to use his money to pay for no funeral. Mama didn't have no life insurance and I didn't know what I was gonna do if she died. I knew of people who had laid up frozen in the morgue for months waiting for their people to come up with some burial cash, and I couldn't even think about nothing like that happening to my mama.

Uncle Suge was a down nigga for me. He came running and dug in his pocket stash with no questions asked. "Don't worry about the money. Just get home and take care of business and get back down here as soon as you can. I can handle everything while you're gone, but I'm gonna need you to sign this proxy form."

"What's that?" I asked, already scribbling my name.

"It's a document that gives me the right to submit your absentee vote to the board so it can still be counted. I'm gonna take it to my lawyer and have him notarize it. We only have two days left before they meet, and I doubt if you'll make it back in time."

I knew damn well I wasn't gonna make it back in time. Yeah, Barron had signed those papers so the board could hold the meeting on schedule and I would get to vote, but that wasn't gonna do shit to help my DNA test results come back saying what I needed them to say. Matter fact, when shit popped off ugly and the results finally did come in I wasn't gonna be coming back to Texas at all. Wouldn't be no reason to. Dy-Nasty would get the whole gwap, which was probably hers to have anyway. But of course I didn't say none of that. As much as I was feeling Uncle Suge, and as good as he loved on me, I still wasn't tryna tell him all my bizz. Yeah, he knew some things about me, but there was a whole lot more that he didn't know too.

Selah rushed over and hugged me before I left. It was good to see her looking all concerned about my feelings again. "Oh, baby. I'm so sorry to hear about your boss. Keep in touch with us, okay? We'll be praying for her to pull through."

Even Barron was decent enough to look like he had a little bit of sympathy for me. At least until he opened his stupid-ass mouth. "What's your boss's name and what hospital is she in?" Mr. Nosy Ass with the shaved-off eyebrows wanted to know. "I'll send her a bouquet of flowers."

"She's in intensive care," I snapped as I headed out the door and toward the limo. "She can't get no flowers in there!" I wasn't worried about him finding out that I was lying. There was so much random violence in New York City that somebody, somehow, somewhere, in some fucked-up borough, had gotten robbed and shot last night.

The whole family followed us outside and Dane put his arms around me. He squeezed me and whispered in my ear, "The board votes the day after tomorrow. What the hell are we gonna do?"

"Uncle Suge's got it covered," I whispered back. "I signed a proxy."

Fallon and Jock both came over to hug me. Jock was frontin' me off a lil bit 'cause he still had the ass with me for busting him out about that dead white girl, but for some reason Fallon held on to me real tight. "I hope your boss pulls through okay, Mink. I can't wait until you and Bunni come back."

The only one who was acting slick and funky was Dy-Nasty. After all the dirt we had gotten down on together there was something crafty about the look in her eye that told me she was operating in full-blown scheme mode. I could already feel the knives coming up outta her pockets and sliding deep into my back, and I just knew that Philly trick was gonna double-cross me as soon as I left. But so what? My *mama* was dying. Wasn't no amount of money gonna make me turn my back on Mama. I was going back to New York. I *had* to go.

I got in the front seat of Suge's truck and Bunni got in the back. Selah stood up on the running board, then leaned into the open window and kissed me good-bye. I felt some kinda way because the last time I left Texas she had broken her neck to ride with me to the airport. She had held on to me and cried like a baby when we got to the departure terminal, and

Bunni almost had to drag my ass outta the whip so we didn't miss our flight.

But this time? Not so much. She had Dy-Nasty to keep her company so I guess all I was good for was a lil kiss and a wave. Selah was still waving when we started pulling off. Dy-Nasty took her by the arm and started turning her toward the house. That scandalous-ass guttersnipe had the nerve to bust on me over her shoulder and flash me a real evil smirk. And then with her free hand dangling at her side where Selah couldn't see it, she gave me the finger down low and mouthed, *Fuck you, bitch!*

We were parked outside the departure terminal at DFW International Airport and Bunni had gone inside to get us checked in. Uncle Suge had come around and opened my door, but instead of getting out I swung my legs around and scooted forward until he was sandwiched between my thighs.

"I'm sorry about your boss getting shot," he said and pulled me closer to him. "Do what you gotta do in New York and then come on back, okay?"

It's my mama! I wanted to scream. But instead I sighed and swallowed hard. I didn't know about all that coming back shit. I knew once those DNA results came in there wouldn't be no reason for me to come back to Texas, and I wouldn't be welcome at the mansion no more anyway. The thought of that kinda hurt me and I snuggled up deeper in Suge's arms. I pressed my face down in his neck and inhaled his strong, sexy scent. Probably for the last time.

"C'mon, lemme walk you inside. I'll be right here when you get back," he said gently.

I knew I might not never see him again, but even still there was no way in hell I could tell him the truth about who I really was, why I had come to Texas, or why I now had to leave. Instead, I raised my head and found his lips. We tongued each other down and I could tell this wasn't the same kinda kiss he gave me when we was just having fun. This was something different and I liked it.

I broke away first.

"I'll call you when I get there, okay?" I lied.

He lifted my chin with two fingers, then pressed his forehead to mine and kissed my lips again. "You can call me anytime you need me, baby. Day or night. And it don't matter what you need neither. Whatever it is, I got you. All you gotta do is say the word."

I stared at him. He was so damn strong. So damn fine and sexy. I had never had no man talk to me this way before. I wasn't tryna make Suge out to be no big-ass liar, but I just couldn't believe what I was hearing him say.

"For real? Are you serious?" I stared in his eyes and hoped.

He touched his hand to his big, strong chest.

"I'm feeling you, Mink. Right in here."

I nodded and reached for his other hand in mine. It was big and rough. A grown-man's hand, and I pressed it to the spot right above my breasts. "I'm feeling you too, Suge," I admitted shyly. "Right here."

Suge left his truck parked at the curb and we walked inside the terminal together holding hands. I felt real good walking next to a dude like him. Like I was safe and I didn't have to work so hard plotting, scheming, or hustling no more. Like he had my back and I would always be taken care of as long as he was around. I looked up at him and we both grinned. I knew me and Suge wasn't family and we never would be, but we were damn sure more than friends.

We landed in New York and me and Bunni left the airport and took a taxi straight to the hospital. Most of my family had already gathered around by the time I got there and it looked like they was having a LaRue family reunion outside in the hallway. All them yellow faces and hazel eyes were looking just like mine.

I couldn't stand they asses. All my aunts and cousins were up there running off at the mouth, and so was my grandmother, my father's scandalous-ass mammy. Everybody tried to hug all on me like they cared about me and shit. I fake-kissed my grandmother and gave her trifling ass her proper respect, but I brushed the rest of them phony-ass LaRues off and went straight to Mama's bedside.

She was in intensive care, and they had her hooked up to mad stuff. She had all kinds of tubes running in her mouth, up her nose, and an IV was stuck in both her arms.

Mama looked real bad. So much had changed about her since the last time I'd seen her. Her lips were blue and twisted. They were clenched extra tight around the tubes in her mouth. The rest of her body looked funny too. She was even more stiff and curled up than before, and her eyes had sunk deep in her face and the color of her skin just wasn't right.

"Mama." I had to bite my lip to keep from crying out loud. It looked like the human part of Mama was dead and the machines was doing all the living for her. There was so much stuff hooked up and going in and out of her body that I didn't know where to touch her. I bent over and pressed my lips to her forehead. "Mama. It's Mink. I'm here now, Mama. I'm right here."

"Well where in the world was you at all this time, baby?"

I whirled around. My grandmother and Aunt Bibby had followed me inside Mama's room. Granny was old but still a fine-ass peach. She had big titties and a plump, wide booty and real soft hair that had gotten thin and gone completely gray. Looking at her I could see exactly how I was gonna look when I got old.

"I was down in Texas, Granny," I answered her. "Working." And then I busted on Aunt Bibby so I could change the subject. "I thought only two people was allowed in here at one time?"

She shrugged. "It don't matter, Mink. Two people, five, or ten. It just don't matter no more, baby."

I turned back to Mama. I was shocked to see that her eyes was open, and I could tell right away that she recognized me.

I got amped. "Mama! Can you hear me, Mama? It's Mink. I'm here now, Mama. Can you hear me?"

I swear to God I saw her nod.

Yep, Mama had nodded her head. It was just a little nod, but she did it. I saw it.

And then I saw something else. Mama's mouth was moving. Not like she was tryna untwist it or like she was messing with the tubes or nothing, but like she was tryna *say something*. Like she was tryna say something to *me*.

"Shhhlll . . . Shhhlll . . . Shhhlll . . ."

Mama's face was getting red. She was squinting her eyes like she was concentrating, and her crooked little hands was reaching out toward me.

"What's that, Mama? What you tryna say?" I held my hair out the way and leaned over until my ear was damn near in her mouth. "Try again, Mama. Say it again so I can hear you!"

"Shhhlll . . . Shhhlll . . . Shhhlll . . ."

It was like she was whistling around that big-ass tube they had in her mouth. I needed them to take it out. I needed them to take it out so I could catch what Mama was tryna say!

A nurse had come in the room. She looked like she was about to tell one of us to get out, but I grabbed her shoulders and turned her toward my mama.

"Can you please take them tubes outta my mother's mouth? She's tryna talk to me. Please! She's got something to tell me. Take them tubes outta her mouth so I can hear her!"

"I'm sorry, ma'am. We'd need a doctor's order before we could do that."

"Well then get a damn doctor up in here!" I shrieked as Mama reached out weakly with her trembling, crooked hands. *"Where's her goddamn doctor?"*

"Someone is on the way. He should be here shortly."

I turned back to Mama. Her face was even redder and now her eyes were locked dead on mine. There was so much damn pain in those eyes of hers that it slammed into my gut. Her hands rose about four inches off the bed. I grabbed them and squeezed them as she held me with her eyes and *shhhllll'd* all around that tube.

"Mamaaaa . . ." I cried. *"Mamaaaa . . ."*

And then it was over.

Mama's hands went limp in mine and the fire in her eyes went totally out. Her body was completely still, and I stood there looking at her in shock and watching all the color slowly drain outta her face.

"Mama!" I screamed. I shook her arms and bent over and pressed my face into her breasts. "Mama! Don't die. *Please* don't die!"

"Jude is gone, baby," my grandmother said. "She's gone to glory."

"Nooooo!" I cried. I was hurt and I was mad and all I could think to do was fight somebody! I was about to wild out! Straight clean shit up! The only thing that stopped me from going bonkers was my Aunt Bibby. She was crying too. She wrapped her strong, manly arms around me and rocked me gently, like I was a little baby.

"It's okay, Mink." She kissed my forehead and tried to soothe me as tears ran from both our eyes. "You gonna be okay, baby girl."

"But Mama was tryna tell me something, Aunt Bibby!" I cried and moaned. "It was her last breath, and she was tryna *tell* me something!"

Outta the blue, my aunt blacked straight the hell out.

"She was probably tryna tell you the goddamn *truth*!" Aunt Bibby turned my shoulders loose and grabbed my wrists and shook the shit outta me. "The truth about your *life*, dammit! Open up your eyes, Mink and stop acting so damn stupid! God knows I loved me some Jude, but that woman was a big-ass *liar*! Why you think she drove her car into that goddamn river with you in it? Huh? Not even the lowest, raggediest, black-hearted *dog-ass* mama does no crazy shit like that! Hell nah, Jude didn't have *no right* to do *half* the low-down shit she did, and what her ass shoulda told you before she clocked out was the goddamn *truth*!"

I stared at my aunt through a haze of confused tears. And then slowly, I glanced down at my mother's still body. Jude Jackson. Even in death she was beautiful. I looked over at my ol' raggedy piece of grandmother and she closed her eyes and nodded, yes.

I couldn't believe it! These bitches was hatin'! My mother's spirit had just flown free, and these trifling-ass Bad News LaRues was *still* hatin'!

I turned back to Aunt Bibby with fire shooting outta my eyes. By all rights I shoulda clocked this bald-headed bitch for calling my mama a liar and talking bad about the dead, but something inside me was frozen, and instead I asked her quietly, "What you mean Mama shoulda told me the truth? What's the truth, Aunt Bibby? What the hell is the truth?"

Aunt Bibby shook her head and wiped at the tears in her eyes. "I don't know everything, Mink," she said, still sniffling. "Hell, I don't think we'll *ever* know everything about all the crooked little stunts Jude pulled over the years. But one thing I do know for sure is that there were two of y'all."

"What?"

Aunt Bibby took a deep breath and let it all out.

"You heard me. There was two of y'all. Somewhere out there you got yourself a sister, Mink, 'cause you was a twin."

To Be Continued . . .

The Misadventures of Mink LaRue continue in *Dirty Rotten Liar.*

SEXY LITTLE LIAR

Noire

ABOUT THIS GUIDE

The suggested questions that follow are included to
enhance your group's reading of this book.

Discussion Questions

1. Con-mami Mink LaRue and her partner-in-grime Bunni Baines have pulled a hundred-grand heist on the Dominion oil family of Texas. Was there any way in hell that Mink was going to do the right thing with that money once she got back to New York City? Or was the dough doomed to run through her fingers like water, setting her up for another crazy misadventure?

2. Bunni is Mink's ever-ready bestie and the brain-child behind most of Mink's calculated schemes. Do you think Bunni is content chilling in the background during Mink's misadventures and picking up whatever scraps come her way? Or is Bunni an ambitious con-mistress who wants some of the spotlight, and the dough, for herself?

3. Dy-Nasty has busted onto the scene ready to knock niggas out with full force. Where did she come from? Who put her up to taking her DNA test? And what kind of gutter tricks does she really have up her sleeve?

4. Mink, Dy-Nasty, and Bunni had a knock-down, drag-out fight in the club. What did you think about the way the three of them banded together to fight off the bouncers?

5. What do you think about the relationship that is starting to blossom between Barron and his kissing-cousin Pilar? Can it go where Pilar wants it to go? Should it?

6. Barron still has a sex jones for Mink that is out of control. Do you want to see the two of them get freaky at least once, just to relieve all the sexual tension?

7. Uncle Suge is a gully cat. Is he getting weak for Mink? Does she have this powerful Dominion man on lock? Between Mink and Dy-Nasty, does Uncle Suge know which one is the liar and which one is the thief?

8. Gutta is out of jail and back in Harlem. Is he going to be satisfied with the deal Barron offered him, or is Mink's neck still in jeopardy if he ever lays eyes on her again?

9. Fallon is being sexually manipulated by her lover. What was REALLY going on when Pilar heard sex sounds coming from the suite on her floor?

10. Mink and Dy-Nasty were forced to come together and work on a scheme to keep Barron off their backs. Did you think they were both willing to put their competing goals aside for the money? Or was one of them, or even BOTH of them, still scheming the whole time?

11. It seems like straight-laced Selah has been getting her freak on with the competition! What kind of marriage does she REALLY have with Viceroy? What do you think is going to happen next between her and Ruddman?

12. Barron has been caught on camera with his balls hanging out! Now that there's some potential dirt floating around on him, how will this affect his control over the board and the vote for power at Dominion Oil?

13. Mink and Dy-Nasty have been going at it head-up. Which one is the more crucial con-artist? The grimiest gamer? The sexiest little liar?

Meet Mink LaRue for the first time in

Natural Born Liar.

In stores now!

CHAPTER 1

The Rip-Off

Pussy sold for pennies on the dollar on Friday nights in Harlem, and if you were looking for a couple of hot whirly-whirlies, then Club Wood was damn sure the place to be. Located on a busy corner off 125th Street, Wood stayed packed out with coochie-sniffin' niggas who were deep on the prowl, and some of the baddest bitches in the city of New York stripped, danced, and hosted private fuck-fests in the club's back rooms.

I had twirled around the strip poles earlier in the day, but I was taking the night off so I could collect some dough from a mark that me and my best friends, Peaches and Bunni, had recently ganked.

We'd schemed up a plan to lure a switch-hittin' old head into a motel room, then we snapped a bunch of shots of him sporting a sexy red bra and taking some real thick pipe up his ass.

Dude was a high-profile principal at a private boys' school and he didn't want no trouble. He didn't want no publicity neither, and in less than five minutes he had agreed to give up twenty g's to stop a picture of his hairy balls from being posted to his teenaged daughter's Facebook page.

The lick had gone down perfectly, and I was chillin' at the

bar sipping slut juice and congratulating myself for a job well done when outta nowhere I caught a funny vibe.

Something wasn't right.

I got the feeling I was being watched. I had a bag full of blackmail dough slung over my shoulder, and something in my gut told me to get the fuck up outta Dodge.

I slid down from the barstool and broke for the door, but Hova's latest banga came on, and every pole freak in the house broke out in a mass stanky stroll. The strippers jumped down from the stage and hit the floor rolling hard, booties twerkin', hips grindin', stroking their pussies and sending a wave of horny niggas rushing down the aisles straight toward me.

WHO GON' STOP ME? WHO GON' STOP ME, HUH?

I crashed into about thirty sweaty niggas as I pushed through the crowd and tried to fight my way outside. I was shaking fools offa me left and right as their horny asses pulled me in all directions and tried to feel me up. A few of my regular customers offered to get me toasted, some wanted me to slide over in the corner so we could smoke some yay, and even more begged me to go in the back room and hit 'em with my patented-move, double-hump lap dance.

Somehow I made it past them, and I was *this close* to getting my ass outta there when a strong hand clamped down on my shoulder and a deep voice boomed, "Excuse me, ma'am."

I almost shit. I didn't know if I should turn around swinging or make another break for the door, but I knew I was busted. The twenty racks I had just hustled from that principal felt like a ton of bricks weighing down my bag. This was supposed to be an easy little gank, and I couldn't believe that greasy old dick-rider had called the cops on me!

Getting arrested was gonna cause some real big problems for me. I was already on probation for writing bad checks, and a thousand lies flew through my head as I thought about the bus ride to Rikers I was about to take.

"I said, excuse me, ma'am," the deep voice boomed behind me again, "but is your name Nicki Minaj?"

I spun around so fast my pink-and-blond Chinese bangs swished across my forehead. I eyeballed the hand that was still gripping my shoulder. It sported a five-thousand-dollar platinum Versace ring on the pinkie finger, and I'd seen that fourteen-thousand-dollar Rolex Prince Cellini on sale at a jewelry store on Broadway.

"Oh! My bad." Dude busted a grin as he checked me out. I was styling pussy-pink from the top of my Glama-Glo wig all the way down to my toenails, and it was real obvious that he was feeling my flow. "You look *just like* Mizz Minaj from the back, but you're even finer than she is in the face."

I stunted on him. I was a con-mami, a pole dancer, and under the right circumstances I could be a big-ass thief. A chick like me had ninety-nine hustles but a rap star wasn't one of 'em.

I breathed a sigh of relief as I checked him out right back. Dude was handling his. He had pretty brown skin and real white teeth. His dome was freshly-lined and he stood at least six-five.

My eyes rolled over his gear as I added up his digits. Chocolate-brown Polo shirt, baggy jeans, Cool Grey Jordans. Uh-huh. He was thuggin' it and I was lovin' it. Papa was stackin' some real mean paper and he wasn't shy about flossin' it. I could almost see the fat money knots swelling up in his pockets and the hard piece of wood that was starting to rock up in his drawers too.

"I'm serious." He grinned again and hit me with his dimples. "I didn't mean no disrespect, shawty. You just look so damn fly, so damn . . . *New York*. For real. My bad."

His mistake was understandable because my shit was put together super-tight. I was rocking Fendi from my diamond-trimmed pink shades down to my tight pink miniskirt. My jewelry was pink mother-of-pearls from Tiffany's, and my pink-polished toenails looked nice and suckable in my peep-toe heels.

"No problem." I grinned and played it sexy-classy. "Men take me for Nicki Minaj all the time."

"Hell, yeah, with that kinda body I bet the fuck they do," he growled. His voice was full of mad appreciation as he introduced himself. "My name is Dajuan," he said. "Dajuan Latrell Sullivan. What's yours?"

"They call me Tasha," I lied, sliding my shades off so he could peep my hazel eyes. "Tasha Pierce."

"Look, I don't mean to come at you, Tasha, but I'm just visiting here tonight. Me and my brother own a club in Philly and we're thinking about opening up a joint around here pretty soon too. You look like you know this city. Can I buy you a drink so we can kick it for a while?"

A businessman? A club owner? I was definitely down for that!

"Nah, I don't think so," I fronted. "I don't drink with strange dudes. For all I know you could be the Harlem River Strangler."

He laughed and pulled out a business card. "I'm a balla, not a killer," he said, passing it to me. "That's real talk. Look, I ain't tryna push up on you, I just want some good conversation, that's all. I ain't askin' you for no lap dance or nothing like that. I got a nice little spot over in the VIP joint, and we can have a few drinks together and then I'll have my driver drop you off anywhere you wanna go. You feelin' that?"

"Your driver?" I played him off, but I had never been the type to turn my back on a knockin' opportunity.

He looked through the glass doors and pointed toward the corner where a shiny black limo was parked right at the curb. An old white man was sitting behind the wheel, and when Dajuan waved at him the old man smiled and waved back.

I glanced down at his business card. The lights in the club were pretty dim, but I could tell it was made of thick, cream-colored card stock with heavy gold trim. The initials D.L.S. were scripted and embossed in large red letters, and a bunch of other words were printed on it real small.

That right there did it. I felt a rush coming on. God, I loved this fuckin' hustle! Hoodwinking niggas felt as good as the first hit on a crack pipe, and I had to stop myself from squealing with excitement. This Philly fool was gwapped out. Swimming in cream! Did I wanna sit in his VIP booth and have a drink with him? Did a wino piss on the stairs?

I shook my head again. I was wide open but I still had a role to play.

"Nah, I can't. I got other plans for tonight."

I was praying he'd push up on me just one more time, 'cause I could tell his deep-ass pockets were dying to get tricked out.

"So that's how y'all treat company around here? A Philly nigga can't get no Big Apple love?"

My bag was already full of dough, but a hustlin' chick like me was always good for one more con. I did the math in my head as I let Dajuan hold me by my waist and lead me back through the crowd. I was in debt with some real dangerous cats for some real crazy cash, and this was gonna be a great opportunity to get my weight up. Between his watch and his ring alone I could probably rack up at least ten grand at the pawnshop around the corner.

I switched my plump apple ass toward the VIP booth while Dajuan walked behind me watching it move. He seemed like an all right cat, but he was on the young side too. He was fine, but he didn't look like no genius. I was planning on getting his horny ass naked and doing a quick little dip and zip. Peaches and Bunni were expecting me to show up at the crib soon, and I figured I could lure Dajuan into the hotel next door and get the whole bizz over and done with in less than an hour.

I slid into the VIP booth just a' crackin' up inside. Somebody's mama shoulda warned him about pickin' up strangers 'cause this was about to be a mismatch. But what the hell *ever*! Niggas these days were just beggin' to get got, and even with a pocketbook full of cash I could always find time to roll an unsuspecting mark with nothing but pussy on his brain!

Barnes & Noble Booksellers #2693
235 Union Street
Waterbury, CT 06706
203-759-7125

STR:2693 REG:006 TRN:6395 CSHR:Krist B

Hood: An Urban Erotic Tale
9781416533030   T1
  (1 @ 15.0)   15.00
Sexy Little Liar
9780758266095   T1
  (1 @ 15.0)   15.00
Subtotal   30.00
Sales Tax T1 (6.350%)   1.91
TOTAL   31.91
VISA   31.91
Card#: XX/XXXXXXXXXX4516
Expdate: XX/XX
Auth: 957760
Entry Method: Swiped

A MEMBER WOULD HAVE SAVED   3.00

Thanks for shopping at
Barnes & Noble

101.25A   10/27/2012 01:15PM

CUSTOMER COPY

Policy on receipt may appear in two sections.

Returns or exchanges will not be permitted (i) after 14 days or without receipt or (ii) for product not carried by Barnes & Noble or Barnes & Noble.com.

in accordance with the applicable warranty.

exchangeable. Defective NOOKs may be exchanged at the store in accordance with the applicable warranty.

Returns or exchanges will not be permitted (i) after 14 days or without receipt or (ii) for product not carried by Barnes & Noble or Barnes & Noble.com.

Policy on receipt may appear in two sections.

Return Policy

With a sales receipt or Barnes & Noble.com packing slip, a full refund in the original form of payment will be issued from any Barnes & Noble Booksellers store for returns of undamaged NOOKs, new and unread books, and unopened and undamaged music CDs, DVDs, and audio books made within 14 days of purchase from a Barnes & Noble Booksellers store or Barnes & Noble.com with the below exceptions:

A store credit for the purchase price will be issued (i) for purchases made by check less than 7 days prior to the date of return, (ii) when a gift receipt is presented within 60 days of purchase, (iii) for textbooks, or (iv) for products purchased at Barnes & Noble College bookstores that are listed for sale in the Barnes & Noble Booksellers inventory management system.

Opened music CDs/DVDs/audio books may not be returned, and can be exchanged only for the same title and only if defective.

NOOKs purchased from other retailers or sellers are returnable only to the retailer or seller from which they are purchased, pursuant to such retailer's or seller's return policy. Magazines, newspapers, eBooks, digital downloads, and used books are not returnable or exchangeable. Defective NOOKs may be exchanged at the store in accordance with the applicable warranty.

Returns or exchanges will not be permitted (i) after 14 days or without receipt or (ii) for product not carried by Barnes & Noble or Barnes & Noble.com.

Policy on receipt may appear in two sections.